Ties That Bind

What ties you to your lover?
Love, need, desire, scarves, rope, ribbons or
something else altogether?

Five short stories of love and lovers that explore
the bonds that bring them together both
figuratively and literally.

Other Erotic Tales from MLR Press

Kimberly Gardner
J.L.Langley & Dick D.
Jet Mykles
and
Laura Baumbach

Ties That Bind

Published by
MLR Press, LLC
3052 Gaines Waterport Rd.
Albion, NY 14411

Visit ManLoveRomance Press, LLC on the Internet
www.mlrpress.com

Cover Art by Deana C. Jamroz
Editing by Maura Anderson
Printed in the United States of America.

ISBN# 978-1-934531-09-9

First Edition
2008

Ties That Bind

Table of contents

'07 Jet Mykles

Ties That Bind

Jet Mykles

Key To Me

"Can't I stay?"

The pillow beneath Noah's face smelled of sweat and musk, with faint traces of citrus shampoo. Breathing it in, he let his straight blond hair obscure his face as he twisted his neck slowly so he could see the man sitting beside him on the bed. Big, almost stocky, with a thick thatch of dark hair covering his chest that was a few shades darker than the short, buzzed hair on his head. He was mostly in shadow since the only light in the room came from the open door behind him, but Noah knew well enough what his big blue puppy dog eyes looked like. A good looking guy. But not the one he wanted. *How did I ever think he might be the one?*

"Probably not a good idea."

Bob's eyes wandered from Noah's face to his bare back. He reached out to pat Noah's shoulder. The pat turned into a caress. The caress spilled down the curve of his shoulder, down Noah's spine, to the dip of his lower back, right next to where the green sheet lay over his ass.

Noah's skin tingled but he was sated enough not to respond. He squirmed aside, not quite out of reach. "Bob."

The hand stopped. Bob heaved a sigh and pulled back, standing. Jeans and dress shirt were back on. He'd even buttoned up. "Yeah, I know. Time for me to leave." His attention returned to Noah's face. Despite the shadows blurring his blunt features, Noah could see the open longing in his face. "Can I see you again?"

No. Guilt tugged at Noah. "Bob, we talked about this." And that should have been Noah's first hint. Noah should have trusted his existing instinct about Bob.

Bob nodded, his face showing that he heard the unspoken negative loud and clear. "I know, I know." He ran a hand over the buzzed dark hair on his scalp. "You're a beautiful man, Noah."

"Thank you." He resisted the urge to pay back the compliment. It'd only give Bob hope where there was none. *Stupid to sleep with him. You knew he couldn't be the one.* But it was too late now.

With a little smile, Bob lifted his hand in a wave. "See you around." He turned and left.

Sighing, Noah closed his eyes and snuggled back down on the pillow, resting for just a bit before he went to clean up. His soft sheets were damp from exertion. The sex had been good. He'd enjoyed it. He knew Bob had enjoyed it as well. He did *not* have to feel guilty. He'd been perfectly upfront with Bob, just like he was with all of his lovers. Bob didn't have to know that Noah had held out a secret wish that he might be someone far more intriguing to Noah's heart.

The sound of voices in the kitchen reopened his eyes. They were faint, but he heard the words loud and clear.

"Hey, Mitch."

Ties That Bind

"Hey, Bob."

Mitch?! Noah pushed up to his elbows, eyes wide on the open bedroom door. The door that had *been* open the entire time he and Bob were…"Ah, shit." He scrambled out of bed and snatched up the soft ivory lounge pants draped over his desk chair. As he stepped into them, he heard the front door open and close. Spearing two hands through his hair and tying it in a quick, loose knot at the nape of his neck, he checked to make sure there was no stray spunk on his skin before heading for the kitchen.

His roommate, Mitch, sat at the kitchen table in one of the uncomfortable plastic and metal chairs, face and remote control aimed at the 13" television seated on the table against the wall. His dark brown curls were freshly trimmed, revealing the back of his neck, and the blue plaid flannel shirt he wore was new. A plastic tub with the familiar pale shapes of lemon bars in it sat at his elbow. So he *had* gone to see his mother.

"What are you doing here?"

Mitch glanced over one big shoulder at him and smiled. "Hey."

Noah stalked over to the table to see Mitch's face properly. Strong square chin, long-ago-broken slim nose, and thick black brows over steely gray eyes. Only the absurdly long eyelashes and curved sensual mouth saved that face from looking too harsh. "What are you doing here? What happened to your mom?"

Mitch continued to channel surf, the smile still playing around his sharply defined lips. "She's fine. She got called in for a late night shift so I came home instead of staying over." He nudged the plastic bin closer to the empty chair beside him. "She sent the sweets you love so much."

"Oh." It was a measure of Noah's distress that he didn't pounce on the plastic tub. He glanced back toward his bedroom, chewing his bottom lip. How had he not heard Mitch come through the front door? "How long have you been here?"

Mitch chuckled, tossing chin-length black curls back from his face. "Long enough."

"Oh. Shit. I'm sorry." He grimaced. "You said you weren't going to be home."

"No sweat. My fault." Mitch paused to listen to the football scores. "Sounded like you enjoyed it." A sly look. "Or, at least Bob did."

Noah went to get a glass from the strainer on the counter by the sink. "Yeah. He's loud."

"I'll say. Damn. He thinks you're something special."

Noah winced. Never having slept with Bob before, he hadn't known how loud he was. And descriptive. Even Noah blushed at hearing some of the ways Bob had described him. He filled his glass with milk from the refrigerator. "Yeah."

Mitch turned in his chair, draping one arm over the back as his steel-gray eyes regarded Noah. "I'm kind of surprised. You don't usually bring your dates home."

Noah put the milk back and closed the fridge. "You weren't supposed to be here."

"Do you bring them back when I'm not here?"

Noah drank down half of his glass then sat in the chair beside Mitch. "Not usually, no." He set the glass down and reached for the tub of pastries.

"That was that guy, Bob, right? The one you said's been after you for years?" Although Mitch was straight, he'd often gone with Noah to his favorite gay clubs. He claimed to like the atmosphere more and was easygoing enough to be flattered rather than offended when guys hit on him. Bob frequented the same clubs, so they had met.

Noah paused to inhale lemony goodness, his mouth watering as he reached for a sticky sugar-powdered sweet. "That's the one."

Mitch leaned forward on the table, setting the remote down and reaching for a bar. "What made you decide to finally fuck him?"

Ties That Bind

Noah eyed Mitch as he chewed. "You're full of questions tonight," he observed, mouth half-full as he licked sugar off his fingertips.

Mitch's gaze dropped to the treat in his own hand as he lifted it. "Not every night I get to hear you getting pounded into the mattress." He laid the whole bar on his tongue then shut his mouth over it.

Noah flushed, but laughed. They'd been roommates for seven years, three in college and four since, and in all that time Noah rarely brought his dates back to the apartment. Mitch was mostly the same way. "Hey, if I'd known that's what you wanted to hear, I'd bring back dates more often."

Mitch laughed, chewing. "Nah. I'm just curious why you'd finally let Bob have you after all this time."

Let Bob have you. It fit. Noah had fended Bob off for years. But tonight he'd taken a chance. Tonight, he had hoped that Bob would turn out to be…

But he wasn't.

Noah shrugged.

"Is he your mystery man?"

Noah slanted a scowl Mitch's way.

Mitch grinned as he sucked sugar off his thumb. "That is why you slept with him, isn't it?"

Noah sighed, reaching for another bar. "Yes."

"Is it him?"

"No."

"You sure?"

"Yes." He held the bar up before him, carefully breaking it in two before bringing one half to his lips. "I thought it made sense for it to be him but…" He popped the treat into his mouth then shook his head.

Mitch laughed. "How did a doormat like *Bob* make sense?"

Noah winced. "He's the only one I know who's really after me."

"You have tons of guys after you."

5

"To fuck me, sure. But none of the guys I know have the romantic streak to pull off the gifts."

"True. Actual *thought* went into them. Other than just getting in your pants, I mean."

Noah stuck out his tongue at Mitch before putting the other half of the lemon bar into his mouth.

Mitch's eyes glittered with mirth as he reached for Noah's glass of milk. "It's driving you crazy, isn't it?" He took a drink.

Snatching the glass back, Noah pouted. "Yes!"

Laughing, Mitch switched off the television and stood. At six foot two he towered over Noah's mere five foot seven, but Noah had never once felt intimidated by his friend. "Cheer up," he said, patting Noah's bare shoulder before he started toward the door to the bedrooms. "I'm sure the mystery man will arrange for you guys to meet soon."

"God, I hope you're right," Noah muttered, reaching for another treat as a balm to his frustrated desire.

* * * * *

"Oh *No*-ah!"

Hearing Kenneth's voice, Noah glanced up from the tequila he was pouring. The hotel clerk was approaching the bar, a familiarly wrapped box in his hand.

Noah's heart thudded in his chest. Nodding to Kenneth, he finished pouring the margarita and lifted it and the glass of Chardonnay onto Rachel's tray.

Rachel's full attention was on the package Kenneth set on the bar. "Damn," she pouted, hefting her tray. She pointed at Noah. "Don't open it until I get back."

Hearing her, Kenneth chuckled as he set the box on the bar. Hitching the legs of his smart gray suit, he slid onto a barstool. He smoothed his tie with one manicured hand and unbuttoned his jacket with the other. "Judging from the last few gifts, you shouldn't open it out here at all."

Wiping suddenly sweating hands on his embroidered pants, Noah tipped a wide glance at his friend. "You think?"

Kenneth shrugged, tapping the little gold box. His gold college ring gleamed softly in the diffused lighting over the bar. "I don't know. After the last one…"

Noah waved his hand to shut Kenneth up, his attention back to the box. "Point taken." The last box had contained an exquisite piece of jewelry, but the fact that it was a nipple chain made it not quite right to display in public. Even if "public" was only The Matador Bar in the Season's Inn hotel at two in the afternoon. He flipped away the long stray hair at the side of his face and leaned his hands on the bar, staring at the box. "It's probably jewelry again." The hair, predictably, fell back against his cheek. He really did need to get that trimmed someday. Either that or let it just grow long enough to reach the tail at the back of his head.

"Yeah. The cuffs were in a larger box."

He scowled at Kenneth. "Say it a little louder, would you?"

Kenneth's hazel eyes lit up as he laughed. He draped one forearm across the padded edge of the bar and arched one perfect brow. His beautiful lips pursed slightly over his smile. "You could get me a drink while you're deciding."

"Aren't you on duty?"

"Nope. Just got off."

Noah raised an eyebrow and gestured at the box. "How long have you been holding on to this?"

Kenneth chuckled. "Just a few hours."

Noah pushed back from the counter and turned to grab a tumbler. "For that, you have to pay for your drink." He scooped ice.

"If I must."

Rachel returned, pressing up against Kenneth's back and peering over his shoulder at the bar. "What's in it? Oh," she pouted at the box as she stepped over to a stool for herself, "you haven't opened it yet."

"You told him not to," Kenneth pointed out, smoothing his hair straight with one hand.

Ties That Bind

She adjusted the frilled off-the-shoulder sleeves of her blouse as she sat. "Oh please, like Noah ever listens to me." She set her tray down and pulled the box closer to her. "It's probably jewelry."

"That's what we suspect."

Rachel leaned toward Kenneth, lowering her voice. "Do you think it's another nipple chain?"

Kenneth leaned closer to her. "No. Noah's mystery man wouldn't be so gauche as to give the same gift *twice*."

"Maybe it's a cock ring," she murmured, eyeing the box. She'd been absurdly delighted with the nipple chain, proclaiming it delightfully naughty. Noah had caught her eying his chest once or twice since then.

"No. That would be in a much smaller box. Although," Kenneth pulled the box closer, eyeing it with new interest, "it could be a 'Gates of Hell'."

Rachel's eyes went wide. "Ooooh! What's that?!"

"Never mind!" Noah snapped, setting the bourbon and club soda on a cocktail napkin before Kenneth. He'd never worn one, but he knew the contraption was a bondage prop consisting of a set of metal or rubber rings that, when worn, would space out evenly over a penis shaft. They didn't need to discuss it here.

Kenneth laughed evilly and patted Rachel's hand. "I'll send you an email with a link."

Noah eyed the box, disagreeing with Kenneth that the box could contain one. Unsure whether he *hoped* Kenneth was wrong. Although, in the right circumstances…

Rachel grimaced. "You'd better," she told Kenneth. Then she pushed the box closer to Noah. "Open it, already. What is that? Like a dozen gifts?"

"This'll be number ten," Kenneth supplied.

Noah eyed him. "You've been counting?"

Kenneth lifted his drink, tilting it in a salute toward Noah. "You're my friend. I need to watch out for you."

8

Ties That Bind

Noah and Kenneth had known each other for two years, both working in the same hotel and both sharing a certain sense of style as well as a liking for men. As two of only four openly gay men who worked in the entire hotel, they had banded together as friends. Luckily, their friendship had progressed beyond just that one tie, although it had never ventured into the sexual. Not that Kenneth wasn't attractive. He was. Tall with straight, light brown hair that he kept in a neat, short cut and devilish hazel eyes over a matching smile. He was probably the best dressed man of Noah's acquaintance, despite the fact that he wasn't the richest. But Noah and Kenneth were not to be an item. They caught on to each other's tricks too quickly.

Drink delivered, Noah had nothing to distract him from the box that lay before him. He bit down on his bottom lip, staring at the box as though that would somehow tell him who had sent it.

"*No*-ah!" Rachel practically bounced on her barstool, leaning forward so that her ample breasts bunched up against the side of the bar. "I'm dying here!"

Noah glanced around. Only the three of them were at the bar. There were customers at two of the tables on the other side of the large room. They couldn't possibly see, even if they might be interested. Only Juan and Eddie were in the kitchen and they weren't allowed to come out front. The rest of the wait staff were busy or out of sight. Mr. Cortez, the owner, wouldn't be in until much later.

With shaking hands, Noah reached for the box.

The nine previous gifts had come in similar gift boxes, wrapped in gold foil and a tied red velvet ribbon. The first few gifts had been candy. Lemon drops and fruit sours, a gourmet kind he'd never before heard of. He'd been tickled to find that his mysterious gift giver knew of his preference for tart sweets. Then there had come the trendy green newsboy cap, then the yellow silk shirt, then the studded denim jacket. All very cool gifts from someone who knew his taste in clothing. Then had

9

come the wrist cuffs. Hand-crafted leather with an intricate design hammered into them. It was Kenneth who'd pointed out that the three big D-rings and the soft layer of fur inside made them exquisite bondage cuffs. Noah had scoffed and worn them as jewelry the following night when he'd gone clubbing. Next came a set of moonstone studs for his ears. Then had come the nipple chain. That one he couldn't deny was both very personal and very sexual. Also very beautiful. The fact that it had hooks for his nipple rings instead of clamps for unpierced nipples meant that the unknown gift giver had, at the very least, seen Noah's bare chest. Unfortunately, that didn't narrow the playing field *too* far since Noah had been known to go clubbing in vests with no shirt.

They had decided when the denim jacket appeared that the gift giver was a man. The fact that he obviously knew Noah and his preferences said that he had to know Noah was gay. A woman, they speculated, would surely have given up.

Setting the paper and ribbon on the narrow counter on his side of the bar, Noah lifted the lid and parted the tissue paper. A folded vellum note was always set just on top of whatever gift was inside. Lifting it away, his eyes widened. There was a thick chain that looked to be either white gold or platinum lying on a padding of faux black velvet.

"Is that a padlock?" Rachel whispered, brown eyes wide in surprise as she pointed at the gold lock that looped through one end of the chain like a charm. A stylized 'N' was engraved on the lock.

"Yes it is." Noah fingered the little ring with two tiny keys that lay beside it.

"Why would he give you a chain with a padlock?"

Noah looked up and met Kenneth's knowing gaze. They saw this thing all the time at some of the clubs they visited. "Because," Kenneth said, looking at Noah and not at the chain, "he wants to own Noah."

"'Own?'"

10

Ties That Bind

Kenneth nodded. He blinked his gaze away from Noah and looked at Rachel. "It's a collar."

"What? Like a dog?"

Kenneth laughed, reaching over to squeeze Rachel's shoulder. "Oh, my dear, you are so naïve."

"What?" Not at all offended, Rachel leaned in to him. "How'm I supposed to know these things if you don't *tell* me?"

While Rachel interrogated Kenneth, Noah unfolded the note and read it:

Noah,

Don't put this on. I want you to have it, but I want to be the one to put it around your neck. And that I won't do until you ask for it. Since that can't happen unless we meet, it's time to do just that.

Rachel and Kenneth abruptly stopped talking when Noah caught his breath, but he read on.

6:00PM tomorrow evening at the Castle Inn. Room 225. A keycard is in the box.

I would appreciate it if you wore the nipple chain.

Yours,

Me

Noah pinched the black, faux velvet lining the box and lifted it, revealing a hotel keycard.

"What's that?" Rachel squealed.

Kenneth plucked the note from his fingers. Rachel leaned on his arm as they both read it.

Noah stared at the keycard, his heart beating wildly.

"Hey," Rachel cried. "How did he know you'd be off before six tomorrow?"

* * * * *

With the gift box and its contents clutched to his heart, Noah left the bar and headed toward the employee break/locker room. He hurried through the kitchen, avoiding Juan and Eddie and kept his head down so none of the wait staff would stop him. He raised his head when he reached the break room and almost failed to hold back a startled shout.

Richard Maeda, the other bartender due to take over for Noah, stood beside the lockers with his back to Noah and his shirt off. The tight embroidered pants that they were made to wear hugged one of the finest asses Noah had ever seen in his life, and the bare expanse of creamy tan skin over mouth-watering muscles was enough to make Noah want to fall to his knees in worship.

As it was, he did stumble, catching himself on the door frame.

Hearing him, Richard turned. "Hey, Noah," he smiled.

The view from the front was just as heart-stopping. Perfect muscles with the healthy start of a six-pack and not a bit of chest hair. Not that Noah minded chest hair, but to see Richard without was a marvel. Noah realized that he'd never seen Richard without his shirt before, although he'd fantasized about it many, *many* times. With short black hair spiked at the top and those vaguely Japanese features, he was gorgeous, and Noah wasn't the only one to think so. If he had to name someone who he *wished* was his mysterious gift giver, it would be this man. It really was too bad he was straight.

Noah took a breath and balanced on his feet. "Hey."

"Sorry I'm late."

Nodding, Noah hurried to the bench that stood before the small bank of lockers. "Brad's covering until you're ready."

Richard slipped into a white tank undershirt as Noah set the box down before turning to the lockers.

Richard sat, straddling the narrow bench. Noah did *not* notice the very nice bulge in those tight pants as Richard tucked in the shirt. "Hey, is this from the mystery man?"

Noah tried to watch him out of the corner of his eye as he spun the combination of his lock. "Yeah."

Richard picked it up and removed the lid. He knew about the other gifts—*all* the other gifts, unlike some whom Noah had only told about the candy and clothing. Noah had let him know mainly to see his reaction. Hoping, in a small part of his heart, that Richard would spill the beans and admit he was the mystery man. It was a small hope but Noah was helpless to quash it.

Richard held up the chain by the padlock and whistled. "Damn."

Noah opened the locker then sat down to remove his slip-on ankle boots. "Yeah."

"You *do* know what this is, don't you?"

Noah gave him a teasing glance. "Do you?"

"This is an *ownership* collar." Seeing Noah's raised brow, he flushed, dropping the collar back into the box. "Hey, I get around."

"In*deed*!"

"Fuck you."

"Any time."

Richard laughed, putting down the box. Like Mitch, he found being hit on by gay men flattering rather than offensive. Unfortunately, it didn't float his boat.

Richard stood back up and pulled his embroidered shirt from a hanger within his locker. "So are you freaked yet?"

"Some," Noah admitted, standing to set his boots on the top shelf of his locker.

Richard snorted. "I don't blame you. Hot little number like you, it's no wonder some guy wants to own you. I'm surprised it hasn't happened before."

His leather oxfords in hand, Noah sat hard on the bench, gaping up at Richard.

In the midst of buttoning his shirt, Richard gave him a blank look. "What?"

"What did you just say?"

Richard smiled, flushing just a little around the ears exposed by the short cut of his thick black hair. "Oh come on, man. I may prefer girls, but I'd have to be blind not to know you're a looker."

Noah grinned. He'd never known Richard found him attractive. It made his heart swell and his hope that Richard was just leading him on and really was the mystery man grew. He batted his eyes coyly. "Why thank you, sir."

Richard laughed. "Don't start."

"What's the matter, big boy? Afraid I might convert you?"

He snorted, starting to tuck in his shirt. "Hardly. But even if you could—" he tipped his chin toward the box lying on the bench, "—your mysterious lover might have issues."

Noah stared up at the box, his shoes still sitting in his lap. Was Richard that good an actor? Could he be the mystery man and still give such a convincing act? Unfortunately, Noah suspected not.

"Maybe you should go to the police."

Lost in his own thoughts, it took a moment for Richard's sentence to register. "What?" He saw Richard's concerned look and frowned. "No! Why?"

"Look at what he's given you."

"They're just gifts."

"Come on, man, you're not that naïve. That chain's a collar. This guy could be a stalker."

Noah blinked, then bent to set his shoes on the floor before him. "No. I'm not. I'm still not calling the police."

"You're turned on, aren't you?"

Noah didn't answer until he finished putting on his shoes. "I'm intrigued," he admitted slowly.

"You ever going to meet the mystery man?"

Instead of answering, Noah plucked the folded note from the box and handed it to Richard.

Richard whistled again after reading it. "Well hot damn." He handed it back, smiling again. "And just a few days before Valentine's Day. How romantic."

Noah stared at him in surprise, neglecting to take back the

vellum paper.

Richard grinned, setting the paper on the bench. "Didn't realize what the date was?" He stood and glanced at the mirror beside the lockers, smoothing a hand over the buttoned front of his shirt.

"No. I didn't."

Richard grinned at him. "I'll betcha it occurred to him."

* * * * *

Hands shaking, Noah inserted the key card and pushed into the room. It was a standard hotel suite with a sitting room, a bedroom and a bathroom off the bedroom. In the sitting room, the low table that usually would sit before the couch had been pushed up against the air/heater unit underneath the window on the far wall. The curtains were drawn and one lit lamp provided illumination. A chair that clearly did not match any other furniture in the sitting room sat square in the middle of the empty space. It was almost plain, but not quite, a well made wooden ladder back with thick, sturdy legs and arms. The seat was wide and thinly padded with shiny leather.

Quickly turning on the light in the bedroom to chase away the shadows, Noah found it empty with the bed neatly made. He was alone in the suite.

On the seat of the chair was a gold wrapped box.

Noah dropped the keycard, his wallet and keys on the shelf of the cabinet that held the coffee maker and supplies. Wiping sweaty palms on his slacks, he approached the chair. The box was maybe eight inches square and half again as deep with an easy lift lid. Biting his lip, Noah lifted the lid and parted the tissue paper.

Underneath the folded note was a wrapped bar of soap, a black silk scarf, folded black silk pajama bottoms, four small votive candles in glass cups, a box of matches, a small bottle of lube and a four inch red jelly butt plug. The last was still in plastic with a picture of a cute guy clearly in orgiastic heaven. The soap and candles smelled strongly of lemon.

15

Ties That Bind

Once he'd identified the contents of the box, Noah unfolded the note:

Noah,
I'd love to smell the lemon soap on your gorgeous skin when I arrive at 7:00PM sharp. Light the candles around the room and turn off the rest of the lights.
When I walk in, I want to see you sitting on this chair wearing the pajamas with the plug in your ass. The blindfold is to be on, so that you can't see. I will check.
If you're not wearing the blindfold when I walk in, game over.
Yours,
Me

Noah set down the note and held the scarf in his hands, twisting it so that his wrists were momentarily pinned. He brought the fabric to his nose, hoping to catch a whiff of the man who had given it. Nothing.

He closed his eyes, hearing the warnings echo through his head. Richard was not the only one to point out how dangerous this was. All of his friends would flip to know what had been demanded in the note, let alone that Noah was considering complying. Did he dare do this?

He opened his eyes and looked down, focusing on the butt plug. Every note from the mystery man had been short but solicitous. Gifts were given with Noah's likes in mind. Even if the man was a stalker, it didn't seem likely that he was a dangerous one.

And chances like this did not occur to everyone and certainly never happened more than once in a lifetime.

He smiled. Yes, he did dare.

Plucking the soap out of the box, he took it to the bathroom. A glance at the clock told him he had almost an hour to get ready. He'd already taken a shower before coming, but clearly the lemon-scented soap had some significance to the man. Or the man knew that citrus scents were his favorite.

He couldn't stop grinning, watching himself as he pulled his straight hair out of the tail at the nape of his neck. Deftly, he used the hair band to twist it all on top of his head. He toed out of his shoes and got out of his slacks, socks and underwear. The nipple chains dangled deliciously across his chest as he unbuttoned the yellow silk shirt. Dropping the shirt atop the rest of his clothing, he laughed at his half erect cock and gave it a fond stroke. "Soon, I hope," he promised it.

He took his time with the shower, letting the hot water ease some of the nervous tension from his muscles. The soap filled the steam with its tart scent as he laved it over his skin.

He was getting hard now, thinking of what might happen. Why must he be blindfolded? What did the mystery man have in mind? He considered jerking off. After all, his anonymous admirer hadn't told him *not* to. But he refrained. He didn't feel like having his own hands tonight, at least not at his own direction. Besides, Noah loved the sense of anticipation.

Out of the shower, he dried himself and used the hotel hair dryer. He suspected the new little hairbrush on the counter was from his secret admirer and used it until his hair practically floated in a yellow-white cloud about his head. Liking how it turned out, he decided to leave it down. Satisfied, he gathered his clothes and returned to the bedroom to lay them on the luggage rack to the far side of the bed. After turning out the lamp, he returned to the main room. The chair beckoned to him and he spent a moment sliding his fingers along the smooth varnish of the back and arm. Experimenting, he pushed at the back and found that the chair was heavy. Delicious ideas of why this was so rolled through Noah's mind.

Whistling to himself, he set the four candles in the four corners of the room and lit them before turning out off the lamp. Immediately a close, romantic feeling settled over him, the shadows around the room subduing the colors of the furniture and splashy artwork on the pale green walls.

Ties That Bind

He picked up the lube and the plug. He glanced at the couch and discarded that as the place to sit to do this. So, instead, he stood by the chair and set one foot on the seat. He poured lube over the plug and smeared it on, then held onto the back of the chair with one hand as he used the other to tease himself. He'd done this before. He loved butt plugs and had a small collection of his own in various shapes and sizes. On a lonely night, they served as an excellent mode of stimulation, and on a not-so-lonely night...well, new lovers usually got a kick out of finding a plug in the ass they intended to fuck. He eased the pointed end of the plug into his hole, relaxing and pushing out as the toy stretched him. He couldn't help a groan, or resist the urge to rub the toy in and out a few times. His dick nodded in appreciation of the pleasure that zinged through him.

A quick trip to the bathroom for a small towel to dry his hands then he was back to shake out the pajama pants and put them on. The silk felt deliciously decadent against his freshly washed skin, not to mention his freshly shaved crotch. Would his soon-to-be lover approve? Too late to worry about that now.

Awash in the warm citrus scent from the candles and his own skin, Noah glanced at the clock. Ten minutes until seven.

Obeying an urge, he went ahead and sat down. He wiggled his ass to jostle the plug, enjoying the rush of pleasure as it rubbed his gland. He lifted the black silk scarf to his eyes. Slowly, drawing out the moment for himself, he tied the scarf around his eyes. The urge to leave peeking room was strong, but he didn't give in to it. He had a feeling that his unknown lover *would* check and just might leave if he disobeyed. He wasn't going to take the chance of losing the man now that he was so close. Not before at least one encounter to give him some feel of who he was. Once the scarf was tied, Noah arranged his hair over it, then sat back in the chair. He placed his heels against the front legs and settled his forearms on the arms.

And waited.

Ties That Bind

The tension was amazing. He almost gave in and removed the scarf a few times just to check the time. But he resisted. He forced himself to sit still. It made him abnormally aware of himself. The smell of his skin. The waft of heated air on his skin, making his nipples pucker. The black silk warming against his thighs and teasing his hard cock. The firm jelly inside his ass, pressing that spot that would keep him erect and aware.

He heard footsteps in the hallway outside the room and hope surged, only to dwindle to disappointment when the walking continued past the door.

How much time was left?

More footsteps. This time they stopped. The lock clicked and beeped.

The door opened.

Noah damn near came at the sound. He clutched the arms of the chair, willing his body to relax. A tiny voice at the back of his head screamed that this could be dangerous, but it was easily ignored in the flood of lust surging through his bloodstream.

Soft footsteps came close as the door quietly snicked shut. Fabric whooshed and sounded like it fell on the couch. A coat? His hyper-aware hearing monitored the sound of footsteps stopping. Was he imagining that he felt the heat of the man's legs right in front of his knees?

The touch of fingertips on his jaw made him jump.

"Shhhh."

Noah swallowed. He tilted his head into the hand, which turned to fully cup his jaw. The thumb stroked the dip between his chin and lower lip. The hand was large and very clearly male.

The man's other hand tested the edges of the scarf at Noah's eyes. Noah's heart beat with pride on hearing a deep hum of approval. Then the fingers circled the rim of his ear, pinched his earlobe above the hoop that pierced it, and then trailed down his neck. The one hand braced on his bare shoulder while the other tilted his face up.

Noah's mouth opened on an inaudible sigh as he smelled

deep, woodsy cologne nearing him. He felt breath on his lips and licked them instinctively.

Lips brushed his, instantly pulling away when he tried to push into the kiss.

He whimpered.

The hand at his jaw slipped down to curve around the front of his neck, palm on his Adam's apple, not squeezing, just holding.

Getting the picture, Noah sat still and merely accepted the kiss bestowed upon him. Soft. Exploring. A tongue darted out to trace his lip before delving between his teeth. He moaned, opening up as the hand on his neck kept him still. He gripped the armrests tighter, wanting to reach up but thinking that might not be acceptable.

Finally, the lips pulled back. The hand at his neck mirrored the other on his shoulder, then both hands slid down his arms until they found his wrists. He realized to be in that position, the other man must be kneeling between his knees. Oh God, he wanted to see that!

The hands left him and there was more rustling of fabric. Then something soft brushed his left wrist. He frowned. Strong hands wafted silk over his arm until he realized it was another scarf, probably a match to the one about his eyes. Deft hands wrapped the scarf loosely about his wrist and the armrest of the chair. He felt the cinch of a simple tie. Fingers grabbed his arm and pulled it up, showing him that he could loosen the scarf if he wanted to.

"Hmmm?"

He groaned. They weren't going to talk, obviously, and he was going to be tied. Tied in such a manner that he could get away if he wanted to. He'd never let a lover tie him before. Never trusted anyone enough. Why did everything in his being want him to trust now?

Biting his lip, he nodded.

With a grunt of assent, the man tied another scarf around

his other wrist. Then the hands gripped his forearms and he felt the weight as the man leaned forward.

A cry tore from his throat when lips pressed his clavicle. Not being able to see turned his other senses into overdrive, and not being able to reach out made him lean into the touch. The man inhaled deeply and let out the breath with a sigh, probably enjoying the lemon scent on Noah's skin. Noah, meanwhile, was dizzy from the lemon in the air and the woodsy scent of the man who now laved attention on his chest. Tongue, lips and teeth explored Noah's shoulders and chest, gradually working toward one nipple. Finally, the wet tip of the tongue touched the achingly sensitive nub, jostling both the ring and chain, and Noah had to cry and arch at the lightning zing to his testicles. Lips closed around nipple and jewelry and suction threatened to pull Noah's beating heart out of his body.

Noah had to make a conscious effort to keep his hands on the armrests. He wished the man had tied him for real instead of forcing him to remember to keep his hands put. The scarves helped, but he had to be careful not to let them get too loose. The attention to his nipple and the rub of the plug in his ass as he writhed wrecked havoc on his concentration.

After feasting on the one nipple, the man switched to the other. As lips and tongue tortured, fingers reached up to tug the chain.

Noah nearly crawled out of the chair. He cried out, head thumping against the back of the chair.

The man stopped. Strong hands gripped Noah's waist, pulling him forward. He whimpered when his chest came up against what felt like a dress shirt, warm from the firm body within. He'd wanted to feel bare flesh. Arms slid around him and a mouth took his again. This time, he was allowed to kiss back hungrily, tilting his head so his unknown lover could take him more deeply. The man was big, his arms easily circling Noah's slighter body. A distant thought suggested he should be worried, but he couldn't bother with it.

Ties That Bind

One hand slipped into the back of the pajama pants. A finger slid in the well-lubricated crack. Parted Noah's cheeks. Checked to make sure the plug was there. Noah felt the smile on the lips that accepted his kiss. The finger at his ass tapped the plug, making him groan.

Moaning, Noah lost track of the kiss, his attention zeroing in on the jiggling toy in his ass. Lips suckled his parted lips as the fingers worked the toy.

"Please," Noah heard himself breathe. He was on fire, trembling with need.

With one pressing kiss and a final push on the toy, the man released him.

"No!" Noah cried.

A hand on his head gently patted him as the man stood. "Shhh," said the voice.

Head falling forward, Noah took a few deep breaths. He was going to come! If he let himself, he could. But he didn't want this to end. He had to control himself.

The unmistakable sound of a zipper made his head shoot up.

The hand gripped his jaw again. The thumb pressed on his chin, opening his mouth. Ever hopeful, Noah opened up.

Something firm tapped his lip. He experimented with his tongue and groaned loudly to taste salty precum. He tipped his head forward and the hand covered his ear as he inhaled a hard, velvety cock shot through with rigid veins. The smell of denim, Irish Spring soap and musky male assaulted him as he pressed for more. He wanted to reach up and wrap his hand around the shaft, but he was a good boy and kept his hands where they were. Moaning, he pulled back up the shaft, laving the underside of the cock with his tongue. It was large and thick enough that he couldn't work the entire thing into his mouth. That made him squirm. He loved large men. He relished the gasp he heard above him. His need for this cock would have surprised him if he allowed himself to think. But he didn't allow that. He dove forward, swallowing as much of that steely rod as he possibly could. He relaxed his throat and let it block his airway. He would have let it plunge down into his stomach if he could have.

A hiss above him and now both hands were on his head. They eased his mouth back, letting his lips slide in the saliva that now coated the hot skin. Then they pulled him forward. Noah relaxed and let his unknown lover guide him, making mental notes as best he could. He wanted to remember the spots that produced those glorious groans or those sharp hisses. He expected to taste this cock again. He was also pretty certain that he'd never had it in his mouth before.

One hand stilled his head and the other pulled the cock out of his mouth. He whimpered, muffled when the cock's head was smeared over his lips. He let his mouth go slack, tilting his head back, letting the man above him slap that tasty dick on his lips and cheek. He moaned, nipping at the head when it pierced his mouth again and whimpering when it was taken away. Sucking cock wasn't new to him, but doing it blindfolded and effectively bound added a whole new dimension since he couldn't see what was coming. He had to trust this unknown man.

Trust.

With a groan, the man shoved into his mouth one last time and pulled out. Noah heard the telltale sound of a palm rapidly stroking wet dick. He whimpered, trying to press forward to recapture the cock, but a strong hand held him still. A grunt sounded just seconds before warm, wet spunk spattered Noah's face. He opened his mouth to catch what he could as more spurted onto his cheek and dripped down the side of his jaw. A satisfied sigh above him told him when the man was done. He felt that amazing glow that always followed making another man come, despite the fact that his own cock was screaming in protest.

Then the hands bracketed his head, tilting it up to accept a wet, possessive kiss. Without breaking the kiss, the man dropped to his knees. One hand descended to pull down the front of Noah's pajama pants, immediately wrapping around his cock. Noah screamed into the other's mouth, instinctively shoving into that hand. He wanted to draw out the moment and prolong it forever but couldn't. This man pulled his control out through his mouth and that hand—together with the plug spreading his clenching ass—yanked the orgasm up and out of him. He screamed again, feeling the warm spatter as his cum landed on the leg of the pajama pants.

The hand kept milking him gently and the mouth kept kissing him until he sank back against the back of the chair. The mouth pulled away, trailing up his cheek to his ear. "Don't move," murmured a voice, deep, dark and sexy.

Noah remained still when the man stood. Truthfully, he was shell shocked by the experience and wasn't sure he *could* move. Footsteps trailed away, accompanied by the sound of a zipper. Water sounded after a moment, placing the man in the bathroom.

Get up, Noah told himself. *Take off the blindfold.*

But he didn't. He stayed in the chair, gripping the arms, just as he'd been told. Warmth suffused his skin and he basked in it.

The man returned with a warm, wet washcloth. He used it to wipe cum from Noah's face and belly and even swiped at what had fallen on the pajamas. Once done, he knelt again, hands wrapping around the scarves at Noah's wrists.

"You're all right?" asked the voice right in his ear. Low. Whispering. Entirely unrecognizable. It could have been any of a thousand men.

"Yes."

Lips pressed the soft spot underneath his jaw. "Start counting. Don't move until you reach one hundred."

Noah jumped, some of the delicious lassitude draining from his skin. "What? You're leaving? No!"

Hands squeezed. "Game over?"

He stilled. Bit his lip. Underneath his immediate ire at his new lover leaving, a warm simmer of anticipation began. This was entirely new and different to him. If it was this good so far, would it be better if he continued to follow? "Will I see you again?"

"Yes." With a last lingering kiss for Noah's mouth, he stood. "Count. Aloud."

Sneering slightly, Noah obeyed. "One. Two. Three…"

He heard movement. Fabric rustling. In a moment, the door opened and eased closed.

Just get up. "Thirty six. Thirty seven…" *He's gone.* "Thirty eight. Thirty nine." *What if it was a test? What if he's standing there? Watching?* That thought made his skin tingle.

He made it to one hundred without any further sound. Removing the scarf, he found himself alone. "Damn." He slumped back in the chair, wiggling as the plug reminded him it was there.

The box was on the table.

Inside was a note and a keycard to another hotel.

Tomorrow night. 10:00PM. Bring the collar.
Yours,
Me

* * * * *

Noah quartered the lemon then lifted one juicy crescent to shove behind his lips. The sour bite shot that shudder that he loved through his neck and chest as his face squeezed up involuntarily.

"Freaks me out when you do that," Richard muttered.

Noah grinned around the lemon rind still held in his teeth.

Seeing this, Richard rolled his eyes and turned to deliver a margarita to a blonde lady who sat at the bar.

It was a slow time on a usually busy night. He and Richard didn't both need to be there, but since Mr. Cortez wasn't around, neither of them was going to give up a night's pay.

Noah finished the lemons and started on limes while Richard filled orders for two of the waiters. He'd just finished when the blonde and her date left to be seated.

"So," Richard turned his back to the bar, using a towel on a glass, "how'd it go last night?"

Noah glanced away, flushed. "It was okay."

Richard chuckled. "Just okay?"

Noah grinned. "More than okay."

"So who is he? Do you know him?"

Noah cleared his throat and stepped up to the bar, smiling broadly at the man who asked for Drambuie on ice.

Richard waited nicely as Noah filled the order, but didn't forget the question. "Well?"

"I don't know," Noah replied softly as he replaced the bottle of whiskey.

"Huh?"

"Well... I was blindfolded."

"Oh now this is getting interesting." Richard settled against the cabinet behind the bar, arms crossed, listening intently.

Sighing, Noah decided that he needed to talk to *some*one. Mitch's door had been closed when he'd gotten home the previous night and his roommate was gone to work by the time Noah got up. He hadn't seen Kenneth yet and since Richard was the first to ask, Richard was elected. "He, um," strangely, he couldn't look at Richard. Noah had *never* felt this bashful, but what he was saying felt so very personal, "he had me sit in a chair and blindfold myself before he showed up."

"Shit, Noah! That could have been dangerous."

"I know, I know. But it wasn't. It was..." He lifted his gaze to the neon clock above the bar, focus misty as his skin vividly recalled his mystery man's touch. "It was amazing."

"I didn't know you were into that kind of thing."

Noah blinked back into focus. "I didn't either. I've never done anything like that before."

"What would convince you to do it now with someone you don't know?"

Noah frowned, starting to rethink talking to Richard. He was not in the mood to hear what could have gone wrong with such a beautiful experience. "He's not dangerous. I know that now. Even when he tied my wrists…"

"He *what*?!"

"Would you shut *up*?" Eyes wide, Noah scanned the nearby tables. A few people looked up at Richard's outburst, but nothing too alarming. They all went back to their dinners. From across the room, he saw Rachel scowl their way. *Great.*

Wincing, Richard scanned the mostly full restaurant himself.

A wave of customers descended on them before they could continue their discussion. Noah filled orders with half a mind, the rest dwelling on Richard's reaction. No doubt in his mind now that Richard was *not* his mystery man. It had been a nice fantasy, but Noah was pretty sure Richard wasn't a good enough actor to fake that last outburst. Ah well, he didn't have any business hoping it was Richard in the first place.

Rachel placed an order for two drinks with Noah, hanging out at the bar as she waited. "What was that about?" she murmured.

Noah opened his mouth to answer, but Richard pressed up behind him, leaning toward Rachel. "He let him tie him up!" He hissed before turning to slide a wineglass into Noah's hand.

Noah glared at his back as he turned to pour a glass of Chablis.

Rachel squeaked, brown eyes wide. "What?"

Noah tutted at her. "Later."

"Oh you'd better *believe* later!" She spun her empty tray around on the end of the bar. "I'll have to go find Kenneth."

"No."

"You don't want him to know?"

Noah opened his mouth, then closed it. He said nothing as

27

he finished pouring her two drinks, then frowned at her as he set them on her tray. "I don't want to talk about it anymore."

She reached out to gently grasp his wrist, concern all over her pretty round face. "You okay?"

"I'm fine. Really. I just… it feels weird to talk about it."

But talking was destined. Business picked up for awhile so there were enough customers that Noah managed to fend Richard off until his shift was almost over. But then there was another lull. As the lone man sitting at the bar stood and dug through his pockets for his wallet, Noah saw Kenneth appear at the entrance to the restaurant. He made a beeline for the bar.

"Great," Noah muttered, recognizing the curiosity on his friend's face.

"Rachel said I had to come talk to you about last night," Kenneth said, taking a seat as the customer set his money on the counter and left.

The restaurant crowd had thinned out considerably. It was close to the end of Noah's shift.

Noah sighed. "It's nothing."

Beside him, Richard snorted, folding his arms on the bar and leaning on them. He focused on Kenneth. "Noah let him tie him up."

Kenneth's hazel eyes blinked repeatedly and he dramatically raised a hand to his throat. "Oh my."

Noah rolled his eyes. "Oh please."

"Noah, this is momentous!"

"No, it's not."

"Yes, it is. Unless there is something you've never told me, you've never been tied up before."

"He didn't really tie me up."

"That's what you told me," Richard proclaimed.

"There was a box waiting for me when I got there." Noah moved closer to them so he could speak in a lower voice. "It had a blindfold in it." He chose not to mention the other contents. "And there was this chair set in the middle of the room. The note said to put on the blindfold and sit there."

They watched him, rapt.

He went on. "So I did. When he got there, he *loosely*—" he gave Richard a pointed look, "—tied my wrists to the arms of the chair. I could have freed my hands at any time."

Richard looked only slightly mollified.

"And?" Kenneth prompted, interest raising his dark sculpted brows.

"*And* none of your business." Noah was so *not* going to share the rest of his night with anyone.

"Well, well, Noah must be feeling something profound if he doesn't want to share." Kenneth spoke of him in the third person, but looked straight at him.

"Don't encourage him," Richard groused.

Kenneth waved a lazily placating hand. "Oh Richard, I seriously doubt that Noah's mystery man is out to harm Noah in any way. Nothing he's said or done has been overtly dangerous."

Richard scowled at him. "Except for not making himself known."

Kenneth smiled, smoothing his tie. "Yes, well, that seems to have worked in his favor, hasn't it? I've never seen Noah so intrigued by a man. That may just be the key to holding Noah's interest."

It was Noah's turn to scowl. "What?"

Kenneth cocked his head to the side. "I've never seen you so taken with anyone, let alone someone you don't even know. You're beside yourself. And you haven't even mentioned clubbing in the past week or so. I'd say that was rather telling."

Noah blinked. Kenneth was right. Normally, he'd be eager to go out. But he didn't *want* to go clubbing. That thought surprised the scowl off his face.

Kenneth chuckled. "You're all tied in knots." He leaned forward, hazel eyes at half mast. "I wish your mystery man could see you now."

Ties That Bind

Confused by both his thoughts as well as Kenneth's words, Noah fidgeted. A check of the clock was his relief. "I've got to go."

Kenneth placed his elbows on the bar and lifted his laced fingers so that he could prop his chin on them. He batted his eyelashes ridiculously at Noah. "Do you need a ride?"

Noah grimaced, hearing the weak double meaning. "No." He briefly extended the scowl toward Richard, then left.

* * * * *

This time it was a single room at the hotel. A big, closed cabinet presumably held a television, and a small table with two chairs occupied the far corner by the window, but the majority of the space was taken up by the king-sized bed. All of the hotel's bedding had been removed and was out of sight, replaced by a shimmery yellow satin fitted sheet. Just the fitted sheet, no top sheet.

Noah stood at the foot of the bed and smiled over the thudding of his heart. Draped across the huge, plump pillows—definitely *not* hotel issue—were two black nylon straps, each with a handle at the end. He could easily tell that the two ends were part of a whole, the sturdy tether draped behind the solid wood headboard. The remainder of his presents lay in front of him, without the wrapped box this time. Another butt plug still in its commercial plastic, a folded black scarf, a bar of the lemon soap and a small gold band were all arranged on the mattress above the familiar folded vellum paper. He picked up the band to see if he could figure it out, but once he saw it he recognized it. He'd never worn a penis crown himself, but he'd been with men who had. The band of gold was made to fit right under the head of his cock and was supposed to make the tip a lot more sensitive. His belly quivered at the thought of wearing it.

Palming the jewelry, he picked up the paper. A small scrap of what looked like copy paper fell out and drifted back onto the mattress, but first he read the letter:

Ties That Bind

Noah,

At 11:00PM. I expect to find you showered and dry, lying on the bed with the blindfold on. The leather straps on the pillows are for you to hold onto. I wouldn't bind you until we both agree, but we can pretend for tonight and see how we like it.

The gold band is a penis crown. Enclosed are instructions for putting it on.

Leave the collar on the nightstand.

As for the plug, I leave that up to you. Wear it if you will. If you don't, I'm going to fuck you.

Wearing everything except the blindfold is negotiable. If you don't wear the blindfold, game over.

Yours,

Me

Noah mused over the line about the plug. He glanced up at the nightstand to where a new bottle of lube and five or six condoms lay scattered. Presumably, his mystery lover planned to use them.

He dropped the letter and crown onto the bed as he toed out of his shoes. Pulling the chain collar from his pocket, he set it beside the lube and condoms. He undressed quickly, draping his clothing over the chair in the corner, then took the soap into the bathroom.

So his mystery lover was leaving the actual fucking choice to him. He rather appreciated that. He wondered if all this careful concern would continue once the blindfold came off. And *when* exactly would the blindfold come off? Tonight?

Once showered, he dried his hair then returned to the room, bringing one of the small white hand towels with him. He retrieved the votive candles from his pack and set them around the room, lighting them. Once the mood was set, he crawled onto the bed and sat in the middle. He slipped on the penis crown and immediately liked it. Looked very classy. Imagining his mysterious lover seeing it on him just made him harder.

Ties That Bind

He picked up the packaged butt plug. This one was black and ribbed. It would feel good, he knew. For a good ten minutes he considered it, watching the clock on the nightstand click from 9:45 to 9:52. But he tossed the package aside. Fucking was what he wanted tonight.

Mind made up, he reached for the lube and ripped off the plastic. He poured some onto the fingers of his right hand and knelt up on the bed to reach behind and prepare himself. He let himself enjoy his fingers, enjoying more the reason he felt it necessary to do this. Wouldn't his mystery lover be pleased that Noah was *really* ready for him?

After wiping his hands dry, he made sure he knew where the restraint handles lay, tied the scarf around his head and lay back to wait. The handles in the straps fell just short of uncomfortable, spreading his arms with a little bend for his elbows. He looped his hands through the straps so they were snug about his wrists, leaving him to grip the first part of the tether, the length of nylon. The straps themselves were slightly padded, clearly meant for this exact use.

Lying there blind and nearly bound, Noah was shocked at the surge of excitement that bubbled under his skin. His cock lengthened over his belly and he tortured himself by not reaching for it, pretending he was unable. A soft moan escaped his lips at the very thought.

If it was like this when he knew he could get away, what would it be like to *really* be bound? To not be able to get away? To be completely at another's mercy? There were two answers that sprang immediately to mind. With someone he could trust, it would be amazing. With someone he didn't, it would be impossible.

How much did he trust this unknown man? Was it really someone he knew? When would he find out?

Mind reeling, he was hardly aware that his lower body was softly writhing until he felt the pull on his wrists. He let his head sink back into the pillows, exposing it to the heated air. On his cock, the gold crown made him far too aware of his erection. He could even feel the little dribble of precum. Damn, he could almost come just from lying there!

The sound of the door opening only made it worse. He tried to stop his hips but only managed to subdue them to a tiny rocking.

Footsteps stopped at the far corner of the bed and there was no sound for a few minutes. *He's looking at me.* Did he like what he saw? A fission of unease speared through Noah's chest, realizing the very real possibility of danger. *Stupid, take off the blindfold. You don't know him. You don't know what he's going to do.* But he remained where he was, spellbound, hard as a rock, his hips still moving just that little bit to make the head of his cock rub his belly. With the crown on, the intensity of the feeling tried to distract him from listening to his soon-to-be lover.

Movement. Some low sounds and a sigh of fabric on skin that Noah chose to interpret as shoes and a shirt coming off. Then the mattress beside him dipped.

A tiny groan escaped his lips at just the knowledge of the other's closeness.

An appreciative sigh sounded just as a warm palm cupped his jaw, turning his face. Minty breath on his lips then the soft press of a mouth on his.

He opened beneath those lips, hungry for a deeper kiss than he was allowed. He tried to capture the tongue that swept his lips but the man evaded him, pulling back.

A chuckle in response to his frustrated whimper. He tugged at the strap handles as the man's hand slid from his jaw down his neck, then slowly explored his chest. Wicked fingers found his nipple rings and gently plucked, teasing.

"Please." The word escaped his lips by surprise.

He felt the hand on his chest tense, heard the sharp intake of breath. The bed adjusted and he felt the brush of an arm on his far side before the weight of a chest was braced low over his. That hot, wet mouth closed over nipple, ring and chain, sucking it all in.

Noah arched into that mouth, shoving his butt into the mattress and pulling at the strong straps with all his strength. He struggled with an orgasm that fought to escape his body, just managing to tame it.

Lips and tongue tormented him, playing with the ring in his nipple, dragging around the sensitive skin surrounding the disk of skin. With a final, playful tug of teeth on ring, the lips found their way to the other nipple to repeat the torment.

The rocking of Noah's hips increased and he stopped even trying to control the movement. "Please," he moaned. He was never this needy. Not so soon, at least. Not after such little actual touch. But he needed…

A warm, dry hand closed around the shaft of his dick.

"Yes!" he cried, nearly catapulting off the bed. "Oh please, yes." He was almost convinced that his death grip on the straps was all that prevented him from hitting the ceiling.

Above him, a moan. Teeth bit down into the meat of the muscle right above Noah's nipple as the hand on his cock squeezed its way up to just beneath the gold crown. A thumb swiped over the copious precum leaking from the tip.

Crying out, Noah's chest twisted toward his lover, his hips rocking away. He had no idea if his first instinct was to press closer or to escape. It didn't matter, since he couldn't escape. The strap bit into his wrist as he yanked. The headboard thumped the wall.

But the hand was steady on his shaft. Another movement of the large body beside him then lips closed around the head of Noah's cock.

"God yes!" Noah bent his knee, the better to shove his dick into the wet, welcome haven of that mouth.

A big hand closed over his hip, stilling him. A heavy chest pinned the other thigh to the bed, preventing much movement.

Pinned, arms restrained, Noah let out an agonized laugh to discover what he felt was delicious freedom. His main frustration stemmed from the fact that one of his legs was mostly free.

His lover's mouth sampled him like a rare delicacy. Lips, tongue and teeth played with the all-too-sensitive head, toying at the rim, exploring the gold band that hugged the pulsing shaft. Then, in response to one of Noah's impatient, aborted thrusts, the mouth slid down, tongue dragging over the vein underneath.

"Oh God, wait," Noah breathed, thrusting in defiance of his request. It was too much. "I'm going to…" He couldn't hold it back. His skin sizzled.

Suction. Glorious, beautiful suction as lips and tongue pulled up then slid down toward the base of his shaft while the tip of his erection scraped the back of that mouth.

He shouted, throwing his head back, shoving his hips against the immovable strength of the chest and hands pinning him. He came, his body exploding, the headboard above him thumping loudly.

A vague corner of his mind registered his lover's start of surprise, the grunt, the clumsy spill of cum from a throat that didn't quite swallow it all. *He hasn't done this much.* If ever. Unable to process it all, Noah subsided with a breathy whimper.

His lover lapped at him, licking up the cum he'd missed. Letting some dribble down over and under Noah's sensitive balls. A cum-wet finger tickled his anus.

Noah moaned, lifting his thigh to afford better access. Despite the mind-numbing orgasm that had just wrecked his body, he gladly invited penetration. When the finger just kept tickling, he pushed down, managing to impale himself on the tip.

Taking the hint, his lover pushed the finger in a little deeper, wiggling it. Lips pressed Noah's belly, lapping at his navel while that one finger pressed in and explored, a welcome invasion but not nearly enough.

The urge to remove his left hand from the strap and lower it onto where he knew his lover's back would be was nearly undeniable. Nearly. With that first surge of lust sated and the second surge building, he wanted to do a little exploring of his own. But judging from this entire experience, he knew he needed to keep his hands to himself until given permission to touch.

He hoped the permission came soon.

When the finger pulled out and the man sat up, he mewled a protest.

A warm chuckle. "Shhh." A wet hand stroked his belly before the man left the bed entirely. Noah listened to the soft susurrus of cloth against skin and decided that it was pants and any possible underwear coming off. At least, he hoped that was what he heard. He definitely recognized the rustle of plastic that had to be a condom packet tearing open.

"Won't you talk to me?" Noah asked, voice soft but the plea was there.

"Not yet," came the whispered response. If the room hadn't been so quiet, if he hadn't been so attuned to this other man, he doubted he'd have heard it. It certainly wasn't distinguishable as any particular voice.

"Soon?"

The mattress dipped down by his knees and a strong hand lifted his leg. "Soon."

Noah smiled. "Fucking now?"

Another chuckle as his ankle was placed on a warm, bare shoulder. Chest hair tickled the back of his calf. "Yes."

Two fingers pushed into him, well-lubed this time. He could have told his lover that such careful preparation wasn't necessary for him, but he chose to enjoy the attention. The fingers scissored inside him and a third was added. He squirmed, loving every second.

Then the fingers came out and the slick tip of that big cock he remembered from the previous night pushed at his hole. Knowing what he wanted and how to get it, Noah rocked his hips, forcing that cock a little bit deeper.

Ties That Bind

A hiss and a squeeze on his thigh stopped him. He gave his own hum of approval when his mysterious lover slowly pushed in a few more inches, finding no resistance, hopefully enjoying the hot confines of Noah's body. He paused when he was fully seated and Noah squirmed, the better to feel the friction within his body. Then when the man started to pull out, causing that glorious rub over Noah's gland, Noah lost his ability to keep quiet.

"Yeah," he cried, "fuck me. Shit, yes, please, oh please…"

Most lovers got off on his begging and this one was no exception. Begging incited groans and got hips to thrust harder. So Noah shamelessly begged and got fucked good and hard like he liked it. He yanked on the straps, writhing, creating as pretty a picture for the man pumping into him as he knew how to make. The knot of the scarf tied about his head drove into the back of his skull but he used it, letting the annoying throb melt into rocking lust as his body was jerked higher and higher toward the headboard by the heavy body between his legs.

Strong hands gripped beneath both of Noah's knees, pushing them back toward his shoulders, tilting his hips up. In that position, Noah couldn't move very much but it afforded his lover freedom to switch up the angle of his thrust. He took Noah fast, then slowed up, making sure Noah felt every inch of hard cock inside him. Noah cried, begging, telling this man how wonderful he felt, making sure his enjoyment was known.

The thrusts got ragged, harder. Fingers bit into Noah's legs. The cock inside him swelled. An agonized grunt preceded a tension in that big body as the man came inside Noah.

He collapsed forward, one arm braced on the mattress beside Noah. Utterly satiated, Noah waited, hoping to receive permission to remove the blindfold. He received a kiss instead. A long, possessive, exploratory kiss that drew out for many beautiful moments. The cock still inside Noah swelled and Noah whimpered in surprise as his lover started thrusting again.

He made an impatient sound and pushed back, pulling out.

Ties That Bind

Noah listened, delighted when the man surged over him and he heard the tearing of another condom packet. *Again?!* So soon?

"Oh you fucking *god* you!" he moaned.

Resheathed, that magical cock pushed back inside of Noah, then his lover was over him again, thrusting. He took Noah's mouth again, slow and overpowering, mating their tongues, thrusting steadily with his tongue, keeping in rhythm with his hips. Noah held onto the straps as rational thought melted out of his pores. His sense of time deteriorated. All that existed was the heated air, the hotter body braced over his and the scorching cock abusing his insides. His own cock swelled without his complete knowledge, made evident only when his lover reached down to palm it. The man's thumb teased the penis crown and Noah screamed into his mouth, coming in hot spurts all over his own belly. On a groaning sigh, his lover came as well.

Noah collapsed into the pillows, hands now hanging useless from the straps. His lover pushed away, staggering a little. He left the bed and Noah distantly listened to water running. *You'll take the blindfold off now,* Noah mused, fighting a yawn. *You'll take it off and I'll finally know who you are.*

Noah's eyes opened with a start. He lay on his back on the hotel bed, hands laid on his chest with a blanket draped over him. The candles were out and the only light came from around the corner in the bathroom.

He'd fallen asleep?

He sat up, tossing aside the blanket. He was still naked but —he glanced behind him—the black nylon strap from around the headboard was gone. The lube and condoms were gone. The penis crown sat on the nightstand beside his wallet and keys.

"Hello?" he called, throwing his legs over the side of the bed.

He stood, wobbling a little. His belly was clean, evidence

that someone had cleaned him up after sex. He rushed into the bathroom but found no one

"You left?!" he cried, his voice bouncing off the tan tiles.

Pissed, dismayed, he stormed back into the bedroom. A familiar vellum envelope lay atop his clothing on the table. He snatched it up and read:

Noah,
Tomorrow I'll make myself known. I'll give you back the collar and you can choose whether or not to accept it.
Yours,
Me

The collar. Noah turned to see that it was missing from the nightstand.

He looked back at the envelope. His lover had planned to leave him mysteriously all along.

* * * * *

"'Mornin'," Mitch greeted him, mouth half full of cereal. He sat in a tank top and sweats on the couch in the living room, watching his flat screen television.

Head still bleary from sleep, Noah grunted at him, shuffling into the kitchen. Thursdays were Mitch's late day. Was it Thursday? Did he care? No.

Listless, restless, Noah opened the refrigerator door and stood in the cold waft of air staring at the contents like something attractive would reach out and grab his balls.

One could only hope.

"Well happy Valentine's Day to you, sunshine," Mitch teased, appearing in the doorway of the kitchen.

Without turning toward him, Noah held up one hand in a middle finger salute.

Mitch laughed. "Who peed in your Cheerios?"

An exasperated sigh exploded from Noah's mouth. Pouting, he slammed the fridge door shut and turned to drop heavily onto one of the kitchen chairs. He let his forehead fall forward onto the arms he folded on the table.

A chair across the table squeaked under Mitch's weight and a bowl clicked on the tabletop. "Did last night not go well?"

"It was fine." He sighed, tilting his head back so his chin propped on his arms. He stared morosely at the pattern of gold and white in the fake granite tabletop. "It was fantastic."

"Wouldn't be able to tell from your reaction."

Noah stuck out his bottom lip. "I still don't know who it is."

"You don't?"

A flash of apprehension made Noah hesitate, remembering what happened when he spoke to Richard the day before. But this was *Mitch*. "I had on a blindfold."

"Dayum. Really?"

He peeked up at Mitch, relieved to see intrigue and not censure on Mitch's smiling face. That made him smile. "Yeah."

"How'd he get you to wear a blindfold?"

"It was in a box with one of those notes waiting for me."

"Both nights?"

"Yeah."

"Damn, I'm sorry I fell asleep before you got home both nights."

Noah frowned. "How'd you know I was out with him last night?"

"I assumed. You haven't gone out with anyone but Bob since the last few gifts appeared."

He squirmed to hear that another friend noted his lack of sociability lately. "True."

Mitch folded his arms on the tabletop, grinning. "So was the blindfold *all*?"

Noah felt the flush creeping up his neck as he stared at the rim of Mitch's bowl. "No."

"Do tell."

"He... kind of tied me up."

"'Kind of?'"

"The knots were loose. I could have gotten away." He didn't mention the tether with the handles.

"But you didn't."

Noah shook his head.

"I'm shocked." But Mitch looked more bemused than shocked, but then it took a lot to throw him, both mentally and physically. "I didn't think you were into that kind of thing."

Noah pushed up, sitting back in his chair. "I'm not. I wasn't."

"And now you are?"

He shrugged. "Seemed like a good idea at the time."

"Could have been dangerous." Mitch's tone was careful, unlike Richard's astonished surprise.

"It could have. But it wasn't."

"Sounds like you enjoyed it."

'Enjoyed' was far too tame a word, but he went ahead and nodded.

Mitch twisted an arm so he could rest his chin on the heel of his palm. Curly black hair crowded his left eye. "So? What happens now?"

"He says he'll make himself known to me today," Noah replied with a frown.

"You don't believe him?"

"I don't know. I don't know what that means."

Mitch chuckled. "Sounds like you'll find out. Pretty cool Valentine's present, I'd say."

"I guess." He stood and went to grab the box of cereal from the counter. "You going out tonight?"

Mitch laughed. "Planning on bringing your mystery man back here?"

Noah glared at him. "No. I'm just curious what *your* plans are. I don't recall you being on a lot of dates lately."

"I've been busy."

"Work?"

"Yeah." With a happy sigh and a big stretch, Mitch sat back. The little chair groaned under his weight as he settled with his hands laced over his belly. "But not tonight. I've got a hot date tonight, too."

Noah reached for a bowl from the cabinet. "Anyone I know?"

"Nope." Nothing new. Noah often didn't meet the women Mitch dated.

"You planning to bring her home tonight?" Noah teased.

"Nope. I've got a whole night of romance planned."

Noah smiled, pouring cereal. "Lucky lady."

"I hope she thinks so."

* * * * *

To say that Noah was on edge when he got to work was putting it mildly.

I'll make myself known. What the hell did that mean? Noah's wild imagination ranged from picturing every black car that approached on his walk from bus stop to bar was going to stop and men were going to jump out and kidnap him, to something as ordinary as a guy sitting down at the bar. He held his breath as each male patron sat down to order a drink. It made it worse that, since it was Valentine's Day, quite a few of the regulars who had expressed interest in him before came by specifically to say "hi."

He jumped when Richard bumped into him. Because of the occasion, they were again teamed together behind the bar until closing.

The taller man laughed, patting his shoulder. "Ease up, man."

He nodded, laughing.

A solemn older man in a dark brown suit hailed Noah from the end of the bar. *Oh please, not you*, he thought. Okay, he wasn't bad looking, but he wasn't gorgeous. It had just occurred to Noah last night that his mystery man might be ugly. Not that it should matter. It *didn't* matter. The man made his blood sing and had almost had him coming at the mere sound of his footsteps. He could look like the hunchback of Notre Dame, right?

But would it be so bad if he were good looking?

Brown suit just ordered a martini, though.

The dinner crowd started to wane. He and Richard spent more time chatting and less time filling drinks.

"You're off soon, aren't you?" Richard asked, setting freshly dried tumblers on the cabinet behind the bar.

Noah checked the neon clock above them. Quarter to eleven. Geez, he'd been on edge all day! "Yeah."

"So where's the mystery man?"

Noah cast his glance over the patrons seated at tables across the restaurant. Mostly in pairs. "Hell if I know."

"You think he's a no show?"

Noah shrugged.

"He's probably just waiting for the end of your shift."

Grimacing, Noah snatched up a rag and started wiping down the bar. "Maybe."

He was filling a drink order for one of the waiters when Kenneth and Mitch appeared at the bar.

He paused, frowning at his roommate. "What are you doing here?"

It was Kenneth who answered. "We came to see the mystery man reveal himself, of course."

Noah glanced at him, frowning. "Well, he's a no show."

Kenneth's grin got wider.

Rachel hurried up to his side, face alight with curiosity.

Noah's frown deepened. He was going to ask Kenneth what was up, but Mitch distracted him.

Eyes fixed on Noah's face, an oddly nervous grin slightly curving his lips. He was dressed up. Well, sorta. Where had that blue silk shirt come from? And since when did he wear shirts like that?

"What happened to your date?"

43

Instead of answering, Mitch reached into the pocket of his slacks—slacks, not jeans—and pulled a familiar, thick white gold chain from his pocket by the small padlock that looped through one end.

Time stopped. Noah gaped, eyes on the chain.

Mitch?!

Somewhere off to his right, he heard Rachel squeal. Kenneth and Richard were laughing. Noah couldn't be bothered to process what they were saying.

Scowling, he looked up at his friend's oddly closed face. "This isn't funny."

Mitch shook his head. "Not a joke."

Noah was trembling, but didn't realize it until he dropped a glass.

Richard caught it. "Hey, why don't you guys go to the locker room and talk? Your shift's almost done anyway."

Noah couldn't for the life of him take his eyes off Mitch. Out of the corner of his eye, he saw his friend wind the chain around his fist and stick the fist back into the pocket of his slacks. Slacks. *Nice* slacks. When did he buy those?

Why did it matter?

"Excellent idea," Kenneth proclaimed, rounding the end of the bar and lifting the partition so Noah could get out. "Better yet, why don't you go on up to the room Mitch reserved?"

Noah's eyebrows shot up to his hairline. "Room?" He managed to switch his gaze to Kenneth. There was too much air brushing his eyeballs, telling him that he had his eyes opened too wide. "How do you know about any room?"

A grin split Kenneth's wide face. "I've been an accomplice."

"You *rat*!" Rachel cried, swatting his arm.

He flinched, laughing.

Noah was going to cuss him out, but Mitch moved and thoughts of Kenneth vaporized. The big man circled the edge of the bar and lifted the pass through at the end of the bar. He looked at Noah, inviting him out. Other than the lack of his normal casual smile, he looked completely composed. Okay, a little tense, but otherwise composed.

Noah snapped his jaw shut and nodded. With effort, he closed his eyes and stalked past Mitch toward the back, trusting Mitch to follow.

Mitch had *better* follow.

There was a door that led into a back corner of the hotel's main lobby, right near the elevators. Noah led the way through it and punched the button. His mind and heart were a jumble of emotions, confusion lacing them all together. He didn't look at Mitch as they entered the elevator and Mitch didn't speak as he hit the button for the third floor. By mutual consent, they said nothing until Mitch had led them to room 315.

Noah stalked to the king-sized bed, noting that the sheets had been replaced with the lemon satin but the restraint straps were missing. He spun to face Mitch as the taller man braced his arms on either wall of the short narrow hall between front door and bed. It made him look big, intimidating. He always looked gorgeous.

Is this for real?

"You're not gay," Noah spat.

That made Mitch smile. "I'm not?"

"No. You've been dating girls as long as I've known you."

"Bisexual?"

"And you never told me?"

Steel-gray eyes gleamed in the light of the lamp. "I've only ever met one man I wanted to sleep with." The heated look on Mitch's face clearly identified Noah as that man.

"Me?"

Slowly, Mitch nodded.

"How the hell am I supposed to believe *that?*"

The teasing smile was gone, replaced with all sincerity. "I'm here to do anything I have to do to convince you."

Noah stumbled back against the table in the corner. His

pulse thudded in his throat, strangling him. He reached down to clutch the table with desperate fingers, bracing his butt between them. "Why?"

Mitch raised an eyebrow. Noah noted that his raven hair was especially glossy and gorgeous tonight, curling around his strong square face. Had he used mousse in his hair? He only did that when he was out to impress. "Why didn't I tell you?"

Noah reeled in his errant thoughts, needing to concentrate on Mitch's words and not his mouth-watering appearance. "That's a good start."

Mitch smiled, making Noah's heart flip. He kept those gray eyes locked on Noah's face. "I didn't realize it for years. Not until we moved out of the dorms and into the apartment. Took me awhile to figure out why I was pissed that you were dating."

"Pissed?"

"Yeah. I felt a lot better when you were home with me. I went out to the clubs with you when it was really bad and I did all I could to keep everyone away from you."

Noah frowned. Searching his memory, he decided that he probably hadn't gotten lucky many of the nights that Mitch had joined him. He couldn't recall minding much.

"Why the gifts?"

Mitch's smile grew. "I thought it'd turn you on."

Noah swallowed in a dry throat.

"All those guys you dated and not one of them ever really took the time to work you, to feed that inner romantic." Mitch grinned, pushing from the wall to stand straight. "But I've seen enough chick flicks with you to know that's what you like."

"What I…?"

"That's your kink, isn't it?" Mitch took a step toward him, eyes gone dark and seductive, shoulders rolling, looking every inch the predator. "To be swept off your feet like some romance heroine?"

Mitch *would* mention that. So far as Noah knew, Mitch was the only person who knew he liked to read romance novels.

46

Ties That Bind

Frowning, Noah raised a finger when Mitch was just a yard away, stopping him. "Bondage is not my kink."

"No?"

Noah shuddered at the suggestive look. "It wasn't."

"Okay. That was *my* kink. When I figured out how I felt, I couldn't get the image out of my head of tying you down. It just kind of grew from there."

Noah shuddered again, blinking slowly, back to clutching the table as Mitch closed the distance between them. Was it getting stuffy in the room?

"I've watched you go from guy to guy the entire time I've known you. You've never settled down once." Mitch pulled the chain from his pocket and held it up in front of Noah with both hands, the gold glinting in the light of the single lamp behind Noah. "I want to tie you up and tie you to me. Forever."

Noah swallowed, lost in a heated, steely gray gaze. "Damn," he breathed. This was so very much more than he'd dreamed. Was this really *Mitch*?

Mitch smiled. Slowly, he lifted the chain up and over Noah's head. The thick links settled around the back of Noah's loose hair, drawing it close against his neck. Mitch brought the two ends of the chain together at the base of his throat in front. Noah didn't need to see to feel the padlock slip through both ends, but he didn't hear the click of the lock. Mitch reached down to pry one of Noah's hands from the edge of the table and brought it up so he could confirm that the lock was looped through the chain but remained unlocked.

Mitch gently lifted Noah's hair from under the chain, allowing the metal to settle against his heated skin. He kept his fingers wound in the straight blond strands as he cupped Noah's jaw. "I love you, Noah," Mitch breathed against his temple, brushing his lips there. "Be mine."

Noah's fingers clenched around the chain and lock. He swayed, suddenly short of breath. "L-love?" Certainly he'd fantasized about his roommate before. He couldn't help it.

47

Mitch was wonderful and gorgeous, the best of friends. He'd never allowed himself to hope for anything more. Certainly not *this*.

Warmth gusted over his cheek. Mitch's hands slid from his hair then closed gently over the ends of his shoulders. "Yes." The scent of Mitch and clean soap surrounded him, devoid of the woodsy cologne from the previous two nights, which had no doubt been used to throw him off.

"Be sure," he warned, tipping his head back to allow those soft lips access to his throat. "Because if we do this, it means no more girls. I won't share you."

Mitch chuckled, nipping the side of Noah's throat. How had Noah not recognized the chuckle before? "Deal. And no other men." How surreal to hear Mitch's voice against his throat. 'Hear against his throat?' Oh God, he was losing it!

"Just us."

"Just us."

"Your mom'll flip."

That made Mitch laugh. Strong arms surrounded Noah, gathering him flush against the man's broad chest. "She loves you. She'll get over it real quick."

Tentatively, Noah lifted his free arm to surround Mitch's waist. Hard muscle underneath cool blue silk. As he let his mind freely think about this, it made perfect sense. Who knew him better than Mitch? Who would have thought of the lemon candy or the clothing? Who was always there when he needed someone? All answers were Mitch. All roads led back to Mitch. He bent his neck, tucking his forehead into the bend of Mitch's throat. It felt right. Good. "Are you sure about this?"

Soothing hands slid over his back. "Absolutely sure."

Fingers still clutching the open padlock, Noah turned his head seeking Mitch's lips. He found smoothly shaven jaw and square chin as Mitch turned to let their mouths come together. It was the sweetest of kisses, a tentative exploration to go with newly voiced feelings. Letting go of the chain for now, Noah turned his hand so he could cup Mitch's neck, stealing around toward the back of his head, slipping fingers into the glorious silk of his hair.

Mitch took that as a sign to deepen the kiss. One hand sank into the hair just above the nape of Noah's neck and pulled his head back, angling him back for deeper exploration. Noah opened willingly, sucking in the tongue that delved deep. He recognized the possession as the same kiss from the previous two nights. *Mitch*. His fingers dug into the heated silk over Mitch's back, hugging him closer.

Mitch groaned. He used the hand in Noah's hair to pull Noah out of the kiss, bending him backwards over the table until he teetered precariously on the edge. Only Mitch's hold kept him steady as his feet left the floor. "God, you're beautiful," Mitch whispered over the side of his jaw. "I knew you were, but when I walked in that first night and saw you on the chair." Fingers unfastened the buttons at Noah's chest, freeing his embroidered white work shirt. "I didn't know. I'd only ever kissed one other guy—"

Who?! Noah thought, but his gasp didn't quite verbalize the question.

Mitch pushed open one side of Noah's shirt then groped to yank up Noah's undershirt, revealing bare chest and the delicate nipple chain dangling from his rings. "—but when I saw you there, I just wanted to devour you."

Noah bent his knees, wrapping his legs around Mitch's waist for some sense of balance. He threw one arm back to brace on the table as it swayed beneath him. The only thing solid in his world at that moment was Mitch's unmovable strength.

Still holding the back of Noah's neck, Mitch bent over his chest. His free hand pulled at the nipple chain just as his tongue found one of the sensitive points.

"Oh God, Mitch!"

"Yeah. Just like that. Call out my name, Noah." He sucked

hard on one little point of sensation.

"Fuck, Mitch!" he clutched at his roommate's shoulders. "Mitch, please, can we... can we move to the bed for this?"

Mitch hummed and let his mouth pop off Noah's skin. "Yes." Without warning, he looped his free arm around Noah's waist and picked him up. Just like that. As easily as he picked up a chair to move it across the room. Noah gasped when Mitch tossed him lightly onto the bed.

Noah yelped, thrown backward when Mitch grabbed one of his feet and slipped off his boot. "Big brute," he complained, pushing up to his elbows as he tossed hair from his face. His head was swimming and the need to joke and lighten the mood was strong.

"No. 'Forceful.'" Noah's boot and sock met with the floor, then Mitch picked up his other foot. "'Masterful.'"

Noah smiled. "'Dominant alpha type?'"

With Noah's feet now bare, Mitch knelt on the bed between his legs, reaching for the hooks that fastened his pants. "Yeah. Just what you need."

Noah licked his lips, watching Mitch's fingers so very close to his cock. "'What I need?'"

"Oh yeah." Mitch hooked his fingers into the waistband of the pants, finding Noah's underwear as well. "I've got exactly what you need." Carefully, he pulled both waistbands up and over Noah's cock, then pulled them down and off his legs. Gray eyes glittered happily. "You wore the crown."

Noah's cock twitched, aching and leaking, against his belly. "It drove me crazy all day."

"Poor pretty baby." Noah got called 'pretty' a lot, but hearing Mitch say it like that while eyeing his cock made things inside him go gooey. "*My* pretty baby," Mitch repeated, glancing at Noah's face to dare him to deny the words.

Noah wouldn't dream of doing such a thing.

Grinning, Mitch tossed aside Noah's clothing. "I'll take care of that in a minute." He turned.

"Why not right now?"

Mitch opened one of the drawers in the cabinet that held the television. He faced Noah again with a long black nylon tether in his hands. This one was different than the one from the previous night, however, in that instead of handles, black Velcroed wrist cuffs were clipped to each end. "Noah, if this isn't what you want—" Mitch began seriously, stepping up to the foot of the bed. He wound the strap around his wrists, the cuffs jangling free. "—we don't have to."

Noah found it hard to breathe over his stuttering heart. He took a good look at his friend-come-lover. Glossy black hair, harshly handsome face, steely gray eyes, broad, muscular shoulders, trim waist. The cock he'd savored the previous night pushed proudly at the placket of Mitch's slacks, taunting him.

He sat up, quickly slipped out of his shirt and undershirt, then held out his wrists, very aware of the still unlocked chain about his neck. Instinct told him to lock it, but he didn't yet. He wanted to make love with Mitch once with his eyes wide open before that final step. "I want it."

Eyes alight, Mitch strapped one of the cuffs around Noah's wrist. "I'll take good care of you."

Noah twisted his wrist, liking the feel of the faux fur inside the restraint. "I know you will." He did. Even without the previous two nights, he knew he could trust Mitch with his life. Now he knew he could trust Mitch with his body as well.

Mitch brushed a quick kiss across his lips before urging him to lie back.

Noah eyed him as he complied. "How is it I didn't know about this kink before?"

"The kink only applies to you."

Noah lay back on the pillows, belly fluttering at the casual seriousness of Mitch's tone. "You never tied up any of your girlfriends?"

Taking Noah's posture as permission, Mitch stepped off the bed and circled around to the headboard. "I have," he admitted, looping the tether behind the headboard and tossing the other end toward the other side of the bed. "You remember Pam?"

Noah nodded as he watched Mitch cross around the foot of the bed to retrieve the tether on the other side.

"She's the one who introduced me to it. She loved being tied up." He grinned as he adjusted the tether behind the headboard. "She also liked to be gagged, so that's why you didn't hear her the few times you were home when we were doing it."

Noah bit his lip, mind reeling as he recalled one of Mitch's girlfriends from when they'd first started living together just out of college. She was older, some type of consultant who'd traveled a lot. He'd liked her and had always wondered why she and Mitch never made it any farther than they did. He guessed he had his answer now.

"Anyone since then?"

"A few." He met Noah's gaze. "I swear, I know what I'm doing. I wouldn't hurt you for the world. If anything makes you uncomfortable, just say it and it stops."

Noah released a nervous giggle and let go of his lip. "Okay."

Completely serious, Mitch tugged the strap, pulling Noah's right arm toward the opposite corner of the headboard. "Comfortable?"

Noah had to smile. So very efficient. Just like the letters, concise and to the point but with a lookout for Noah. It made him feel even more comfortable. He snuggled back into the pillows and took a deep, calming breath. "Yes."

Mitch nodded, then picked up Noah's free arm. He paused, staring at it. "You've got such slim wrists," he purred, bestowing a kiss on Noah's pulse point. "Beautiful hands." He lapped at the palm.

"All of these compliments are going to make me light-headed."

Ties That Bind

Mitch nipped the end of his thumb. "Good." He wrapped the restraint around it then fiddled with adjustments on the tether until Noah was secure.

Bound. If he worked at it, Noah could probably get the strap out from behind the headboard, but until or unless he could do that, he was at Mitch's mercy. He stared up at the ceiling, unnerved.

Mitch's handsome face appeared in his line of vision, all shadows from the light behind him. "You okay?" he asked gently, smoothing a hand over Noah's heart.

"Yeah. Just... kind of caught me off guard."

"Want me to take them off?"

"No."

Mitch sat at Noah's side, one arm braced on the mattress to Noah's other side. "You're so sexy," he purred, eyes trailing from Noah's bound wrists to his chest to his face. "All spread out and trusting." He leaned in to kiss Noah, softly, full of promise. "I love you. I want you to feel good."

Noah let his head sink into the pillows, his trepidation melting under the simmer of heat Mitch's touch and words caused. "I feel good."

Mitch nipped at his throat. "I'll make you feel better."

"I can't wait."

Lips trailed down his chin to find his neck, then lower. Mitch closed his mouth over the skin above Noah's heart and sucked hard, making a mark. "Mine," he whispered over it, laving it wet with his tongue before inching down to find Noah's nipple. His tongue toyed with the nipple ring and the chain rustled softly against Noah's chest.

He moaned, pulling at his wrists. The taut strap and sturdy cuffs kept his hands where they were. Cooling peace laced through the simmering lust, shutting down his capacity to think beyond the body above him and the lips devouring the small nub on his chest.

He dragged his eyes open when Mitch pulled back. Lips

wet and red, Mitch stood, never taking his eyes off Noah. His hands went to the buttons of his blue silk shirt. "I've got matching ankle cuffs at home," he told Noah as the silk parted to reveal the dark patch of hair that covered his chest. "I've been dreaming of strapping you to my bed and having my way with you."

Just the words put vivid, erotic images in Noah's head. He groaned, writhing. His cock dripped warm precum on his belly.

The blue silk shirt flew aside. Noah enjoyed an eyeful of taut muscle under a light ruff of black hair as Mitch started on his pants. "We'll have to get a bigger bed," he said, leaning from side to side as he toed out of his shoes. "One of those expensive, pillow-top deals. A California king with four posters." He pushed his slacks and underwear down powerful legs. "And we'll rig it with straps, just for you."

Noah's heart beat faster at the sound of his words, but his attention centered on the truly gorgeous cock that was revealed. How had he gone through so many years of knowing Mitch and not really noticed his cock? He'd seen him naked, but never aroused. To be honest, Noah had probably avoided noticing, an unconscious survival mechanism so that he wouldn't lust after his friend. Because if he'd gotten a good look at that baby all hard and curved up like it was now, he didn't think he could have avoided begging.

After quickly shucking his socks, Mitch stood at the side of the bed and wrapped fingers around the thickly veined shaft, pulling the skin up and over the flushed, mushroom head. "You like?" Mitch asked, pulling back to reveal the head again and the clear bead of liquid at the tip.

Noah licked his lips, nodding. "Let me taste." He leaned toward Mitch as far and as best as he could. "Please."

Mitch purred, kneeling on the bed. "Since you asked so nice." He threw a leg over Noah's chest, straddling him. With one hand braced on the headboard above Noah's head, he reached down to again grab his cock, angling it for Noah's mouth.

Noah opened up, rolling his eyes so he could see Mitch's expression as his cock touched Noah's tongue.

Dark, possessive desire lit Mitch's face, an expression Noah had never seen before and was instantly addicted to. Humming happily, he bent his neck so he could take in more.

Mitch's hand cupped the back of his head, supporting its weight as Mitch slowly pushed more of that delicious rod into Noah's mouth. "So pretty," he crooned, "your mouth looks so good wrapped around my dick, Noah."

Noah lapped at the firm edge of the head of Mitch's dick, rubbing underneath as Mitch pulled slowly out. He watched the muscles of Mitch's firm belly roll as he thrust slowly in and out of Noah's mouth.

"I could come in your mouth," Mitch growled, stopping with as much of his dick stuffed in Noah as possible. "But I'm not going to." He pulled all the way out, despite the desperate suction Noah applied to try and keep his tasty treat. Mitch dropped back to brace on all fours above Noah, a wicked gleam in his eyes. "I've finally got you exactly where I want you, hot and horny." He pressed a kiss to one of Noah's nipples. "I'm going to fuck you. I need to be inside you."

"Oh God, Mitch."

Noah again lost track of time and place as Mitch nipped and lapped at every inch of his chest and belly. He even ran his tongue along the groove of Noah's hip. He shoved Noah's legs apart and settled down between them, laving at the crease between thigh and groin before applying that wicked tongue to each of Noah's balls. "Smooth," he murmured, pushing Noah's thighs up so he could lick the sensitive skin behind Noah's testicles. "Did you shave just for me, Noah?"

"Yes."

"Mmmmm." He bit down on that small strip of skin and Noah cried out, bucking up into the bite of pain that turned into a luscious wash of pleasure. "Like that, do you?" Mitch asked, doing it again. And again. He pushed Noah's thighs up even higher, forcing his hips to tilt up. "Jesus, Noah, you're fucking gorgeous, even down here." Noah didn't think he'd do it, but he did. His tongue edged down to tickle Noah's anus.

"Mitch," Noah cried. Normally he was far more coherent during sex, but the combination of the restraints and the fact that it was his best friend who started to eat him out made speech impossible. He was stuck with Mitch's name, rolling over and over with it, stretching it out to two and even three syllables. His neglected cock bounced on his belly, the gold crown just under the head making it so that the very air was a goddamned caress. The thick metal chain rubbed against the base of his neck, the padlock a heavier weight on his clavicle.

"Mitch, oh God, Mitch, I'm gonna come!"

Mitch stopped, pulling back. Eyes closed, a look of pure bliss on his face, he turned into Noah's thigh, pressing kisses there. "Not yet," he breathed. "Not without me."

"No." Noah agreed, panting. "But please hurry."

His legs dropped back to the mattress. Mitch surged up over him, reaching for the nightstand. Noah opened his eyes to hungrily take in the expanse of bare chest. His mouth watered for a taste of one of those tiny little nipples peeking through a shallow forest of black hair.

"I'm clean," Mitch told him, sitting back on his heels, bottle of lube in hand. "Please believe that I'm clean."

"I do," Noah assured him, spreading his legs wide as he watched Mitch smear liquid on that gorgeous cock. "So am I."

"We don't need a condom?"

"No. Please, just fuck me." Words suddenly returned to him. He looked up into Mitch's gray eyes and put on his best seductive face. One that had compelled plenty of other lovers to fuck him silly. "Shove that big, gorgeous cock inside me, Mitch. Take me. Fuck me. God, now!"

Mitch shook, dropping the lube onto the mattress. He bowed his head, breathing, his fingers in a death grip around his cock. "Fuck!"

"Please, Mitch," Noah begged, knowing he had him, needing this to work. He grabbed the straps above the wrist restraints and undulated his body, making sure Mitch got a good look at everything.

Groaning, Mitch pried his wet hand from his dick and reached for Noah's hole.

"No. Just put it in me. Please! I need to come. I need your dick deep inside me when I come. Please, Mitch. Please, Master."

The 'Master' had Mitch's head flying up, his expression full of fire as he searched Noah's face.

Gotcha! Noah undulated again and added a whimper. He'd used the title for other lovers on request but had never, ever meant it more than he did at this moment. "Master, please."

With a sexy little sneer, Mitch grabbed his cock in one hand and one of Noah's thighs with the other. "Fucking evil minx," he muttered, rubbing the head of his cock against Noah's hole. "If I come before I'm all the way inside, it's your fault."

Before Noah could think of more to say to spur him on, Mitch pushed in. Noah threw back his head on a cry of pure bliss as the thick crown of Mitch's bare dick popped inside of him. He'd never gone bareback and just the thought—let alone the feel—of Mitch's bare, velvety skin pushing inside him nearly blew his control. Mitch stopped, face drawn in a rictus of fierce concentration and Noah was glad for it, needing a moment to compose himself as well.

"God, Noah," Mitch groaned, dropping Noah's leg and leaning forward to brace his arms on the bed. "So hot." He pushed in another inch, the wiry hair of his thighs scraping the soft curve of the bottom of Noah's ass. "So fucking hot."

Noah opened his mouth, needing it to suck great gouts of air into his lungs as fire lit within him. He pulled his hands, wrists aching where they were securely held.

Mitch stopped, his entire cock sheathed inside Noah. Sweat dripped from his forehead onto Noah's belly, mingling with the sheen that already coated the skin. Noah wanted to touch him, wanted to dig his fingers into those strong shoulders. The fact that he couldn't frustrated him, made him writhe, made him do what he could to rock his body on that cock.

"Master please, please, please, fuck me, Master, please…" He kept babbling, rocking to fuck himself as best he could while Mitch held still.

Then Mitch moved. Abruptly, he pulled back, almost out of Noah. Which made Noah gasp. Then he shoved back in one smooth, hard glide. Which pushed a scream out of Noah.

"God yes!" he shouted. "More."

Mitch did it again with the same deliberate precision. And again. Too slow to push Noah over the edge but enough to keep building the fire hotter and hotter. His cock slapped his belly and the padlock slipped from his chest to nestle somewhere on his shoulder.

"Noah." Mitch shifted his weight to one arm, freeing the other so the hand could wrap around Noah's cock.

"Oh God, wait! Yes!"

It only took a few firm strokes and a swipe of a thumb over the too-sensitive tip and Noah was coming. Spunk splashed over Mitch's hand and onto Noah's skin in a surprisingly long series of spurts. His chest contracted and his spine exploded through the back of his skull. Cries bled from his lips while his insides clamped down on the gorgeous invader.

"Noah!" Mitch shouted, losing control. As Noah's orgasm spurted to a halt, Mitch's hips thrust in earnest, spearing that cock into Noah's body, nailing his gland in such a way that Noah wasn't sure he had stopped coming. Then warmth filled him when Mitch stuttered to a halt, crying wordlessly as his cock spent deep in Noah's body.

Ties That Bind

Noah's hips sank slowly to the mattress as he fought for breath. Mitch fell in a near collapse over him, braced on elbows on either side of Noah's chest. His lover pressed an open-mouthed kiss on Noah, stealing his breath until he wrenched his head to the side with a whimper.

Shaking, Mitch pushed up higher and reached for one of Noah's wrists. Velcro ripped and Noah's hand dropped to the pillow. A moment later, the other hand did the same. Noah groaned when Mitch gently, carefully placed one, then the other hand on his chest, rubbing the wrists and kissing the red marks. "I love you," he murmured, holding Noah's palms to his chest. "God, I just love you more."

"I love you too," Noah breathed, drinking in Mitch's flushed, sweaty face.

"You mean that?"

Noah gently dislodged his hands from Mitch's. As Mitch watched, he reached up to right the chain about his throat, finding the padlock and bringing it forward. He turned it correctly and clicked it closed. "Yours."

Mitch slid hands up under Noah's shoulders, dropping down chest to chest. "Mine," he agreed, sealing their mouths.

Although his arms were sore, Noah wouldn't let that stop him from wrapping them around Mitch for the first time as lovers.

* * * * *

"That's so romantic," Rachel sighed, elbow on the bar, cheek on her palm, dreamy smile on her face. "After all those years, finally finding each other."

Noah smiled big, eyes on the drink Richard handed to him. His shift was over and he wore street clothes rather than his work outfit, but he was still hanging around, waiting for Mitch to pick him up.

"Oh, look at you *smile*," she squealed. "You're so cute."

"All right, cut it out."

She laughed. She, too, was out of her work outfit. Unlike

Noah, she could leave at any time. She was hanging around to bug him on his first day back after Valentine's Day. "So, where are you two off to? Romantic dinner?"

Noah flushed, sipping his rum and Coke. "Nowhere special."

On the other side of the bar, Richard snorted. Noah glanced up to see the other man finish rolling his eyes. "You might as well tell her. Or she'll ask Mitch when he gets here."

"Ask me what?"

Noah and Richard both jumped at the sound of Mitch's voice. He'd come through the side entrance with Kenneth, who was right behind him.

Not pausing for an answer to his question, Mitch slid an arm around Noah's shoulders and planted a kiss on his upturned face. His tongue swiped Noah's bottom lip, but when Noah opened up, he pulled back with a smile that made promises for later. While he straightened to look at Richard, Noah took a brief moment to admire his profile.

Mine, he thought, happily slipping an arm around that trim waist and hooking his thumb in Mitch's belt.

"Where are you taking Noah?" Rachel asked.

Mitch smiled big. "We're going bed shopping."

Noah closed his eyes, smiling over a groan when Rachel practically screamed.

When he opened his eyes again, she had her hands laced over her mouth and her eyes were simpering sweet as they darted from his face to Mitch's.

"Oh man," Richard sighed, shaking his head. "Too much information." But he was smiling.

"Speak for yourself," said Kenneth, standing beside Rachel with a big grin on his face. "I, for one, think it's absolutely wonderful that Mitch found the key to Noah's heart."

Noah's hand crept up to close fingers around the small gold padlock that lay at the base of his throat. *The key to me? I guess so.* Happily, he tucked his head under Mitch's chin.

Ties That Bind

Laura Baumbach

Roughly Tied Together

Excerpt from the award winning, best-selling novel
A BIT OF ROUGH

The restaurant was busy, filled with Saturday night patrons. There was a spattering of families with children present but the majority of the diners were couples.

A short, swarthy man in a dark suit rushed toward them as Bram and James entered.

"Mr. Lord! How wonderful to see you. Mrs. Giovani and I were beginning to wonder if everything was well with you. It has been weeks since you were last here, weeks!"

Giovani shook Bram's hand, clasping the big man's wrist and pumping his arm hard.

Bram grinned down at his energetic, rotund host. "Been

busy with a new contract, Vito. Living on fast food and candy bars."

Vito gasped. "We will not mention that to Mrs. Giovanni or neither of us will hear the end of it for months. I'm just glad to see you back." Vito smiled at James, standing silent at Bram's side. "A special occasion tonight, maybe?"

"Someone special." Bram rested his arm around James' shoulders and gave him the lopsided smile that never failed to touch a flame to James' libido. "Vito Giovanni meet James Justin. I wanted the best for him, so I brought him to 'Via Emilia' and Mrs. Giovanni's manicotti."

James shook the man's hand, surprised at the powerful grip in the stubby fingers. "Hi. Pleased to met you, Mr. Giovanni."

"Vito, please! You are welcome in my humble restaurant anytime, Mr. Justin." Vito began walking toward the back of the restaurant, gesturing for the two men to follow him. "Come, come. I will have to get Mrs. Giovanni. She will want to know you have finally reappeared in one piece."

Bram leaned down and whispered conspiratorially in Vito's ear. "I actually had a dream about her sauce last night." He leaned a bit closer. "Sauce everywhere. Very messy, but satisfying."

Vito jumped back and roared with laughter. His eyes darted back and forth between Bram's unabashed grin and James' embarrassed blush. "We will not tell her that either. It will be our little secret, yes? Just between the men."

"I think that's wise, Vito. Save us both from some bodily harm." Bram smiled at James. He walked closer, and brushed hand over James' hip as they came to a halt in front of a u-shaped booth.

Without comment, Vito shoved the table to one side to create a bigger opening for Bram's large frame. Bram nudged James onto the curved bench seat, then slid in close beside him.

Vito snapped his fingers and a waiter appeared from

nearby. He turned back to speak to Bram. "Your usual or would you like the menu for Mr. Justin?"

"You know what I like, Vito. Make my dream come true." Both men chuckled then Bram touched James' knee under the table. "How about you, Jamie?" Expectant, Vito and Bram both looked at James.

The warmth from Bram's hand seeped into his leg and distracted him. James felt his heart rate quicken and he had to resist the urge to squirm. It was nice being in a place where the fact that he was on a date with another man wasn't an issue, but all the personal attention was unnerving.

Biting his lower lip, James considered his options. "Well, I like just about anything. Bram trusts you. What do you recommend, Vito?"

He had apparently hit upon the right answer. Vito beamed and clapped his hands. "I have just the thing, a special dish. You will think you have died and gone to heaven. Be patient."

Vito addressed the waiter. "A bottle of our best red. You know the one, Angelo." The young man scurried off and Vito excused himself. "Now I must see to things." He bowed and hurried away, leaving the two alone.

James leaned back into the deep leather of the booth, feeling its butter-smooth texture beneath him. Bram's hand still rested on his knee. It felt good, a gentle reminder he wasn't alone, possessive, but not too much. James liked this mountain of a man more and more with each passing hour.

Darting a quick look around the room to see who was watching them, James was relieved when all he got was a shy smile from a young woman who happened to look up from her plate at the same moment. He placed a hand over Bram's on his knee and felt his fingers instantly laced between Bram's longer ones.

"How do you like the place? I usually eat here a lot. The food is fabulous and atmosphere is homey. Vito and wife are terrific hosts. They always make me feel welcome, like one of the family." A passing waitress smiled and said a bright, "Good evening, Mr. Lord." Bram nodded and smiled at her.

"I think it's a great place." James watched the innocent exchange between Bram and the woman. Her glance lingered and James was surprised when a jolt of jealousy rippled through him. "Friendly." James frowned at the waitress. "Very friendly."

Incredulous, Bram squeezed James' hand. "Are you actually jealous?"

James blushed and tried not to duck his head. He half-heartedly tried to pull his hand away, but Bram refused to let go.

"That's such a compliment, Jamie." Leaning in closer, Bram lower his voice to just above a whisper. "I'll be sure to take the time to thank you properly later tonight. I may have to thank you several times."

Now James did squirm, his dress pants suddenly too tight and too warm for comfort. Bram winked at him and sat back as the waiter returned with the wine. Bram tasted it and nodded his approval before handing James a glass.

James took a sip and let the mellow tang of the grapes ease the dryness in his sore throat. Some of his unease melted away it. "It's nice here. Comfortable."

"Yeah, I think so." Bram leaned back, but kept hold of James' hand, bringing it with him as he settled more comfortably into the curve of the booth. He sipped at his wine and winked at another waitress as she greeted him.

He knew it was next to impossible for a man of Bram's size to go unnoticed, but James was amazed at how many people went out of their way to say hello. Bram was very well known and liked here. James' comfort level with the physically intimating and powerful man went up a few more notches.

James glanced down at their intertwined fingers and noticed a couple of Bram's knuckles had fresh abrasions on them. James brought their hands up from beneath the table and run his thumb just under one of the raw knuckles. "I've been so whacked out over the whole thing in the hall, I didn't even notice you were hurt. Christ!"

Guilt and shame over the incident with Williams came rushing down on him and bile rose to the back of his throat. "I'm sorry you had to get involved in that."

"I'm not." Bram frowned and took a deep breath before admitting, "I'm glad."

"What?" James' voice cracked on the word.

"I'm glad I was there. Glad I got the chance to stop that asshole from hurting you. Glad I was the one there for you afterwards." Bram smiled his lopsided grin and looked sheepish. "And yeah, I'll admit it. I wasn't lying when I told that creep I was possessive and protective of you." Bram's tanned face darkened a shade. "Maybe it's kind of early to say this, but I like how you make me feel when I'm with you."

Swallowing past the residual burn in his throat from earlier, James decided to plunge ahead and go through the emotional door Bram had left open. "How *do* you feel when you're with me?"

Leaning an elbow on the table, the big man hunched forward slightly and studied the wine in his glass. He swirled the liquid around and then took a sip, setting the glass back down on the table before answering.

James began to think he had misread the situation then Bram raised his head and smiled. "Needed. You make me feel needed. Appreciated. You let me have control, but you aren't dependent on me." Bram took another sip of wine then stared James in the eye, his voice suddenly very serious. "I don't want to be consumed by someone who wants me to orchestrate his entire life for him."

James let out the breath he had been holding and released his bottom lip from the tight hold his teeth had on it. "I don't like being told what to do outside of the bedroom. I can run my own life just fine."

"Then we're good, because I don't want to be your

'daddy'." The big man gripped James' hand tighter. "But honestly, it does give me a rush to see you all flustered and unsettled. Like in the alley last night, when you weren't sure what was happening. And earlier tonight, at your apartment, when you needed someone to anchor you down. I'm glad I was there."

"I'm glad, too, Bram. I don't want to think about what would have happened if you hadn't shown up." James stared off into the distance. He felt a cold knot of anxiety ball up in his stomach at idea of Williams being allowed to finish what he had implied he wanted to do.

"The apartment building is up for sale. I might have to move soon, anyway." James was suddenly very glad he had meet Bram. Pushing the incident aside, he smiled at Bram. "I don't think I thanked you for earlier."

The lopsided grin on Bram's lips turned into a gentle leer. "Oh, I don't know. You felt pretty grateful to me on the couch. My leg thought you were grateful, too."

A strangled snort of laughter escaped James and Bram joined him. James laughed until tears blurred his eyes. He had to wipe them away to see his food as their waiter placed a large tray of appetizers on the table and disappeared again.

"Okay, I guess we're even. We're both glad to be with each other." James brushed away the last of the moisture from his eyes and looked over the food tray, trying to decide what to sample first.

"Yeah." Bram's tone was considering. "We go well together. I knew that last night. That's why I asked you out. I had a feeling about us being right together."

James popped a marinated shrimp into his mouth and sucked the sauce off it. He looked up to see Bram watching his mouth as he savored the shrimp. Feeling playful, he sucked slowly and ran the fleshy part of the shrimp over his lips once before he ate it.

Bram's breathing increased and his hand was back on

James' leg, this time higher up. His large, hot palm slid around to James' inner thigh and his fingers boldly stroked the sensitive skin there, but didn't move any higher.

James tightened his buttocks and fought the urge to push his groin into the man's hand. He grabbed his wineglass and took a sip, while his brain scrambled for conversation to distract him from the tantalizing pressure under the table.

"Your business card said you work for 'Eclipse Construction'. They're a pretty impressive company. Even the architectural firm I'm at, 'Dunn & Piper', does a lot of business with 'Eclipse'. What do you do there?"

Bram relaxed into soft leather and tilted his upper body so that their shoulders touched, all the while tapping lightly on James' inner thigh with his fingertips. "Well. . ." Bram sighed.

Thinking Bram's hesitation as a sign he might be reluctant to admit he was a blue-collar worker after James had admitted at the apartment to being an architect, James hastened to let the big man know it didn't bother him.

"Hey, as long as you can support yourself," James smiled, "and can pay for dinner, I don't care what you do for a living." He popped another shrimp in his mouth, enjoying the way Bram's eyes immediately darted to look at his mouth while he chewed. "But I'm thinking, they wouldn't be so nice here if you couldn't pay the bill."

James delicately licked a tiny spot of cocktail sauce off from one fingertip. He felt a thrill race down his spine when Bram swallowed hard and licked his own dry lips.

His half-lidded gaze never strayed from James' face as Bram said, "I'm thinking of making someone pay right now, but it's not the bill." The long fingers on his leg tightened and James squirmed. Bram murmured seductively into his ear, "Bad boy tonight, is it? Maybe we need to rethink that punishment idea."

James' heart pounded in his chest and his mouth went dry with excitement, but remained silent. It would be interesting to see what direction Bram took this, whether he had been honest about his expectations from James.

"I think you'll have to owe me a kiss, a real kiss," Bram reached up and ran his thumb over James' lower lip, "for each time you cocktease. You're up to two right now."

Gaze locked on Bram's face, James dipped forward and captured the man's thumb in his mouth. He gave it the same treatment he had given the shrimp beforehand. He sucked on it, swirled his tongue over the callused pad then slowly pulled it from between his lips, letting his teeth rake over the surface on the way out.

"Would you like more wine, gentlemen? Dinner will be ready in just a few minutes." Not having heard the waiter approach, James jumped and pulled back from Bram.

The waiter glanced at the uneaten tray of appetizers. "Was there something unsatisfactory with the food, Mr. Lord? Would you like something else instead?"

Turning, Bram cleared his throat and shifted in his seat. He grabbed a canapé from the tray and prepared to stuff it into his mouth. "No, no, Angelo. This is fine. We just. . . got caught up in the moment." He put the delicacy into his mouth, chewed and swallowed, but his eyes were on James the whole time. "It's perfect. I've never had better."

His blush deepened and James dropped his gaze to the table. He picked up a breadstick and began tearing it into pieces.

"Ah." Angelo smiled at the blush creeping up James' cheeks and nodded. "Excellent, Mr. Lord." He poured more wine into their glasses, then left, a knowing smile on his twitching lips.

The two men looked at one another and burst out laughing, the sudden awkwardness dissolving away.

James was surprised the hand on his leg never left. Bram might have been caught flirting with another man, but he didn't appear to be embarrassed by it. The man's self-confidence was rock solid.

"You never answered me. What do you do at 'Eclipse'?

I had this fantasy of you in jeans and a work shirt, all sweaty and covered in concrete dust, but now I'm having trouble seeing you that way."

"Why?"

"You're too self-confident, too take charge, to be a worker bee. I'm guessing management -- supervisor or project lead."

"Close." Bram smiled. "Owner."

"Owner?" James nearly choked on the piece of salmon he had just swallowed. "Of 'Eclipse'?" He looked at Bram's self-depreciating smile. "Wow. I'm impressed."

Finishing off the last bit of wine in his glass, Bram shrugged. "Majority stockholder." He set the empty glass down and fingered with the edge of his napkin. "I have people who run the day-to-day nuts and bolts of it, but I stay involved in all the major contracts and have final say on what projects we take on. I work a site now and then, too."

"'Eclipse' does a fair amount of charity work. Is that your doing?" James was impressed. Bram's company was a leader in promoting fair housing standards.

"We do some low-bid contracts for public housing and a lot of high priced bids to help pay for them." Bram shrugged off the compliment again. "I try to keep a balance between what's good for public interest and what's good for the company."

"A man used to being in charge, but knows how to compromise. I like that." James bit at his lower lip, then soothed it with a lick. "It's . . . sexy." The hand on his leg inched higher, then stopped. James flexed his thigh muscles in an unspoken acknowledgment of the thrill the movement produced.

Bram refilled his wineglass and took a large sip. "It was my father's company and he liked a hands-on approach. He loved to create beautiful buildings. For him it was more art than construction. I took over when he passed away four years ago, right after my mom. I've tried to follow in his footsteps with the company."

A melancholy tone had settled into Bram's voice and James felt a need to erase the small frown from the big man's furrowed brow. "Well, he did a good job of creating beautiful art with you. He must have been a good man." James let every ounce of attraction growing inside of him for this man show in his voice. Bram responded with a shy, appreciative smile that James cherished.

"Thank you, Jamie. And he was a good man." Bram took a steadying breath and stopped playing with his napkin. "I miss him." He sat up straighter and turned his full attention on James. "But the real guiding force in his life was my mom. She was petite, just a little thing really, quiet and intense. Kind of like you."

Bram reached over and brushed a strand of dark curl back from James' forehead, softly caressing the smooth skin with his thumb as he talked. "Same sapphire eyes, too. They both would have liked you. I'm sorry they aren't here to meet you."

James swallowed down the lump forming in his throat. The big man's sadness was almost palpable, making James' chest ache with the desire to share it and make it less of a burden for him to carry alone. "I would have liked to have met them. They sound great. They wouldn't have minded? That I'm a guy, I mean?"

"They wouldn't have chosen this lifestyle for me, if there had been a choice to be made, but they accepted it as something that just was. It was never an issue between us. Sure, they worried about me when I was younger, but as soon as I filled out, they figured I could handle any problems that cropped up."

Bram dropped his hand and lightly touched the red mark still visible on James' throat. "There haven't been any Williams in my life, I'm relieved to say. Not that there haven't been the odd coy remark or cutting comment when my back was turned, but not very many people come at me head on."

"I can understand that. I thought twice about just talking to you."

Bram snorted and stretched his long legs under the table, hitting the bench seat on the other side, a good four feet away. "It's one of the detractions of being so big. I even had to find a hundred year old house with nine foot ceilings and seven foot doorways to live in so I didn't have to duck every time I went from room to room."

James' eyes lit up and he turned in the seat, careful not to dislodge the warm hand working its way up his lap. "I love old houses. They have some of the most outstanding architectural designs ever made."

His hands moved in the air in front of him, emphasizing and expressing his feelings better than his words could. "The Brant Hill District on the north side of town is wonderful. It's not as swank as the Talbot Oaks area, but there's one block of homes, from Cypress to Evergreen, that's amazing. I'd love to live in one of those homes."

James realized Bram had been staring at him as he talked non-stop, a delighted grin on his face. "Sorry, I get a little over-enthusiastic sometimes." He picked up his glass and took several sips from it, hoping to blame the heat in his face on the wine.

"No apology necessary. I like seeing some of that passion you keep bottle up inside come out." Bram slid his hand into James' crotch and lightly caressed the growing bulge he found. "I want to know what makes you passionate. What turns you on, what pushes your buttons."?

James began to pant. His hips pushed up of their own accord, seeking more, but Bram kept the pressure to a steady, light stroking.

The big man picked up a pastry from the tray with his unoccupied hand and fed a cheese-filled morsel to his date. His thumb became covered in the creamy mixture. As he pulled back, James grabbed it. He swallowed, and licked the fallen droplets from Bram's thumb. He scoured the digit carefully with his tongue before taking it into his mouth and sucking it clean.

His own breathing uneven and rapid, Bram shifted so his broad back blocked their activities from view of the rest of the diners. "If this is what just talking about old houses does to you, I'll have to show you my place. It's full of interesting angles and miles of elaborate detailing."

James actually felt heat radiate off the big man in waves. He found it difficult to breathe.

"Especially my bedroom."

The pressure at his groin increased and James bucked up into Bram's hand. He took a couple of deep breaths through pursed lips to dispel the dizziness rippling through him.

"Lots of interesting . . . architectural features?" If he passed out right now, James wondered if he could blame it on the lack of air in the room.

"Uh-huh. My bed, for one is a great eighteenth century design. Only one I could find that I could fit in comfortably. You'll like it. It has plenty of room to stretch out. Lots of places to hold onto, sturdy enough to be tied to." The slow stroking kept rhythm with the soft fluctuations in Bram's voice.

James let out a soft, strangled moan. His eyes darted around to make sure they weren't making a public display of themselves, but all he could see was Bram. Every broad, muscled inch of the man filled James' sight. "Tied? Me or you?" James managed to pant out.

"Either. Both." Bram moved the last few inches needed for them to make contact and whispered against James' lips before he gave him a chaste kiss. "Does it matter, baby?"

"I think the only thing that matters to me right now," James swallowed hard and wet his lips, "is how soon can we be there?"

A soft, but distinct clearing of a throat jarred both men. Bram stilled his hand, eased back and turned, making sure James was protected from any prying eyes.

The younger man knew he was flushed, and he could feel a fine sheen of sweat on his face. His breath still came in short, shallow gasps over chapped lips and his pants visibly tented. He wouldn't be standing up anytime soon. James made an effort to pull himself together, then peeked past Bram's shoulder to see who had interrupted them.

Vito stood at the table, a large bag of take out containers in his hands and a rakish grin on his face. He chuckled at James' soft moan of embarrassment and extended the bag to Bram. "Dinner for two, to go. I thought maybe this night would be better spent at home, yes?"

Bram laughed and accepted the bag, nodding. "I think you maybe right. Thank you, Vito. You're a very intuitive man." Fishing out his wallet, Bram tossed three fifties on the table.

Vito shrugged and tilted his head to indicate their waiter at a table several feet away from them. "Thank Angelo. He said you were distracting him too much for him to work."

James dropped his chin to his chest and mumbled a distressed, "Oh, God, Bram. He'll never let us eat here again."

Bram just laughed again and tapped the top of James' fallen head. "It's okay, Jamie. I think he'll forgive us as long as we leave quietly. Right, Vito?" Bram stood and motioned for James to join him.

Vito chuckled. "Not to worry. The biggest catastrophe of the evening will be if Mrs. Giovanni's cooking goes to waste. See to it that it doesn't, my friends, and all will be forgiven." He patted Bram's arm, tucked an unopened bottle of red wine under it and walked off, humming a love song James recognized from a popular Italian opera.

Picking up the loaded bag, Bram waited for James. James inched out of the booth then awkwardly gained his feet, trying to unobtrusively rearrange himself in his pants.

A sudden, painful pinch to one butt cheek made him jump, muttering a string of oaths under his breath. "What the hell did you do that for?" Shocked, James rubbed at his abused ass, trying to soothe away the deep ache.

"Just trying to help." Bram took James' arm with his free hand and began leading them to the exit.

"How did bruising my butt help anything?" Confused, but wanting to leave, James let the other man guide him out the door.

"Easy." Bram glanced down at the front of James' pants. "You can walk just fine now."

James suddenly realized the uncomfortable fullness was gone from his trousers. His erection had subsided the moment the pain had jarred through him. "Crafty bastard."

Bram grinned and let his voice take on the rough, sexy tone that had sparked James' interest from the beginning. "Don't worry, baby. I promise I'll make it up to you. I know a few uses for Mrs. Giovanni's sauce she probably hasn't tried yet."

* * * * *

The drive to Bram's house took fifteen minutes, much of which James spent pressed against the passenger window, commenting on the structural style and elegance of the long established neighborhood.

They ended the drive on a short, circular driveway in front of a graceful, two-story, red brick home. Wrought iron rods, spirals, fence posts and grates adorned much of the building. There was even an elaborate weather vane topping the patina-colored, copper roof of an octagonal tower. The approaching twilight hid the rest of the home's period features.

Awed, James climbed out of the truck and followed Bram up the steps of the wide porch. He waited while Bram opened two heavy-duty locks on the entry door, and then preceded his host inside.

Once they passed through the marble-floored foyer, the adjoining rooms became massive, all boasting nine-foot, domed ceilings, stylized, ten-inch baseboards and oak hardwood floors.

Ties That Bind

Ancient oriental rugs accented leather and dark oak furniture groupings and numerous original landscapes done in oils and watercolors hung on the walls.

They passed through one large, open room completely bare of furnishing. One wall was almost completely glass, a series of lead-paned French doors that opened out to a courtyard. James could see a small fountain and several stone benches outside. "What a great room! The natural light in here must be outstanding. Why don't you use it?"

"I was going to make it into an office, but it's just too big. It would be a waste." Bram looked around the mahogany-paneled room admiringly. "So now, I'm waiting for inspiration to hit me."

"Wow. It would be a terrific place to work. You should reconsider." James' gaze drank in every feature of the room, from its carved ceiling rails to its massive marble fireplace and built-in ceiling to floor bookcases.

"I'll think about it." Taking in James' delighted, awed reaction to the room, Bram's expression became thoughtful. "Something will come up."

Bram led James down a long hallway, pausing to hang up their coats on the way. They emerged in an updated, gleaming kitchen complete with granite-topped counters and a gourmet eight-burner stove.

"I don't know about you, Jamie, but I'm starving. What do you say we eat some of this before it gets too cold and then I'll give you a tour of the old place?" Bram set the bag of food on the center island and began to unpack their dinner.

James rubbed his hands together and sniffed the air. "I can't wait to see the place, and as much as I'd like to take up where we left off in the restaurant," he patted his stomach, "I'm running on empty here."

James joined him at the counter, taking a plate Bram offered, filled with Mrs. Giovanni's spicy-smelling, cheese-filled pasta sleeves covered in a thick layer of rich, meaty sauce.

Ties That Bind

"Those appetizers were great, but they only got me warmed up." James smirked and seductively licked a smear of sauce off his index finger.

Bram reached over and pulled the finger from James' mouth. He wrapped his hand around the enticing digit and shook it. "Put that thing away. At least until we've eaten."

Picking up his own plate and the bottle of wine, Bram pulled out a stool with his foot and kicked it toward James. "What time did you eat lunch?"

James slid onto the stool and started eating. "Skipped it. And since I don't eat breakfast," he chewed and swallowed a huge bite of manicotti, "this is the first decent food I've had since yesterday." He forked up another mouthful and chewed. "This is fantastic. Good thing Vito's open-minded. I could get addicted to this."

"We like the same foods. That's good." Smiling, Bram poured two glasses of wine and handed one to James.

The younger man accepted it, but took three more bites of pasta before sampling the vintage. "Sorry." James worked the solitary words in between bites. "Hungry."

"Don't apologize, eat." They ate in silence for several minutes, devouring the meal Vito had packed.

Bram hunched forward and wiped a speck of cheese from James' chin. "Make sure you're full. You'll need your strength for later."

Gaze locked on James' face, he licked the speck off his finger, and then pulled back and dug into his food. "We both will." Bram cleaned his plate in only a few hefty bites.

"That a promise?" James teased.

Bram's eyes became hooded and his voice dropped to that low, sultry tone that made James' stomach do somersaults. He hooked a boot under the rungs of James' stool and dragged his lover over to him in one swift yank, sliding his knees between the other man's slender thighs. He pulled James into an embrace and tilted the younger man's face up. His lips brushed against James' skin as he talked.

"A promise," he kissed the tip of James' nose, "and a threat. I believe," he placed another kiss on James' chin. "Someone has some punishment," he kissed one corner of James' mouth, "coming," then the other corner. "Don't you, baby?"

James groaned and closed his eyes, completely seduced by the gravel-rough sound of Bram's demanding whisper and the teasing, feathery touch of the man's lips. Food was forgotten.

James relaxed into Bram's tight embrace, arching his neck so the unmoving fingers laced through his hair had to tug harder to keep their grip. A thrill of anticipation rocketed down his limbs as the pressure from Bram's hand increased, and he was forced to angle his head back a few inches more.

"Oh yeah, baby, fight me. I'll remind you who's in charge." Bram yanked James' hips off the stool and onto his lap.

James' swelling cock rocked into the other man's stomach. He couldn't resist bucking against the hard ridge of solid muscles, and letting out a low grunt. "Fuck!"

Bram chuckled and clamped one long arm around James' bucking hips and pulled them in tight to still them. His meaty hand massaged and kneaded James' ass as he promised, "Soon, baby, soon. But when I say we fuck, and not before." He continued raining light, almost-caresses over James' mouth with his lips, occasionally snaking out the tip of his tongue to moisten a section of chapped skin.

Before long, James was panting and moaning, unable to do more than endure the erotic pleasure of Bram's embrace and slow attentions. The tingling warmth centered in his groin grew, turning into a smoldering delight.

When the slow, steady pace remained unchanged, James began to resist the confines of the other man's restraining hold. He squirmed, gratified by the feeling of Bram's iron-hard erection digging greedily into his ass with each tiny shift of his hips. Hoping to encourage his lover to move faster, James contracted and relaxed the tight muscles of his buttocks, milking the curve of his ass over the growing bulge under him.

The results were instantaneous. Wiping food off the countertop with one sweeping motion of his arm, Bram lifted them both from the stool and slammed James down on his back on the counter.

"Uh!" James' breath was forced out of him. His head smacked down hard, but met a protective palm instead of granite.

Bram easily pinned James in place with his long body. He let go of James' hair long enough to grab both of his lover's wrists. He then pressed them onto the countertop, held imprisoned in one massive, sandpaper-rough hand.

"Oh, no, baby. Not yet." Bram settled his body between James' spread legs, covering the smaller man from hip to chest. He held himself up on one forearm to allow his partner just enough room to catch his breath. "I think it's time your punishment started."

Gathering his captive up, Bram slid one arm under James' shoulders and used his other hand to grip the younger man's smooth jaw line. He trailed hot, wet kisses along James' neck and up into his ear, then licked a path down James' profile from forehead to his Adam's apple. Nuzzling and sucking at the convulsively, bobbing knob, Bram raked his teeth over it, dragging a strangled moan from his lover.

A shiver racked through the body under his and Bram leaned up to whisper into James' ear. "That's my baby. Shake for me. Let me feel what I do to you. Share it with me, baby."

James shivered at the command. A sharp gasp pushed warm, oregano-scented air to swirl in and past his ear. Intent on pulling even more of a response from his unhurried partner, he arched and wiggled, then pulled one leg up to brace his heel on the countertop, bringing Bram's erection more firmly into contact with his own. His eager cock pulsed and strained against the added pressure.

"Jesus, fuck! Do me, just do me. Right here. Please!" James panted and strained against the hold on his wrists, desperate to touch and be touched.

Gripping the thin wrists tighter, Bram nipped James' lower lip and let his voice rumble up from deep inside his chest, sultry and hot. "Oh, I'll do you. I'll do you so hard and so deep, you'll swear to God you can taste me."

James' insides quivered and he felt the head of his cock leak and grow larger. One continuous tremor shook his entire body and his lover groaned into his mouth.

"Soon, baby, soon. Let's get your 'punishment' out of the way first." Bram captured James' mouth with his own and began ravishing it, biting the fullness of swollen lips. He sucked James' willing tongue into his own wet mouth to stroke it, then licked and bathed every millimeter of tender flesh on the inside of his mouth until James' entire awareness was centered there.

When James was breathless and shaking, Bram released him, and turned his cheek to brush rough stubble over James' gasping mouth. "That's one kiss. I believe you owe me three."

Bram released James' wrists and pulled his partner's shirt up and off in one powerfully swift motion, tossing it to one side. He reached out and snagged the large plastic bag the food had been packed in off the edge of the counter. He pulled the bag through his hands, forming a long twisted strand of white.

James' gaze darted from the bag to Bram's face. "What's that for?" His voice trembled.

Staring down into James' wide eyes, Bram tied the bag around the smaller man's unresisting wrists, still obediently lying where he had left them. He stretched James' arms up to hook the tied wrists over one faucet handle of the sink in the long countertop.

"I want to use my hands." He yanked James' hips down so that his arms were fully extended. "And you're not allowed to." He nipped at James' lower lip and stared intently at him. "Don't. Move."

Bram grinned at the unintelligible grunt and whimper that answered his command. He raised himself up slowly, dragging his hands down James' body, stroking the lean frame as he stood up. "Good boy. I like that." He rubbed his erection against James' wide-open crotch and ran his hands up James' tense thighs.

"Come on, man. Do me!" James whimpered.

"Not yet, baby. You don't want it enough." Bram kissed James' twitching cock through his tenting pants. "You haven't begged yet."

His zipper was tugged down and his belt unfastened. James felt hot fingers slide under the waistband of his boxers. His hips were lifted and within seconds, he was divested of every scrap of clothing, socks and shoes included.

Looking up through half-lidded eyes, James watched as the tanned and weathered man above him raked his hungry gaze over his tied and splayed body.

The big man's expression softened and his pale blue eyes suddenly mirrored more of the light in the room as moisture filled them. Gritty palms slid down the flesh of his thighs, brushed over his dripping cock, then crawled up his out-stretched, trembling torso, grating over the aching peaks of his nipples along the way. Bram's upper body followed his hands and his warmth settled over James again.

"God, you're so beautiful. Every fuckable inch of you, baby. Mine. Mine to have. Any way I want, any time I want."

Bram's whispered breath puffed across James' neck and gooseflesh broke out on the younger man's skin. The scent of wine, mixed with a sweaty musk that was all Bram, invaded his mind and a shudder of desire hit him so hard both men shook with the force of it.

Bram's palms caressed his face, forcing James to look up into his eyes. "Isn't that right, baby? Only mine. Say it for me." The last was spoken in a gravel-filled hiss of command that traveled straight to James' trapped cock.

He moaned and bucked up, panting his frustration into Bram's mouth as his engorged and neglected shaft was suddenly wrapped in a sandpaper-lined vise of heat and muscle. James gave a strangled scream as the rough, mauling grip worked him hard and fast. He tugged on his arms and felt the plastic dig into his skin, using the burn and pressure of the bonds to keep him grounded.

This was the second time this man had denied James the use of his hands during sex, denied him the pleasure of touching his partner, denied him an outlet for his need. Kept him on the edge, kept him wanting, kept him in a haze of passion and desire. James moaned and tugged harder on his arms, thrilled by the helplessness of his position.

But guttural, needy moans and pain/pleasure filled screams weren't enough for his lover.

"Say it for me, baby. Tell me to whom you belong. Say it. *Say it!*" Despite his demand, Bram made it impossible for James to respond, sealing their mouths tightly together in a devastating, consuming kiss that left them both gasping and flushed when he finally broke away.

Hand still milking his lover's cock mercilessly, Bram rolled his forehead against James' sweat covered brow and harshly whispered, "Say it, baby, say it. For me."

Swallowing hard to relieve the burning dryness in his throat, James gasped into the sweaty mass of honey-blond hair hanging down in his face. "Any time. Any way. Yours."

Gritting his teeth against the dual sensation of raw burning and fiery ecstasy Bram was creating at his abused groin, James closed his eyes and moaned, then begged. "Please!"

His eyes popped open when the rough, gritty sheath around his cock suddenly disappeared then turned into a satin lined fist and the strong smell of garlic filled the already spice-laden air. The abrupt change in sensation sent James reeling as his lover ruthlessly pumped, massaged and squeezed his newly slicked erection.

"Fuck-fuck-fuck-fuck-fuck!" His climax raced to the edge of near-eruption and hung there, sizzling down his nerve endings, but never setting off the major explosion.

"My baby needs more, doesn't he? I'll give you what you need. Come for me, baby, now." Bram tongued one of the healing brick-and-mortar abrasions on James' chest, then latched onto a taut, rosy nipple with his teeth, biting lightly and flicking the peak with his tongue.

James screamed, his climax spiking along with the warm burn of pain. He went rigid as fire swept through his body. Bram took no pity on him, milking his erupting cock until it was limp and James was shuddering and groaning with each new stroke.

"That's it. That's the way I like it, baby. Shake for me. Show me what I do to you. Show me." Bram sighed into James' neck, gathering the still shuddering man into his arms. Not waiting for James to recover even the power of speech, Bram unhooked the bag from the faucet handle and stood, pulling James' limp and unresisting body with him.

Still deeply buried in a euphoric, sex-induced stupor, James didn't object when his arms and chest were draped over Bram's shoulder. "Bram?"

"Don't worry, lover. I just thought it was about time we took this to a bed." Bram lifted James' slight weight, balancing the man on one shoulder, grabbed the open bottle of wine and left the room.

Startled, James grunted and grabbed at Bram's sides. "Hey, put me down!"

Laughing, Bram jogged up the stairs to the second story of the house. "Uh-huh. This is my caveman ritual. Get used to it, baby."

"Bastard." James grunted at each jostling step. "And you can kiss my ass, Caveman."

Ties That Bind

Bram brushed his hand over the taut, bare globes by his head, then planted a loud, wet kiss on the bruise spreading over the ass cheek nearest to him. He ignored James' indignant yelp. "Anything you want, baby. Just ask."

Ties That Bind

Ms. Gardner would like to thank Steve Hays, whose speech, "The Enemies of Eros in Antiquity," she discovered while doing research on the Internet. Though not quoted verbatim, it provided valuable inspiration and authenticity for the dialogue and classroom commentary of Dr. Anton MacDonnough. Gift of Eros

Kimberly Gardner

Gift of Eros

"The classical cannon of Greek and Latin literature does not treat Eros with particular reverence." Professor Anton MacDonnough stepped out from behind his podium. He paced across the front of the classroom, his eyes alighting first on one student, then another. "In fact, any sensible reader will come away from a careful reading of the ancient texts with the clear impression that, rather than a god to be adored, we would do better to treat Eros as…" Here he paused for effect, "Frankly, a psychopath."

Laughter rippled through the room. MacDonnough

smiled. Val sighed.

Of course he'd heard this line before in Mac's other lectures over the last four years. Mac had been his faculty advisor since his freshman year, and was now advising on the writing of Val's senior thesis. Mac always delivered the psychopath line in that exact cadence, always paused at that exact place and always smiled when the students laughed.

Just like he was smiling now.

Val sketched a stickman in the margin of his notebook; a sleeping stickman.

What the hell was he doing here anyway? He should have taken a class where he might have actually learned something to make up the three literature credits he needed to graduate. Instead, he'd let Mac talk him into this class, an intro course made up mostly of freshmen and sophomores, on the role of gods and monsters in ancient literature.

A total snoozer, but three easy credits for his final semester.

Val slid his gaze to the left and eyed the little hottie sitting at the next desk over. Dark hair pulled back in a stubby tail, skin so smooth it looked like he couldn't grow a beard and a face prettier than three quarters of the girls in the class. Not that Val was into girls. He hadn't even thought about girls that way since that day in junior high when Rickie Garcia had given him his very first blowjob behind the bleachers after gym class.

The little hottie slumped in his chair and yawned hugely without even covering his mouth.

Val smiled. He sketched a bed for his stickman, then he drew a yawning mouth as Mac droned on.

"Let's talk about the Iliad for a moment, and the coming together of those legendary lovers, Helen and Paris." He paused and lifted a hand to his ear. "Ah yes, I can hear the dreamy sighs even now."

A few of the students laughed.

"But set aside, if you will, our modern view of a magical

and romantic Eros. Instead, try seeing him as a destructive force that feeds off the lust and weakness of the lovers."

Val glanced up from his doodling, his gaze locking with the hottie in the next desk. The greenest eyes Val had ever seen watched him intently. A tongue slipped out to wet full lips.

Val's prick stirred. He dropped his gaze back to his notebook. With a few strokes of his pen he gave his stickman a raging hard-on, then a hand to wrap around it.

Oh, he was so going to fuck, or be fucked by, Green Eyes before this semester, and maybe even this day, was over.

From the corner of his eye he saw a slender hand. It reached across the space between the desks, dropped something on Val's notebook, then retreated. A scrap of paper. Val picked it up, unfolded it, and read.

What are you doing after class?

Hopefully getting your cock up my ass, or down my throat, Val thought. *Whatever you want, baby.*

He was supposed to be going to a wine and cheese reception in the classics department, had promised Mac he would go. But…

Picking up his pen, Val scribbled his reply.

Wait for me outside.

Refolding the paper, Val flipped it across the narrow space between the desks. It skidded across the surface and was caught just before drifting to the floor.

Val watched as the note was unfolded and read. Green eyes lifted to meet his and the kid gave an almost imperceptible nod.

Oh yeah!

The stickman began jacking as Val wove a little fantasy starring slim hands and big green eyes and a long, thick cock. Of course, by the look of him, the guy was probably a bottom. No big deal. Even though he would rather get fucked than do the fucking, he could be flexible.

To his cartoon he added a balloon coming out of Sticky's

mouth. In it he wrote, "uh, uh, uh, aaaaaahhhh!"

Oh yeah, for this he could be as flexible as need be.

For the next half hour, Val occupied himself by sneaking sideways glances at his future hook-up. The hottie wore a baggy T-shirt with some sort of faded image on the front and long sleeves pushed up to reveal sinewy forearms lightly dusted with dark hair. Graceful hands toyed with a pen, long fingers idly stroking the shaft and — no, that part of a pen was called the barrel, not the shaft.

Was he even conscious of what he was doing? Or were those actions nothing more than the fidgeting of bored hands?

In an attempt to accommodate his growing erection, Val shifted in his seat. The chair creaked and the hottie looked up.

Oh, he knew what he was doing all right. The curve of that beautiful mouth and the wicked gleam in his eyes made that perfectly clear.

"Next time we'll pick up with Helen and Paris." Mac paused, his gaze settling on Val. "I hope to see many of you at the wine and cheese reception sponsored by the department."

"When is it?" A girl with short brown hair lifted her backpack and slung it over her shoulder.

"It starts at five, which gives you…" Mac looked at his watch, "…fifteen minutes."

Val flipped his notebook closed and clipped his pen to the cover. Glancing sideways, his eyes met those of his hottie. Val swore he felt the spark jump between them. As casually as he could, he tugged his sweatshirt down as he got to his feet. His prick, which had never gone entirely soft since they'd first made eye contact, was now a very noticeable bulge in his jeans.

"Val, can I see you a moment?" From where he stood amidst a clutch of students, Mac crooked a finger at him.

Val nodded and sat down to wait for Mac.

His hottie was already halfway to the door.

Mmm, nice ass.

Gradually, the classroom emptied, students drifting away in

twos and threes. But the group surrounding Mac never seemed to get smaller. One person would leave only to be replaced by another.

C'mon. Val tapped his foot. He did not intend to miss his hook-up with Green Eyes.

After ten seemingly endless minutes, Mac shooed away the last of the students and walked to where Val waited. "Sorry about that." He smiled at Val and held out a book. "I brought that book you and I were talking about the other day."

What book?

Val took it. "Thanks."

"I hope it's helpful." Mac was looking at him, one salt-and-pepper brow lifted.

Val glanced down at the book in his hand. *The Path of Eros: Passion and Despair in Classical Mythology.* "I'm sure it will be."

"Good." Mac paused. "If you can wait a few minutes more, I'll collect my belongings and we can walk to the reception together." He smiled. "I hope you have your ID with you. The dean is quite adamant about no underage students being served alcohol."

"Actually, I need to make a stop before I head over to the reception." Val stuck the book in his backpack. "So maybe I'll just see you there."

The hallway outside the classroom was mostly deserted except for a few stragglers; none of them was his green-eyed hottie.

Damn.

Val took his time descending the two flights of stairs that would take him to the front entrance of the classroom building. All the while he kept an eye out for his hook-up. Pushing open the outer door, he stepped outside. The February wind kissed his cheeks and slid chilly fingers inside his jacket. He shivered. He searched the faces of the students who chatted and milled around despite the cold. No hottie.

Shit.

Ties That Bind

Well, it wasn't like he'd never see the guy again. They were in class together, so that was something. Consoling himself with the promise of other chances on other days, Val hefted his backpack and turned down the path that would take him to the classics department building, and the wine and cheese reception.

* * * * *

"But Dr. MacDonnough, Odysseus *was* ruled by Eros. He even fought off a goddess's affections to return to his wife. I think that's very romantic."

Mac caught Val's eye as the girl from the Gods and Monsters class, the one with the short brown hair who always sat in the front row, continued to argue her point. Mac's eye-roll was anything but subtle.

Val hid his grin in his glass of chardonnay. Even as he did, a part of him pitied the girl who was about to be ridiculed. She seemed so earnest. Mac could be a real prick when he thought you were talking out your ass, which happened most often when you weren't agreeing with him.

"Hey, are you really drinking that shit or just being polite?"

A prickle of awareness raced down Val's spine and straight to his dick. Even though the soft male voice was unfamiliar, he knew who it belonged to before he turned around. His green-eyed hottie stood just behind him, close enough to touch, a small smile playing around his lips.

Standing like this, the two of them were nearly eye-to-eye, the other man maybe an inch taller than Val's five-feet-nine. Perfect.

Val let his gaze slide down that slender body. The baggy shirt—the faded image on the front was Bob Dylan, he now realized—did nothing to conceal the whip-cord leanness of his form. Yet he wasn't skinny, not at all. He had the arms and shoulders of someone who worked out regularly and was no wuss when it came to the bench-press. Those arms would feel just right around him.

"So, are you?"

Tearing his gaze and his thoughts away from his lithe form, Val met those amazing green eyes. "Am I what?"

"Drinking that cheap-shit chardonnay."

"Not really." Using his body as a shield, Val flicked the other man's nipple, only just visible through his t-shirt. "Why, you want some, Dylan?"

Green eyes flashed. "How'd you know my name?"

"Your name's really Dylan? Like Bob?"

"Just like. Mom was a huge fan. I am too." Taking the glass from Val's fingers, Dylan turned it so his lips touched exactly where Val's had and sipped. He scrunched up his face and, without asking, turned and dumped the rest of the wine into the dirt of a nearby potted ficus tree. Setting the empty glass aside, he held out his hand.

"Let's get out of here."

Val glanced around, then down at the hand held out so invitingly. No one seemed to be paying them any attention.

"Okay." Sliding his hand into Dylan's, Val let himself be led out of the department and down the nearly deserted corridor.

"What's your name?"

"Val." The hand was so warm, long fingers twined with his so possessively, he could hardly wait to feel those hands on other, more intimate parts of his body.

"Like Valentine?"

"No, like Valentin. I was named after my grandfather."

"Yeah?" Val was treated to a heart-stopping grin. "Was grandpop a beautiful blondie, too?"

Val returned the grin. "Nope. He was dark and swarthy, from what I remember, and built like a fire hydrant."

In fact no one in his family possessed either blond hair or blue eyes. As for his willowy slimness, where that had come from was also anybody's guess. His mother, to this day, still called him her little changeling babe.

Val's hand was squeezed. "Well, I like your looks,

Valentine."

It was nearly dark when they emerged from the classics building, lights coming on all over campus, and the wind had picked up. Val shivered, though whether from the cold or anticipation he couldn't say.

"Let's go this way." Dylan tugged him to the right.

"Where—"

"Do you live on campus?"

"No, I share a house with some guys just the other side of City Avenue."

"That's kind of far."

They passed the utilities management building, then a series of sheds that were little more than cinderblock huts used for storage. Without warning, Dylan veered off the path and turned down a narrow alley, dragging Val with him.

Pausing before one of the sheds, he shoved open the door, yanked Val inside and behind a pallet stacked nearly to the ceiling with boxes.

"Hey, man, what are you—uh!" Val was shoved hard against the wall, trapped against the chilly cinderblock by the press of Dylan's lean body. Slender hands framed his face, fingers spearing into his hair.

"I can't wait that long." Dylan's breath fanned over Val's lips. "Gonna fuck you right here, my pretty Valentine."

"My name's not—" Dylan's lips slammed down on Val's, cutting off the words, stealing his breath. His lips were forced apart by the tongue that invaded his mouth. Pinned in place by hands and lips and body, Val was helpless to do anything but kiss Dylan back.

Dylan's hands left Val's face and insinuated themselves between their bodies. Long fingers jerked open the button of Val's jeans while the other hand unzipped his jacket and rucked up his sweatshirt. Fingers pinched his nipple, sending an electric shock of sensation straight to his prick.

Val gasped into Dylan's mouth.

Ties That Bind

The cold, rough brick scraped against his back as the kiss went on and on. His jeans were shoved down his hips, the chill extending to his ass as his dick sprang free.

"You smell so good, baby." Val's cock was grasped and lightly squeezed, Dylan's thumb swiping the head. "You want this, don't you?" Clever fingers rolled his balls. "Say you want it, or I'll stop."

Val gripped Dylan's shoulders for balance while only yards away on the other side of the door the business of the college went on unaware.

He won't stop, no matter what I say.

The thought that his choice could be taken away in the blink of an eye thrilled him, even if it was just an illusion.

"Say it." Releasing Val's cock and balls, Dylan crushed their bodies together. The ridge of his denim-clad erection rubbed against Val's naked prick.

"I want it." A hand slid around behind him and a finger pressed against his entrance. He gasped.

"Like this? You want my finger?"

Val shook his head. "Not like that. Your cock. I want your cock up my ass. Please?"

In the space of a heartbeat, Val found himself spun around and facing the wall, hands gripping his hips. Lips brushed his ear.

"Put your hands on the wall. Don't move them or I'll stop." Teeth scraped the vein in Val's neck. He shivered. "Don't come until I tell you. And don't turn around."

Yes. God.

Obediently, Val placed his palms against the wall. The cold stone contrasted with the hot breath on his neck and the warm body at his back. He could have come from sheer anticipation. He was about to get fucked in a public place by a guy whose last name he didn't even know, whose delicate beauty hid the heart of a dominant. That, in itself, would have been enough to push him over the edge. But being taken and controlled and

94

commanded not to come was more exciting than he could have imagined. He wasn't about to do anything that might risk his not getting this man's cock inside him within the next five minutes.

The hands on his hips disappeared suddenly and Val started to protest. Then he heard the unmistakable sound of a condom packet being torn open. Shaking his hair out of his eyes, he turned his head just a little. He was dying to see Dylan's cock. Just a peek was all he wanted.

Oh my fucking God!

Val's anus clenched in anticipation and pre-come dripped from the head of his prick.

"You aren't being a bad boy and peeking, are you, my little Valentine?" Dylan smoothed the Day-Glo orange condom down his shaft, taking his time, not looking at Val.

With a groan, Val rested his forehead against his upper arm and silently recited Latin verb conjugations. It didn't help. God, he was so close.

"Gonna get you ready now." A cool, slick finger pressed into his ass. A moment later a second finger joined the first, twisting to find then stroke his gland. A moan was torn from Val's lips. He pushed back, fucking himself on the fingers, enjoying the penetration. He didn't bother to tell Dylan that he didn't need much preparation. Those fingers felt so fucking good. And how they must look, the two of them—Dylan fully clothed, his cock jutting proudly from his jeans, and him half naked, fucking himself on Dylan's fingers.

Then the fingers were pulled out. "Brace yourself, baby."

Val braced. The blunt tip of Dylan's cock pressed, warm and slick, against his entrance. Gripping Val's hips, Dylan pushed. Val gasped as the head popped through the tight ring of muscle, stretching him just enough to sting.

"That's it, baby. Gods, but you're tight. Tight and hot and sweet." Dylan grunted and thrust, shoving his cock in then pulling out just a little.

Ties That Bind

"Oh God, please." Val braced with his forearms to keep from being smashed into the wall. Another thrust shoved him forward, his arms scraped against the stone, burning a little. It was nothing compared to the burn and stretch in his ass. Another thrust and Val felt the prickle of Dylan's pubes, his hole stuffed and stretched around the thick base of Dylan's cock.

Dylan rested his chin on Val's shoulder. "You okay, my little Valentine? My big cock too much for your sweet little hole?" Val's sweatshirt was yanked aside and his shoulder nipped. "Want me to stop? Shall I pull my dick out?"

"No," Val sighed. "Fuck me. Fill me up. Let me come for you."

Dylan's chuckle rumbled against Val's back. "Okay. You asked for it, sweetheart. Gonna fuck you so hard you'll remember me for days."

Dylan pulled out almost all the way then shoved in, nailing Val's gland. Val whimpered and bit his lip to keep from crying out. Again and again Dylan thrust hard, shoving Val nearly flush against the wall.

Val's skin prickled with goose flesh, his nipples standing out as hard little points even as sweat dripped in his eyes. He blinked against the sting. The muscles in his arms strained to keep his face from smashing into the stone as Dylan fucked his ass. One hard thrust after another. God, it felt amazing.

The tingling began low in Val's belly, the first signal that he was going to come. His knees shook. The scent of his own arousal mixed with Dylan's musky aroma filled his head.

Not yet. He would not come yet. He wanted to feel that gorgeous cock pulsing inside him, wanted Dylan's permission before he blew his load.

"Ah, gods, but you're sweet." A hand closed around Val's cock, stroking and teasing the sensitive glans, dragging the orgasm ever closer to the base of his prick.

Val's stomach muscles clenched and his balls drew tight

against his body. Dylan pulled out, leaving just the head inside his ass. His muscles fluttered and clenched, every spasm trying to draw Dylan's thick shaft deeper inside his sensitized passage.

"Oh God, please," Val whimpered. "Please, I need it. I want it. Fuck me. Give me all of it."

He shoved himself back, impaling himself on Dylan's prick until he swore he could feel the head in his throat.

And the shed door opened.

Val froze.

"Hello? Somebody in here?" The voice came from just the other side of the pallet, the boxes the only thing shielding them from discovery. Footsteps scraped along the cement floor, the beam of a flashlight tracked along the ground, illuminating the shadows. Something squeaked and scurried away from the light.

Oh my God!

Val held his breath, Dylan's cock still balls deep in his ass. Quietly, he tried to pull away, but Dylan held him pinned. He was crazy. They would be caught.

"Be still." The command was little more than a breath. Teeth nipped his ear, hard. The hand on his prick began stroking again. The cock in his ass was dragged over his gland then thrust back in.

Val swallowed and heard the click in his throat. He had zero spit left in his mouth. Shutting his eyes, he waited for the light to expose them.

From the other side of the pallet came the sound of a walkie-talkie.

"Frank, it's Roger. You there?" An indistinct reply mixed with static. "There's nobody in here but the rats, man. You're seeing things."

Frank said something indecipherable.

"I did look." Footsteps retreated. "You fucking dickhead." This last was muttered just under Roger's breath. The door opened then closed.

Silence, except for the sound of Dylan's breathing in Val's

ear.

Dylan began to move again. Harder and deeper, he fucked Val's ass, matching his rhythm with the stroking of his hand.

"That's it," Dylan breathed. "Give it up for me. Be my slut, you know you want to." Val's cock was squeezed, Dylan's thumb rubbed over the head, a sharp little pain as he pressed his thumbnail lightly into the slit.

God, he did want to.

Fingers gripped his balls and squeezed, yanking him back from the edge of orgasm. The biting edge of pain blended with pleasure, ramping up his need as Dylan shoved in deep. Val fought not to groan.

Faster and harder, Dylan worked him, the grip on his dick punishingly fierce as Val rocked into the motion, the sound of Dylan's balls slapping against his ass drowning out everything else.

"Come for me now," Dylan whispered. Teeth sank into Val's shoulder as Dylan's cock swelled and pulsed against his hole.

Val choked back a scream as the orgasm raced down his spine and exploded out his cock and he sprayed the wall with pulse after pulse of spunk.

As the last of the come drained from his prick, Val's knees buckled. A slender arm wrapped around his waist, holding him up. Dylan's cock slipped out of Val's ass. Lips brushed his ear as he rested against Dylan's chest.

"Are you okay, my Valentine?"

"Don't know." He tried to stand and found he was still shaky. "We almost got caught."

"No way." Dylan laughed. "That wasn't even close."

"God, you're a lunatic." Val's lips curved and he leaned his head back against Dylan's shoulder.

"Maybe." Lips nuzzled just under his ear. "But it was exciting. And you liked it, didn't you?"

Val rubbed his cheek against Dylan's. "Yeah, I liked it."

Liked it, hell. It was fucking heart-stopping. And he'd come so hard he nearly passed out.

Gradually Val steadied and regained his feet. Turning in Dylan's arms, he wrapped himself around the other man and nuzzled the side of his neck. He inhaled the scents of sweat and sex and Dylan's skin. "That was fucking fantastic."

Dylan chuckled. "Yeah, it was pretty great, wasn't it?"

Val's jeans were pulled up, his cock tucked gently away before he was buttoned and zipped. His shirt was straightened, his lips kissed.

"Okay?" Dylan brushed Val's hair back from his face.

Val nodded.

"Where did you say you live?" Dylan took Val's hand in his.

"Just across City Avenue, maybe four or five blocks from here."

"C'mon then, I'll walk you home."

"You don't have to."

"I want to." Tugging him to the door, Dylan pushed it open a crack and peered out. "Let's go." He shoved it open the rest of the way and stepped out.

"Are you a classics major?" Val fell into step beside him.

"I'm undeclared." Dylan kept Val's hand in his as they walked along the alley.

"What made you take Mac's class?"

"Mythology is sort of a hobby of mine."

When they reached the street, Dylan paused. "Which way?"

Val pointed to the left. "That way."

Dylan squeezed his hand. "Lead the way then, my pretty Valentine."

* * * * *

"Don't tell me you're all out of the Arabian coffee." The woman in the white polyester pants huffed out a breath.

"There should be some over there on the rack. Let me just…" Val started around the counter.

She rolled her eyes. "I already looked. There isn't any over there."

Val stopped. "Well, then I guess we're out."

She let go a long-suffering sigh, like he had just pissed in her cheerios. "Well, do you think maybe you could look in the back?"

Not for you, bitch.

"Sure." Val pasted on a smile and turned to the manager. "Eddie, I'm going in the back." Without waiting for Eddie's reply, Val left the drinks station and the obnoxious woman and escaped into the stockroom at the back of the shop.

"Fucking bitch." Val scanned the shelves, looking for the beans the customer wanted. Somebody should tell her those pants make her look like an albino elephant. Unfortunately, it couldn't be him. Too bad.

Why did people have to act like that anyway? Or maybe it was just him. Eddie, the friend and housemate who'd gotten him the job at the Bean Bar, never seemed to have these problems with the customers. Maybe he just wasn't cut out for the service industry.

They were out of the beans she wanted. Crap. He was about to return to the counter to break the bad news when he caught sight of the boxes stacked in the corner that had yet to be opened and stocked. Checking the labels, he found the Arabian beans. He opened the box. The redolent aroma of the dark roast assailed him. Even though he didn't drink coffee, he loved that smell. He took out two bags and, feeling good, headed back to the front of the shop.

The woman was nowhere in sight.

Val turned to Eddie. "Where'd the lady in the white pants go?"

Eddie glanced up from his magazine. "What?"

"The customer who wanted the Arabian."

"Oh, her?" He turned a page. "She said something about not having all day and she left."

"Bitch." Plunking the bags of coffee down on the counter, Val picked up the nearly empty decaf pot.

"Where were you anyway?" Eddie flipped the magazine closed and slid off the stool behind the register. "Some guy was just in here looking for you."

Val's heart leaped and his hands stilled.

Dylan.

No. Don't be an idiot. Dylan was a hook-up, nothing more. No matter how hot the guy was, a single fuck in an equipment shed did not a relationship make. Though in the two days since that encounter, Val had thought of little else. Especially when he was alone with only his hand for company.

He kept his tone deliberately casual. "Who was it?"

"How should I know? I didn't ask for his ID."

It wasn't Dylan. Couldn't be Dylan.

"What did he look like?"

Eddie shrugged. "About your height. Black hair in a ponytail. Young."

"Did he have green eyes?"

"Dude, I was not checking him out."

Dylan.

"Why didn't you call me?"

"I did." Opening the pastry case, Eddie selected a chocolate frosted donut, bit in and chewed, delivering his next words around a mouthful of pastry. "You didn't answer. I figured you were taking a leak or something."

Fucking great.

"Did he give you a message or anything?"

Eddie shook his head. "No message. But he left something for you."

"What?" Val bobbled the coffee pot he was filling. Water splashed over the counter and onto the floor. Setting the pot down, he lowered his voice. "He left something for me? What is it?"

"Hey, man, watch what you're doing." Stuffing the rest of

the donut into his mouth, Eddie reached under the register, withdrew a small bag with handles and held it out.

Val took it. "What's in it?"

"How the hell should I know?" Eddie grinned. "It looks like a present. I looked, but it's all wrapped up." His gaze dropped to the water puddled on the floor. "I'll get that if you want to take your break now."

God, Eddie was human after all.

Val opened his mouth to say thanks, but before he could speak, the door opened and a gaggle of teenage girls entered, all talking at once. Val counted nine of them, all wearing their little Catholic schoolgirl uniforms.

So much for his break.

Stashing the bag back under the counter, he took his place at the register. "What can I get you ladies today?"

A girl of about fifteen with bright pink hair eyed him up and down then licked her lips. "I don't know…" She cracked her gum. "I think I want something hot and sweet. You got anything like that?"

Her friends giggled.

Oh brother. This was going to be a long day.

A half hour later the door closed behind the last of the girls, leaving the shop blessedly empty and quiet. Val sighed just as Eddie wiped imaginary sweat from his brow.

"I didn't think they'd ever leave." Eddie grinned. "That one with the pink hair had the hots for you, dude."

"You think?" Grabbing a paper towel, Val wiped down the counter.

"Hell, yeah. Wonder what she'd say if she knew you'd rather go out with her brother."

Val chuckled, imagining himself telling the little hussy he was gay. Not that it hadn't crossed his mind to do just that. She'd been relentless, flirting outrageously the entire time he was making her drink, then when he went to hand it to her, leaning way across the counter and giving him a perfect view down her shirt at her perky little breasts.

Tossing the paper towel in the trash, Val returned to the register. He reached under the counter and pulled out the bag.

"I'm going outside for a smoke."

"You don't smoke."

"I just started." No way was he opening the package in front of Eddie. Not without knowing what was inside.

Val pushed open the back door and stepped out into the alley behind the shop.

The bag was smallish, about the size they used to hold two pounds of coffee. Val opened it and pulled out the box. About eight inches long and four or five inches wide, it was wrapped in white paper printed with gold and silver bows and arrows. He shook it. No sound. He was dying to rip into the pretty paper but forced himself to go slow, picking at the tape then carefully peeling it back before he unwrapped the box and raised the lid. Inside, a card lay atop neatly folded tissue paper.

Setting the box on the window ledge at his elbow, Val picked up the card. It was small, made of heavy white paper, the front embossed with the same gold and silver design as adorned the wrapping. Slowly Val opened the card.

Wear it for me.

He turned the card over but that was it. No date, no signature, not even an initial, just a command to "wear it for me."

And it was definitely a command.

What was in the box? And was it something he would want to wear?

Heart pounding, Val gazed down at the bold loopy scrawl and savored the delicious anticipation. Closing his eyes, he recalled Dylan's eyes, and Dylan's mouth, and Dylan's hands, and the way Dylan took charge. And how much he, Val, had liked it. Liked it, hell, he'd come so hard he'd just about passed out.

Oh yeah, he could do with more of that.

Val reached for the box at his elbow and slowly unfolded the tissue paper.

Oh. My. Fucking. God.

It was a corset.

Val's hand shook as he lifted it from the box. White leather, about seven inches wide, with long laces to cinch it snug around the wearer's waist. Around his waist.

And he would wear it, just as he'd been told to. For Dylan.

* * * * *

Val studied his reflection in the bedroom mirror. The corset, laced up and holding him tight, accentuated the arch of his spine and his taut, flat belly. Aside from that, it was impossible to tell, unless you knew, that he was even wearing it.

But Dylan would know. Not that he would be seeing Dylan. Maybe. Probably. He was going to the library to do homework, not to look for Dylan.

Val's cock twitched at the thought of Dylan. Ever since he'd opened the box and slid the cool, supple leather around his waist, his prick had been more than a little interested. Now that he was laced up tight enough to feel it with every breath, his prick was throbbing and wet at the tip. He'd thought about jerking off, then hadn't done it. He liked the feeling of edgy anticipation that wearing the corset gave him. Not that there was anything to anticipate, not at the library.

Val straightened the loose tails of his shirt and checked his reflection one last time. With his shirt out, you couldn't even tell that he had a hard-on. Good.

Now, where were his books and his laptop?

***

Val ran a fingertip along the edge of the shelf and scanned the spines of the books. The translation he needed wasn't there. He glanced down at the note in his hand. Maybe he had copied the info wrong. He would have to go back to the computer and check the reference again.

Fuck. He didn't have time for this. His translation was due

in the morning and despite an hour of tedious labor—Greek wasn't his strongest subject—he still had pages left to translate.

Turning, he left the dusty stacks and ran straight into another person.

"Excuse me. I didn't…"

His words were cut off as strong arms closed around him and he was pulled against a lean body. He barely had time to register the identity of his assailant before lips claimed his in a fierce kiss.

Dylan.

On a sigh, Val's lips parted, Dylan's tongue sliding in to tease his.

Mmm, so good.

Val allowed himself to linger a minute before he broke the kiss. But when Dylan didn't release him he pushed at the other man's chest.

"Dylan, let me go. We can't make out in the library."

"Why not?" Rather than letting go, Dylan walked him backward, deeper into the stacks. Val's back was pushed against the shelf he'd been perusing only moments before. Pressing in against him, Dylan took his mouth again. This time the kiss was slow and soft, the kind of kiss that made Val's insides go all hot and gooey, the kind of kiss that made his dick hard, the kind that was uniquely Dylan's.

"We have to stop." Val shoved at Dylan.

"Don't want to stop." Hands slid under Val's shirt. "Mmm, you're wearing your present. Good boy." Fingers traced his ribs. "Do you like it? Does it make you feel sexy?"

Val's breath caught. The heat from Dylan's palms seared him right through the leather. "Yes." He licked his lips. "Yes, it does."

"And does it make you hard, my little Valentine? Is your dick hard for me right now?"

"Yes," Val breathed, "so hard for you right now."

"Show me."

"Not here."

"Yes, here." Val's nipple was pinched.

His cock jerked. "Ow. Stop that."

"You don't mean that." Dylan pinched the other nipple. His thigh slipped between Val's legs.

"I do mean it. I have work to do. I can't fool around. I shouldn't even have worn this…" Val stopped, his cheeks going hot.

"It's called a corset, Valentine." Dylan nipped Val's lower lip. "C'mon, say it with me. Cor-set."

"Shhh. Be quiet. Somebody will hear."

"Yeah? Like who? Nobody ever hangs out back here except you classics majors."

"I don't know. Somebody might come." Almost against his will, Val rubbed against Dylan's thigh.

"If we're lucky, somebody'll come." Dylan pressed his leg up against Val's crotch. "Mmm, you are hard for me." Reaching down, he gave Val's prick a squeeze.

Val groaned. His head fell back and bonked against the shelf. "C'mon, man. I really do have work to do. I have this translation due tomorrow and it's not even close to being done."

"Latin or Greek?"

"Greek." Val rocked against Dylan's leg. "God, you're making me so horny."

"Where's your stuff?"

Val's jaw dropped.

"Not that kind of stuff." Dylan laughed. "I meant your books and stuff, Valentine. Geeze, is sex all you ever think about?"

Val grinned. "Over there in the study cube." Dylan stepped back and held out his hand. Val took it. "You can't stay, though. You'll distract me."

He led Dylan over to the study cubicle where his books, papers and laptop were set up. Leaning over, Dylan frowned down at the page. "Homer. Cool."

"You can read Greek? I thought you weren't a classics major. Why are you taking Greek?"

And how had Dylan known that was Homer just from those few lines? Had he told Dylan that's what he was translating? The man got him so turned around he very well might have and just forgot.

Dylan didn't answer. Hooking the single chair with one booted foot, he pulled it out and pointed. "Sit. Work. I won't bug you."

Val sat. "What are you going to do?"

"Watch you." He leaned back against the cubicle wall and crossed his arms over his chest.

"You're just going to stand there and watch me translate Greek? Don't you have anything better to do?"

"Nope. Go on. I promise I'll be good." The look he sent from under his lashes spoke of anything but goodness.

Val dropped his head to the desk and thumped it once, then again. Dylan was going to be the death of him. But what a way to go.

Aeolus entertained me for a whole month, asking me questions all the time about Troy, the Argive fleet, and the return of the Achaeans.

Val read the line again, then the entire passage, changed the order of two words and erased half of what he'd written.

"No wonder I'm bombing Greek." Totally disgusted with himself, he threw down his pencil.

"You aren't bombing Greek." Dylan leaned over Val's shoulder and read what he'd just written. "What are you pulling, like an A minus?"

"No." He was pulling a B, but he didn't have to say so.

Dylan picked up his pencil and wrote something in his notebook.

"Hey, man, that's my homework. What are you doing?"

"I'm helping." Dylan kept writing, but when Val tried to look, he nudged him away. After several minutes, Dylan put down the pencil and slid Val's notebook under his nose.

Ties That Bind

Val read what Dylan had just written, then he read it again. He had crossed out several of Val's phrases, rearranged others and rewritten one entire line. His changes were not only correct, but they made more sense and flowed more smoothly than the lines Val had agonized over.

Val met Dylan's gaze. "How the fuck did you do that?"

"Do what?" Dylan blinked. "I didn't do anything."

"Bullshit. You just fixed my translation so it makes more sense, and you did it without a dictionary or anything. How did you do that?"

His answer was a shrug. "I just tweaked what you had. You're the one who did the work." He picked up the Greek text and flipped pages. "How much of this do you have to do for tomorrow?"

"Mac said to do as much as I could."

"This is for one of MacDonnough's classes?"

"It's an independent study. Mac's working on a translation of Homer and I'm assisting him. For credit."

Dylan's lips thinned briefly then he shook his head. "Okay, let's do some more. Another couple pages should do."

"You can't just do my homework for me." He didn't bother to ask again how Dylan had even managed to do as much as he had. Clearly, he wasn't getting an answer.

"I'm not doing it for you. I'm just helping."

"Why?"

"So you'll be grateful." Dylan smiled. "You will be grateful, won't you?"

Val lowered his lashes. "How grateful do you want me to be?"

"Grateful enough that you'll let me suck your cock."

The suggestion went straight to Val's prick. He swallowed. "I don't... You want to suck my cock?"

"Unless you have your heart set on sucking mine." He leaned down close. His breath fanned over Val's lips. "But I really, really want to taste you. I'll bet you taste sweet."

Ties That Bind

He should back away and not let Dylan distract him. He really should. He had a ton of work to do. Work that wouldn't get done if he let himself drown in those merman eyes.

Instead of backing away, Val leaned forward and brought their lips together. He drank in Dylan's sigh and returned one of his own. Long fingers slid into his hair and angled his head so the kiss could go deep.

Soft lips teased his, teeth nipping, tongue sliding in to taste and explore. Dylan took his time, fucking Val's mouth with his tongue, drawing little breathy moans from him until Val could do nothing but let Dylan have his way.

Sliding Val's chair back, Dylan nudged his thighs apart and stepped between them.

"What are you doing?" Val tried to get to his feet but Dylan pushed him back.

"Sit and be quiet or someone will hear." He sank to his knees and dropped a wink. "People are trying to study, you know?"

"You can't." Aware that his voice had gotten much too loud, Val shut his mouth. Dylan wouldn't stop anyway, and truthfully, though he would never admit it out loud, Dylan's brand of public affection was thrilling beyond anything Val had ever imagined.

Scooting backward under the desk, Dylan rolled Val's chair in close. "Put your hands on the desk, baby. And don't move or I'll stop. Understand?"

Val nodded.

"Good boy." Dylan buried his face against Val's crotch, nuzzling his prick through his jeans. Green eyes rolled up to meet his. "Gonna make you come so hard you'll see stars."

Oh God.

Val strained his ears, listening for approaching footsteps. But the library remained quiet. Thank God. If anyone did walk by they would surely hear his thundering heartbeat.

Nudging his thighs farther apart, Dylan settled into the

intimate vee of Val's thighs. Strong hands slid up his legs, fingers kneading his muscles. Dylan mouthed Val's erection through his jeans as he drew the zipper down inch by agonizing inch. Fingers slid between denim and flesh, wrapped around his prick and drew it out.

The walls of the cubicle pressed in close on both sides, the back of the chair high enough that anyone passing by would have trouble seeing the surface of the desk let alone the action underneath.

Warm breath ghosted over his cock. A drop of moisture welled from the slit and was quickly licked away.

Val squirmed, inching his ass closer to the edge of the chair.

"Don't move, Valentine, or I'll stop." Dylan's voice was low, pitched for Val's ears alone.

Shutting his eyes, Val flattened his palms on the desk and forced himself to be still. Sitting there with his cock exposed and Dylan kneeling between his legs, he wanted nothing more than to shoot his load in that hot, silky mouth. Wanted to feel his lover drink him down then watch as he licked him clean.

In one smooth motion Dylan gulped him to the root. Val's eyes rolled back and he stifled a cry as Dylan's throat constricted around the head. Teeth scraped his shaft. A tongue teased his slit. Val's hips jerked and Dylan's hands tightened on his thighs. Be still, the move said, and Val struggled to obey.

Dylan's head bobbed as he set up a rhythm, laving with his tongue, teasing with his teeth, sucking hard, calling the orgasm up from Val's balls.

On the desk Val's hands curled into fists. He gripped his pencil hard as he fought to stay still. Biting the inside of his cheek, he panted through his nose. If he dared to open his mouth he would moan for sure.

With each glorious suck his thigh muscles tensed and need coiled tighter in his belly. God, how he wanted to fuck that beautiful face. Fist his hand in that glossy hair and come in that luscious mouth.

"Close," Val whispered.

Dylan doubled his efforts, licking and sucking like he was starving and Val's cock was the best thing he'd ever tasted.

Val squeezed his hands tighter and tighter until his nails bit into his palms. Blood pounded in his ears, his dick swelled and throbbed against Dylan's tongue as the orgasm exploded up from his sack and out his prick. The pencil snapped in two in his hand, the sound as loud as a gunshot.

* * * * *

"Your translations are really improving, Val." Mac's desk chair creaked as he sat back. A smile curved his lips and crinkled the corners of his eyes. "Your progress this semester is very impressive."

They were seated in Mac's office, just the two of them. The morning sun poured through the window behind Mac's head, bathing everything in a clear golden light.

"Thank you." Val grinned, recalling how Dylan had "helped" him with his homework.

After the blowjob of a lifetime, they moved from the cubicle to one of the large tables. Dylan had located an online copy of the very translation Val couldn't find on the shelves then sat with him while he worked, tweaking and refining Val's assignment until late into the night. But when Val invited him home, Dylan shook his head and muttered something about having his own stuff to get done. Then he'd dropped a light kiss on Val's lips and left the library.

"Val?"

"Hmm?" Shit, Mac was talking to him. Val's cheeks heated. "Sorry, Mac. I was just thinking."

"Oh? Care to share?"

Not really.

"I was thinking about the translation."

It wasn't a total lie.

Mac nodded as if this made perfect sense and was just

111

what he'd expected. "I asked if you found the Butler translation helpful." He glanced down at the pages on his desk. "It certainly seems so, judging from the quality of your work."

"Very helpful." He ignored the prickle of guilt at not telling his mentor about his special tutor. Not the details, of course, but that he was getting outside help. But even if he'd wanted to tell Mac, which he didn't, how could he explain Dylan's facility with Greek when he couldn't even reason it out for himself?

As they sat together working, he had tried once again to quiz Dylan about his life—where he came from, what high school he'd gone to, did he have any brothers or sisters? But all he got were the same noncommittal answers and evasions as before. Just when he'd begun to feel like a total pain in the ass, Dylan had told him he'd transferred from a small liberal arts college called Olympia State where he had indeed been a classical studies major. So that explained at least a little.

"I'm going to hold on to these pages, if that's all right." Mac tapped the edges of the papers together and slipped them back in the folder. "You do have another copy, don't you?"

"I do." He had the copy with Dylan's notes scribbled all over it. He'd kept it, liking the way the bold loopy scrawl looked next to his own small, tight script.

Mac opened his desk drawer and slid the folder inside. Folding his arms, he leaned forward, elbows resting on the desk blotter, blue eyes keen on Val's face.

"I'd like to put aside our usual discussion of Homer for a few minutes. I have something else I want to discuss with you."

Val glanced from Mac's face down to his own text, already open on his lap, then back. "Is something wrong?"

"No, no, it's nothing bad. It's…well, it's rather good, at least I think it is."

Despite Mac's assurance, apprehension slid through Val and coiled itself tight in his belly. He closed his book, giving his teacher and friend his full attention.

"In June, I'm going to be leaving for Greece. It's a sort of combined sabbatical and research trip. I expect to be there for three months, returning in time to teach again in the fall. I find myself with a need, and a moderate budget, for engaging a research assistant and I was hoping you would consider the position."

Val opened his mouth but no words came out. He swallowed and licked his lips. Mac was asking him to go to Greece for the summer as his assistant. It was almost too good to be real. So why did the sensation in his gut feel more like dread than elation?

Mac lifted a hand. "You don't have to answer right now. I know it must be something of a surprise." He smiled. "I must confess, I've known for a couple of weeks that I was going to ask you. I was just waiting for the right time."

"Why me?"

"Why not you?" The chair squeaked as Mac leaned back. "You're the perfect choice, Val. You're a graduating senior. Your work ethic is unquestionable. Your interest in the classics closely mirrors my own. And you are my best and brightest student in years."

This brand of unvarnished praise, coming from a man he liked and respected, should have had him dancing in the street. And he did feel a warm glow of pride at Mac's high opinion of him. Add to that the fact that ever since high school, when he'd first fallen in love with classical literature, he'd harbored a secret desire to go to Greece. He should be jumping at this opportunity.

But if he said yes and accepted Mac's offer and went to Greece for the summer, what would happen to his relationship with Dylan? A week ago the question would not even have occurred to him. A week ago he hadn't even known Dylan. And now? What was so different now that it should cause him to hesitate to accept Mac's generous and flattering offer?

"Val? Are you all right?"

Val jerked himself back to the conversation at hand. "I'm

fine. I'm just…I don't know what to say."

"As I said, you don't have to answer me today. Take some time, perhaps talk it over with someone whose opinion you trust. Then you can let me know."

Val nodded. The trouble with that suggestion was that Mac was the person whose opinion Val most trusted. Briefly, he let himself imagine that discussion.

Yeah, so Mac, there's this beautiful man I've been fucking for the last week or so. I don't know much about him but I think I might be just the tiniest bit addicted to him because I can't get him out of my head. And now I'm thinking about not going to Greece because I don't want to leave him.

Yeah, that would be good.

"So, I suppose we should spend just a little time with Homer." Mac opened his text.

Val did likewise, but after only a few minutes spent with Odysseus on his ship, Mac returned to the subject of Greece.

"I don't think I mentioned that if you decide to take the position, you'll be paid a small stipend for living expenses. It won't be much. Of course, you won't need much, I shouldn't think. We'll be staying in a small villa just outside Athens." Mac's cheeks colored just a little. "I mean…well, it's a two bedroom house that belongs to a colleague, a man I've known for years and who is spending the summer in London. I'll be working a good deal of the time, completing my translation, and you would, of course, be expected to assist me with that. But we would certainly have ample time for leisure activities, seeing the sites and so on." He paused. "Not that I'm trying to unduly influence your decision."

Val said nothing.

A villa. Just outside Athens. The Acropolis. The Parthenon. Hadrian's Arch. And the monastery at Kaisariani.

God.

For the rest of the hour Val heard little else that Mac said, too caught up in his own thoughts.

Ties That Bind

At last, Mac looked at the clock on his desk, the way he always did, and said, "Well, it seems our time together is at an end." Pushing back his chair, he stood up and rounded the desk.

With a sense of relief that far out-stripped the situation, Val stuffed his belongings into his backpack, stood up and slung it over his shoulder.

Mac walked him to the door, then paused with his hand on the doorknob. "I meant what I said about not wanting to unduly influence your decision. But I do hope you'll accept the position."

"I'll give it very serious consideration." God, why was he suddenly sounding like a stiff-necked old fart?

Mac laid a hand on Val's shoulder and squeezed. "I know you will. You're very sensible and focused on your goals. And I know you'll make the right decision."

Val stepped out into the hallway and paused as the door clicked shut behind him.

Mac was right. He was sensible. And most of the time he did make good decisions. As for keeping his focus, of that he wasn't so sure.

* * * * *

"You do know I could lose my freakin' work study if anybody finds out I did this for you." Eddie's fingers flew over the computer keyboard as he logged in to the university's student database.

Perched on the end of his housemate's bed, Val watched as Eddie signed on. "I swear I won't tell anyone." He crossed his heart. "Scout's honor."

"They don't let gay guys in the boy scouts, man."

"I was ten."

"You didn't know you were gay when you were ten?" Eddie squinted at the screen.

"Did you know you were straight when you were ten?"

"Hell, yeah. I tongue-kissed Caitlin O'Connell behind the swing set when I was six."

115

"Perv."

"I was an early bloomer. What can I say?" He hit a few more keys. "What did you say his name is?"

"Dylan. He's a transfer." Val leaned back on one elbow.

Of course he knew it was wrong, checking up on Dylan like this. Not only morally and ethically wrong, but Eddie was right, they could get in a lot of legal trouble if anyone found out they'd been rummaging around in the student database. Still, Dylan was so secretive, avoiding Val's questions, never answering directly when he answered at all, not letting Val walk him home. How else was he supposed to find out about the guy? And he needed to find out, especially if he was basing his future plans on their relationship.

Val paused. Could he even call it a relationship after so short a time?

"What's his last name?" Eddie scrolled through the list of new students.

"I don't know."

Turning all the way around in his chair, Eddie looked at Val. "You've been fucking for how long now and you don't know his last name? Man, you really are a slut." Eddie grinned. "You got a sister?"

"Sorry, no sister." Val sat up. "But I always thought you were kind of cute…" He winked.

Eddie's eyes went huge and he scrunched up his face but his grin never wavered. "Oh man, you so did not just say that to me."

Val laughed and Eddie joined him.

"Okay," Eddie turned back to the computer screen. "Let's find out about this guy you're so hot for." His fingers danced over the keys. "Nobody with the first name Dylan who transferred in this semester. Where did you say he went to school before?"

Val told him.

"I never heard of that school. Where is it?"

"I don't know. Can you search for it?"

More typing. "I'm not finding anything, man. Could his last name be Dylan? You know, like Bob?"

"Maybe."

Val fought down his growing apprehension. He knew Dylan was a student. They had a class together. Just because they couldn't find him in the database…

"There's nobody in the freshman class with the last name Dylan. Let me try the sophomores." They sat in silence, the only sound the tapping of keys. "Dude, I'm not finding anything. Is he maybe an upper classman? Do you know his major? What dorm he's in? Anything like that?"

"He's undeclared. I don't know what dorm he lives in."

Or even if he lives in the dorm at all.

"What class did you say you have with him?"

"Gods and Monsters. It's a lit class."

There was more typing then silence.

"Huh."

"What?" Val leaned forward and peered at the screen over Eddie's shoulder.

"I can't get into the class list. I keep getting an error. That's really weird." He twisted around in his seat. "I can try again later, if you want. But for right now I don't think I can help you, man."

"Would you? Try again later, I mean?" Val got to his feet.

Shoving back his chair, Eddie stood too. "Sure. It's probably just some glitch in the system. It would also help if you could get a little bit more information. A last name, a major, a dorm."

"Yeah. Okay. I'll see what I can do."

"Dude, you know you really should be more…" He made some vague gesture with his hand.

"Selective?" Val suggested.

"No. Not selective. Just maybe you should know the guy a little better before—"

117

"Thanks, mom." Val grinned. "I'll try to be less slutty in the future."

In his room, Val got his books together and shoved them in his backpack. He would go to the library and work for a few hours, maybe get a jump on his reading or work on his thesis. Yeah, that's what he would do.

But his feet didn't take him to the library. Instead Val found himself standing in front of the building that housed the classics department. Since evening classes were still in session, the building was brightly lit and students milled around or sat quietly studying in the various alcoves designed for that purpose.

Val pulled out his student ID and showed it to the girl at the desk. She glanced at it and nodded.

"Have a good evening."

"You too." Val stuffed the ID back in his pocket and hurried down the hall. He climbed the stairs to the second floor and made it to the classics department without seeing anyone he knew.

The door to Mac's office was closed, as he'd expected. Even though he knew Mac was in class at that hour, and would probably remain there for several hours more, Val knocked anyway. No answer.

Heart pounding, he reached into his pocket and took out the key Mac had given him at the beginning of the prior semester when they'd started working together on the translation.

"This way," Mac had said, "you can drop off assignments without me having to be here. And you'll also have access to my personal reference books."

Of course this was strictly against university policy and the administration would have a fit if they ever found out. So he and Mac had agreed to keep the key as their own little secret.

Val fitted the key into the lock and tried to ignore the sick feeling in the pit of his stomach. He was betraying Mac's trust by letting himself in when he had no business here. The act was inexcusable. But he had to know. As he pushed open the door, Val promised himself that he would be quick and he wouldn't look at anything but the class list for Gods and Monsters, and once done, he would get the hell out of there. And he would never do anything like this again.

Inside the office was dark, the only light came from the streetlights; thin bars of illumination that slanted through the nearly closed blinds.

Val walked to the desk and opened the top drawer where he knew Mac kept his attendance folders, one for day classes and one for evening. Removing the day folder, he set it on the desk and flipped it open.

"You won't find me in there, Valentine."

Val yelped and stumbled backward, nearly falling over the desk chair. It tumbled back with a crash, wheels spinning in the air.

Dylan stood in front of the desk, face half illuminated and half in shadow. He reached across the surface and closed the folder, the expression in his beautiful eyes unspeakably sad.

Val pressed a hand to his racing heart. "What the hell are you doing in here?"

"I guess I could ask you the same question." Reaching across the desk, Dylan picked up the folder.

"Hey, give me that. You're not supposed to be looking at that."

"Oh, you mean like you are?" He tossed the folder back onto the desk. "Why did you have to do it, Val? Why couldn't you just…"

"I don't know what you're talking about." Because he didn't want to look into Dylan's eyes any longer, Val turned and righted the desk chair.

"C'mon, Valentine, we both know you came in here to check up on me, to try to find out more about me. Why couldn't you just leave well enough alone?"

119

Shit.

How had he known? And what was the point in denying it anyway? Not that he'd wanted a confrontation, but at least now he might get some answers.

"I don't know anything about you, Dylan. Hell, I don't even know if that's your real name. And how the fuck did you get in here anyway?"

Dylan laughed. "You're really something. Of all the questions you have, how did I get in here is the first thing you ask me? Of course, not everyone gets a key to their prof's office, so I guess it's a valid question. What do you think Mac would say if he knew you came here and went through his desk?"

Val felt his cheeks go hot. "I hope he won't find out." He glanced at the closed door. "We better get out of here before
—"

"Relax. He won't be back for a while yet. We have some time to talk."

"How do you know?"

"We'll get to that. Why don't you start with asking me my real name?"

"So Dylan's not your real name." Val's heart sank. "Why'd you lie to me?"

"I never lied to you, Valentine. You called me Dylan. I just let it go. People have called me a lot of things over the years. Dylan's as good as any. So it wasn't technically a lie." He propped one hip on the corner of the desk. "What else?"

"Who the fuck are you then?"

"I'm Eros."

"Excuse me?"

"C'mon, man, you're a classicist. Eros. God of love between men. Born out of chaos. Maker of matches for mortals and immortals alike. You know, Eros."

"Nice try, dude. And a pretty creative line, too." Val laughed. He had to, the whole thing was just too absurd to do otherwise. "Are you sure you're not a classics major? Oh wait, I forgot, you're not even a student here. You're just some—"

"I told you, I'm fucking Eros." He slammed his fist down on the desk. A framed photograph fell over, the glass cracked.

"And I'm the freakin' Queen of England. Right. At least if you're going to lie, don't treat me like a moron." Val stood the picture back up. "Or maybe you're just a lunatic."

"Or a psychopath. Isn't that what Mac calls me, Eros the psychopath? Is that what you think too, Val? That I'm the Eros of disaster, death and madness? That's your thesis topic, isn't it?"

Val said nothing. A thread of unease slid through him. What if Dylan really was mentally unbalanced? What if this wasn't just a big joke? Val eyed the telephone. Would he have time to call campus security? And if he did call, how would he explain his presence in Mac's office?

"Stop looking at the phone like that. You're not in any danger from me." He reached across the desk and touched Val's cheek. "I'd never hurt you, Valentine."

It took all Val's strength not to lean into that touch, but somehow he managed. Hell, maybe he was the lunatic.

"How did you know my thesis topic? I never told you that. Are you a stalker or something?"

Dylan shook his head. "Not a stalker. I told you, I'm Eros."

"This is nuts." Val raked shaky fingers through his hair.

"You got that right." Dylan sighed. He straightened and walked to the window and peered out between the blinds. "I should have left well enough alone. I should never have tried to…"

"What do you mean?"

"You and MacDonnough. The two of you are meant for each other. I should never have interfered with that."

"I don't know what you're talking about."

Dylan turned from the window. "C'mon, Val. Don't try to

tell me you didn't spend your entire freshman year beating off to thoughts of Mac bending you over that desk and fucking you till your brains ran out your ears."

Val's jaw dropped. How the hell had Dylan known that?

In his freshman year he'd had a major crush on Mac. It was true. And that particular sex on the desk scenario had been one of his favorite jacking off fantasies.

"Don't know what to say to that, do you?" Dylan smiled. "That's all right. You haven't had that little fantasy for a while now, have you? Guess maybe you grew out of your crush on the teacher. Mac still has them about you though, did you know that?"

"I don't think I want to hear this." Val stepped around the desk and picked up his backpack.

"I think you need to hear it." Dylan stopped him before he got halfway to the door. "You're trying to decide about Greece. Well, I think you need all the facts before you do."

"How did you know—"

"I'm a fucking god. I just know stuff." He pointed to a chair. "Sit. And listen."

Dropping his books at his feet, Val sat. He would listen to what Dylan had to say then he would get the hell out of there.

Dylan sat across from him. He scrubbed his hands over his face. His beautiful eyes held a haunted expression. "Mac's been dying to fuck you for years, Val. Almost since the day he met you. But he's an honorable man, for the most part, and he wouldn't ever violate the student-teacher relationship like that. But now you're graduating and that barrier won't be there anymore." Dylan sighed. "He's planning on getting you to Greece, then making his move."

"You're lying."

"I'm not."

"That's why he asked me? Because he wants to fuck me?"

"Yeah. It's not the only reason. He really does think a lot of you. But yeah, he definitely wants to fuck you."

"What does all this have to do with you?"

Dylan shrugged. "I guess I want to know if it's what you want. It's not just the sex, he's half in love with you." Dylan's smile was sad. "Do you want to be in love with him, Val? Because I can make that happen."

Val stared at the one who, he suspected, had stolen his heart. The man who, despite his wild assertions about Eros and his disturbingly intimate knowledge of Val's life, was still the single person he most wanted to be with, in bed and out. "How can you do that?"

"It's what I do, man. You know, gold-tipped arrows and all that. I can make your match. It's what I came for. Then I saw you, met you…"

"Fucked me."

"Yeah, that too. But it's more than that. I'm sort of hooked on you, Valentine. It's why I'm still here. Why I haven't done my job and made your match. As long as you didn't know, I could hang around and keep you for myself a little while longer. Now that you do…"

"Now that I do what?"

"Now that you know who I am and what I'm doing here, it's time to choose. Do you want to be in love with Mac? Do you want him to fall in love with you? Greece is a very romantic place. Chances are even if I do nothing, the two of you will have a long, hot summer together. Is that what you want, Valentine?"

Why can't I have you instead? Val swallowed the question.

"This is crazy." He got to his feet. "Dude, I think you need medication or something." He picked up his backpack and started for the door.

Suddenly Dylan was beside him. He grabbed Val's arm and spun him around. "You believe me. Don't tell me you don't."

"You're a lunatic. Get out of my way."

"Not until you answer me. Is this what you want?" Dylan blocked Val's path, his face set in stubborn lines.

Val did his best to glare, though his pulse was pounding

wildly. "You expect me to believe that all this time I've been getting fucked by a mythical deity?"

"I'm not a myth. I'm as real as you are."

"Prove it." Val couldn't believe he was having this conversation.

"What about when I helped you with your Greek homework?"

"Big deal. You can translate Greek."

And Latin too, Val guessed. Without a dictionary.

Growling low in his throat, Dylan seized Val's upper arms and dragged him close. Val's backpack crashed to the floor just before Dylan's mouth slammed down on his.

His lips mashed against his teeth, the kiss tasting of blood and frustration. Dylan's fingers bit into his arms, hard enough to bruise.

Val moaned.

The kiss broke as suddenly as it had begun. He was pushed away and held at arm's length, Dylan's gaze burning into his.

"Is that real enough for you, Val?"

With fingers that weren't quite steady, Val touched his bruised lips. "Eros is a myth. He doesn't exist. In the classical cannon—"

"Put a lid on it, man. You sound just like MacDonnough."

"Leave Mac out of this."

"Yeah, fine, whatever." Dylan shoved a hand through the hair that fell in wild waves around his face. "I'm sure the two of you will be very happy together in Greece."

"I haven't said I was going." He'd never seen Dylan's hair loose before and hadn't even noticed it till that moment.

God, he was so beautiful.

"You'll go."

"Is that another bit of godly knowledge? Can you look into the future and know what I'll decide, too?"

All he got this time was a shrug.

"I haven't decided. I don't know if I even want to go."

Dylan laughed. "You're fucking creaming your jeans to go to Greece."

He was too, or had been, before he met Dylan.

"I don't want to hear anymore."

"Do you want him to fall in love with you?"

"C'mon with the falling in love crap, man."

"I can make him fall in love with you. It'll be easy. Would that be enough proof for you that I am who I say I am?"

"You're a lunatic." Val backed up.

"Am I?" Dylan snapped his fingers. There was a flash like a million light bulbs all coming on at once.

Val stumbled back, shielding his eyes against the blinding glare. Blinking to clear his vision, he gaped, unable to believe what he was seeing.

In Dylan's hand, he held a bow and arrow. A gold-tipped arrow. Without breaking eye contact, he fitted the arrow and drew back the string.

"Just say the word, my little Valentine, and I'll get you the man of your dreams."

Raising his hands as if warding off a blow, Val backed up. His foot caught on the leg of a chair and he tumbled backward. His head thudded against the edge of the desk, pain exploding at the back of his skull, then he was swallowed up by darkness.

* * * * *

Beep. Beep. Beep.

Shit.

Reaching out blindly toward the sound, Val slammed his hand down on the alarm clock, cutting off the obnoxious beeping before it made his head explode.

The inside of his skull felt like it was filled with broken glass. He rolled over.

Ow! Fuck. Fuckfuckfuck.

Gingerly Val probed the back of his head. A lump the size of an egg poked out from his skull.

What the hell?

125

Ties That Bind

Careful not to move too suddenly, Val rolled his head to the side, slitted his eyes open and squinted at the clock. Seven-thirty. He had class in half an hour. And unless he got his ass moving, like right fucking now, he was going to be late.

God, but his head was killing him.

Slowly, Val shoved himself to a half-sitting position against the headboard. The jagged shards of glass inside his skull ground together. He moaned and slid back down.

Okay, so he wasn't going to class, not the morning classes anyway.

What the hell had happened to him last night?

Think, man, think.

He remembered packing his stuff for the library and ending up at Mac's office instead. He remembered letting himself in and looking for the attendance file. And he remembered Dylan showing up.

Dylan. Eros. God.

I'm fucking Eros. I told you.

Mac's been dying to fuck you ever since you met. He's planning to get you to Greece then make his move.

Do you want him to fall in love with you, Valentine? Is that what you want? Because I can do make that happen.

Bit by bit the conversation came back to him. The stuff Dylan had said. The stuff he had said. And that kiss. That brutal, bruising, frustrated kiss.

God.

Maybe he'd hallucinated the whole thing. Maybe he'd fallen, banged his head and…

Pulling his arm out from under the covers, Val held it up. The pale gray light from the window was just enough to make out the bruises in the shape of fingers marring his flesh. Hallucinations did not leave bruises. And there was no way those marks were made by anything but fingers.

But how had he gotten home? He had no clue. And that scared him more than a little. More than a little? Hell. It scared the shit out of him.

Someone knocked on his bedroom door.

"Go away."

The door opened just a crack. Eddie's head poked through the opening. "You okay, dude?"

"No. I have a mother of a headache."

The door opened the rest of the way and Eddie came in. "You look like shit, man. You didn't look that bad last night."

"You saw me last night?" Ignoring the pain in his head, Val sat up.

Eddie nodded. "Yeah, don't you remember? I opened the door when that guy brought you home. I guess he couldn't find your key."

"Who brought me home?"

Eddie shrugged. "Dark hair, about your height, I didn't get his name. He said you and him were out walking and you slipped on the ice, fell and hit your head. He said you were knocked out for a few seconds. You were conscious when you got here but you were pretty out of it. He seemed really worried about you."

"Who put me to bed?"

"He did. I thought maybe he'd stay but he said he couldn't. Made me promise to wake you up in case you had a concussion or something."

"Did you?"

"What do you think I'm doing now?" He paused. "So do you want me to take you to the hospital?"

Val shook his head. It was a mistake. Slumping back against the pillows, he shut his eyes.

"Do we have any aspirin?"

"Yeah. You want some?" Without waiting for an answer, Eddie turned and fled.

So Dylan had brought him home—brought him home, put him to bed, and taken care of him.

God.

Ties That Bind

Val spent the day in bed, swallowing aspirin every few hours and dozing on and off. His head hurt like fuck and his dreams were vivid and troubled.

He was in Athens. How he knew it was Athens in the dream, he had no clue, but he did. The brilliant sun beat down on him as he walked through narrow, ancient streets. He could feel it burning his skin. He glanced down, expecting to see the red of sunburn but did not. All the same, he knew he should get to a shady place before he burned too badly. Yet something called to him, compelling him to keep going and not to stop, not even to rest or find the shade. Like a beacon, it drew him, closer and closer, whispering his name in a soft, coaxing murmur.

His head ached. His feet hurt. His skin tingled with sunburn. Yet still he trudged on.

Then suddenly, the dream shifted and he was lying in a lush meadow, cool breezes caressing his face, soft grasses pillowing his head and a lithe male form leaning over him.

"I've waited so long for you," his dream lover whispered. "Touch me. I need you to touch me."

But when Val reached up and tried to wrap his arms around the man, his hands passed through the image as if through thin air. He tried again and the same thing happened.

"Please," his lover begged, "I need you. Touch me. I've been waiting so long."

Again and again Val tried to embrace the man. Again and again the figure dissolved and reformed just above him. Again and again that pleading voice begged for his touch.

Crying out in frustration, Val reared up and clutched at his lover's lithe body... And the dream shattered around him.

Jerking awake, Val sat straight up in bed, head and heart pounding, the sheets in a damp tangle around his legs.

What the hell was that?

He pushed sweaty hair out of his face, his gaze seeking out the clock.

128

Ties That Bind

Shit. He had ten minutes to get his act together and get to class. Today of all days, he did not want to miss Gods and Monsters, not when it might be his only chance to see Dylan.

Somehow he made it with two minutes to spare. Pulse racing and skin drenched with sweat, he collapsed into his usual seat. Dylan wasn't there.

He'll show up. He has to.

"Mind if I sit here?"

Val glanced up. The girl with the short brown hair, the one who was always sparring with Mac, smiled at him. Without waiting for an answer, she plopped into the desk next to his, where Dylan should be sitting.

He opened his mouth to tell her that the seat was taken. But before he could get the words out, Mac walked in and closed the door behind him.

Walking over to the desk, he set down his briefcase, opened it and took out his books. Reaching in again, he withdrew a folder. The attendance folder.

Val's pulse sped up.

"Now that the add/drop period has officially ended," Mac said, "I'd like to take a moment to go through the class list and find out who's still with us." He flipped open the folder. He began reading off names.

Val held his breath and waited.

You won't find me on that list, Valentine.

Please, Val prayed, though to whom he was praying he had no idea. Who was the patron saint of lost boyfriends anyway?

"Sierra. Max. Jackie. Leslie. And Val." Mac looked up and smiled. "All right. That's everyone. We've got a full house so let's get started, shall we?"

* * * * *

After class, Val went straight to the library. He told himself it was simply a matter of needing the quiet to work on his thesis; that he wasn't looking for Dylan. Except he'd never been very good at deluding himself.

129

Ties That Bind

Rather than his usual study cube, he settled at one of the large tables on the first floor, a place from which he could see everyone who came through the entrance. He'd been there only a few minutes when a shadow fell across his laptop screen.

He looked up and found the girl from class, the one with the short brown hair watching him.

"Mind if I sit here?" Again without waiting for an answer, she pulled out a chair and joined him. "We're in Gods and Monsters together. I'm Leslie."

"I know. I recognized you." Was she stalking him, or what?

He took out the notes for his thesis. Maybe if he looked busy she wouldn't try to talk to him.

She leaned over and looked at his laptop screen. "Is that your senior thesis?"

"Yeah, the start of it anyway. It's nowhere near a thesis yet, just some notes."

"I'm writing a paper for one of my other classes on Eros and Thanatos." Hopeful brown eyes met his. "Maybe we could talk sometime? I'm majoring in philosophy and classics."

She looked like a hopeful puppy. All she needed was a wagging tail to make the image complete.

Before he could think of an excuse to blow her off, she went on. "I'm writing about the duality of Eros and Thanatos in art and classical literature. And I'm having trouble with my classical references. I wouldn't take up a lot of your time."

"Is Mac your advisor?"

She nodded.

"He could probably help you more than I could."

Her smile, firmly in place until now, evaporated. "He doesn't really have the time. I've made two appointments with him and he had to cancel both. I don't think he likes me."

"He's pretty busy, being head of the department and all."

"I know but…"

Val took pity on her. "I guess I could spare a couple minutes."

Ties That Bind

Her smile reappeared. She really did have a nice smile. "That would be great." Reaching into her book bag she produced a sheaf of papers and slid them in front of him. "It's a little messy but I think it's readable."

It was more than a little messy and her handwriting was nearly indecipherable. Val sighed inwardly and began to read.

Myths are present in everything we do. Eros is the creative, warm energy within ourselves, like Faust's cultural creativity in the second part of Goethe's masterpiece.

Something clutched tight in Val's chest, like a fist squeezing his heart.

Eros is the creative, warm energy within ourselves.

He reread that single line several times and thought of Dylan.

"Is something wrong?" Fingers brushed the back of his hand.

Val opened his mouth to say of course there was nothing wrong, but no words came out, so he just shook his head. He could see she didn't believe him.

"The paper is about the duality inherent in our experience of Eros in art and mythology." She paused, but when he said nothing she continued. "It's like how you can't experience real despair unless you've experienced real love. And how, when you do experience despair, it can only go as deep as the love that came before it." She paused, looking at him. "You don't believe that though, do you?"

Before he met Dylan, Val would have said no, he didn't believe that. Now he wasn't so sure.

"I don't know."

"Eros is passion. You believe in passion, don't you?" Her cheeks flushed. "I mean…"

"I know what you mean. Yeah, I believe in passion."

"So you can't possibly think that being in love is all bad. That it leads you to ultimate destruction. Sometimes, sure, but not always." She clicked her pen. "See, it's a duality. Like if you

131

believe in God then you have to believe in Satan. If you believe in love you have to believe in hate. If you believe in passion…"

"I get you."

"Do you?"

"Yeah, I do."

And he did.

They sat together for a long time, talking in hushed tones about Eros. Val thought he could almost hear Dylan laughing and saying, "See, she believes me. Why couldn't you?"

And he knew what he had to do.

* * * * *

"I don't understand, Val." Mac looked up from the papers in his hand and met Val's gaze. "You want to change your thesis topic now? When we're nearly halfway through the semester?"

They were seated in Mac's office. But this time the light that filtered in through the window was a pale, ghostly gray; the clouds, just visible over the tops of the buildings, heavily pregnant with snow.

Val sighed inwardly. They weren't nearly halfway through the semester. It wasn't even mid-February yet.

"But what did you think of the new proposal?"

Mac shrugged. "It's fine, I suppose. Technically correct, as far as that goes. I just wonder why the sudden change."

"I want to explore the positive portrayals of Eros in classical literature." Val fidgeted with the notebook in his lap, running his fingers up and down the spine.

"Now you're starting to sound like Leslie from the Gods and Monsters class. You're not turning into a romantic on me, are you? Should I be referring you to Dr. Passow for your thesis? The two of you can discuss Sappho's poetry over tea and cookies." Mac chuckled but the smile didn't reach his eyes.

Val felt the sting of the rebuke.

"I'm just saying there's more to Eros than disaster, death and madness. I want to explore that duality, to look at how the depth of the passion, the Eros, that we experience is directly proportional to the despair we feel when that passion disappears."

"And how does this relate to classical mythology?"

Mac grilled him for over an hour, picking apart his new thesis proposal, questioning every point, calling him on every assertion. By the time Mac looked at the clock and made his usual statement about their time being up, Val felt like he'd been through a war.

Just as Val was getting to his feet, Mac spoke. "I think you're making a mistake, Val."

"What do you mean?" Val let his backpack slip from his shoulders. He rested it on the seat of the chair he'd just vacated while he waited for Mac to make his point.

"Passion is a fleeting thing. Love even more so. No one knew that better than the Greeks. By switching your thesis topic, you're setting yourself a difficult task. I think when you review the classical cannon, you'll see that I'm right."

"I respectfully disagree."

"Have it your way, then."

Val picked up his backpack and shrugged the straps over his shoulders. "There's one more thing. It's about the trip to Greece."

* * * * *

He should be working on his new thesis, or catching up on his reading, or sleeping off this headache, not dressing himself like a slut and going out on what would probably amount to a fool's errand.

In his room, Val opened the dresser drawer, took out the box and lifted the lid. His cock stirred and began to fill even before he touched the corset. The leather should have been cool under his fingers. Instead it was warm and supple, almost alive. He lifted it out of the box and raised it to his face. Closing his eyes, he inhaled the rich scent of leather as he stroked it along his cheek.

Yanking off his sweatshirt, he let it fall to the floor in an inside-out tangle. His jeans went next and were joined by socks and briefs. When he was naked, he slipped the corset around his waist. Slowly he laced it up and, taking a breath, pulled it snug.

His cock jerked, a drop of pre-come welling from the slit and slicking the head.

Val closed his eyes and pictured Dylan/Eros. This was probably a stupid waste of time. Dylan was gone. He had no idea how he knew, but he did. And he couldn't accept it, refused to accept it.

Dressing quickly, Val grabbed his notebook from the desk and closed the door to his room. He pulled on his jacket as he descended the stairs. Eddie was in the living room, a book open on his lap, the TV on with the sound turned down low. He looked up.

"You going to the library?"

"Eventually." Val scooped his keys off the top of the TV and headed for the door.

"Maybe I'll see you there later."

"Yeah. Maybe." Opening the door, Val stepped outside.

The night was still, like Mother Nature herself was holding her breath, waiting for something. Val inhaled, the icy air stinging his nostrils. He pulled his collar up around his face and turned toward campus. He'd gone only a block when the first fat snowflakes appeared in the glow of the streetlights. Ducking his head, Val quickened his pace.

The windows of the classroom building glowed with a warm and welcoming light. Val opened the door and sighed with relief when the warm air embraced him. He passed one open door after another as he hurried down the first floor hallway, the drone of lectures and the quiet hum of class discussions hardly registering, he was so focused on his goal.

Up the two short flights of steps, his sneakers squeaked on the worn tiles as he made his way along the second floor hall. He reached room 210 and paused. The door was closed, the room dark. Glancing quickly around, he opened the door, slipped inside and closed it behind him. Enough light filtered through the window that he didn't need to turn on the overhead fluorescents.

He walked to his usual desk, sat down and opened his notebook. He flipped through until he reached the right page, the page with the cartoon of the stickman. The cartoon he'd drawn the day he met Dylan.

Val stared at the empty desk beside him, like maybe if he looked hard enough he could conjure the man from thin air. Given everything else that had happened recently, was that really such a crazy thought?

He sat for a while in the dimness and quiet, recalling the instant flash of attraction between them and the silent flirtation that followed. He wished he still had Dylan's note.

He wished he still had Dylan.

Time passed. Maybe minutes. Maybe as long as a half an hour, but nothing happened. At last Val got to his feet, picked up his notebook and left the empty classroom.

Outside the snow was falling faster. Large wet flakes blew against his face, melted almost immediately and ran like icy tears down his cheeks. He wiped them away with the back of his hand and turned down the path toward the equipment sheds.

The area was dark and quiet when he reached the row of little cinderblock buildings. Which one did he want? He didn't know.

Val opened the first door and peered into the darkness. If only he'd thought to bring a flashlight. Then he remembered the light on his key ring. Through sheer persistence and with the help of that tiny beam, he found the right shed and slipped inside.

The boxes were still there, stacked on the pallet just the way they'd been that night. Val stepped behind the stack, leaned against the wall and closed his eyes. Even through his jacket and sweatshirt the chill reached him. He shivered.

He remembered the way Dylan had shoved him against

this very wall and kissed him, the feel of those long-fingered hands cupping his face and Dylan's words. *Gonna fuck you right here, my pretty Valentine.*

"Where are you?" Val whispered into the darkness.

There was no answer.

After the frigid solitude of the equipment shed, the library was warm and busy. Val went up to the stacks and found the shelf where he'd been searching the night Dylan had shown up. He read the spines of the books just as he'd done then. Except tonight the Butler translation was right where it should be on the shelf. Uncertain why he was doing it, Val took the volume down and left the stacks. But when he reached the study cube where Dylan had given him the blowjob, he found it occupied-by the girl with the short brown hair. What was her name? Leslie.

She glanced up from the book she was reading and smiled. "Hi, Val."

"Hey, how's it going?" Val shifted from foot to foot. How the hell was he supposed to ask her to move without looking like a jerk or a lunatic?

"Those references you gave me were really helpful. My paper's really coming along. In fact it's almost done."

"Cool. Glad I could help."

An awkward silence settled between them. Val opened his mouth to ask if she'd mind moving to another cubicle but she cut him off.

"Since you helped me so much, I was sort of wondering... would you mind reading over my paper before I turn it in?"

"I guess I can do that." Val paused. *Oh, just suck it up and ask.* "Would you do something for me?"

"Sure. If I can."

"Would you mind moving to another cubicle so I can sit here?"

Her eyes widened a little. "Sure. I guess."

Please, don't let her ask why.

Ties That Bind

She didn't, just gathered up her stuff and left.

Setting his book on the desk, Val sank into the chair and closed his eyes. This was it, the last place he'd been with Dylan except for Mac's office, and he couldn't go there. Could he? No, there was no way he could go there. So this had to be it.

Val opened his eyes, scooted the chair in close to the desk and reached for the book. Something stuck out from between the pages, a slip of paper someone had used to mark their spot. It was as good a place to start as any. Val opened the book and the slip of paper slid out. He picked it up and glanced at it.

Sweet mother, I lack the power to strike the loom. I am consumed with love from Aphrodite for a slender boy.

Val recognized the quote. It was from Sappho's poetry, said to have been written about Eros.

Was he consumed? Maybe. What he was doing tonight didn't exactly bode well for his sanity, did it? Another fragment of Sappho came back to him.

Eros shook my soul like the wind, attacking trees on a mountain.

Yeah, shaken was just about right. Maybe he really was losing it.

Folding the scrap of paper, Val stuck it in his pocket.

He stayed there in that cubicle for the rest of the evening, the book open in front of him, the slip of paper tucked safely away like a talisman. He didn't read. He tried not to think, just waited.

And nothing happened.

When the lights blinked, indicating that the library would soon be closing for the night, Val returned the book to the stacks and walked home through the snow. The house was quiet and dark when he got there, his housemate either still out or already asleep. He let himself in and went straight to his room, pausing only long enough to hang his jacket over the back of a chair.

He'd wasted an entire night on a whim. He was cold and tired and wet from the snow and his head was beginning to ache again, not to mention how ridiculous he felt. Consumed, that's what he was, and it was doing him no good.

Shoving open the bedroom door, Val groped for the light. His fingers found the switch and he flicked it on.

Dylan sprawled across his bed on his stomach, chin resting on his hand, a book open in front of him. He looked up and smiled.

"It's about time you got back, Valentine."

Dylan was here. In his room. On his bed. Waiting for him.

Forgetting everything else, Val crossed the room in two long strides and flung himself on Dylan.

"Ugh."

Somehow Dylan caught him. They rolled together across the bed and off the opposite side, crashing to the floor in a tangle of arms and legs. Fisting his hand in Dylan's hair, Val crushed their mouths together and drank in the taste of the lover he'd been so sure was gone for good. He could have gone on like that all night, kissing Dylan, touching Dylan, but it was Dylan who broke the kiss.

"Easy, Valentine. Gods, but you're freezing."

"So warm me up." Val, who had somehow ended up on top when they fell, ground his hips down on his lover.

Dylan's back arched, his body responding, the growing hardness in his jeans pressing up into Val. "We can't." He gasped, the movement of his body belying his words. "Val, stop. We have to talk."

"I don't want to talk." Val shoved Dylan's legs apart and pressed his thigh up against Dylan's crotch. "I want you. Fuck me."

Dylan laughed, the sound a little breathless. "I want you too, baby. But we have business first. Now, let me up."

Gazing down into that beautiful face, Val saw the seriousness in Dylan's eyes. "What's wrong?"

"Nothing." Dylan took a quick hard kiss. "But you need to let me up so we can talk."

Ties That Bind

He did not want to talk. They had talked last night in Mac's office and it had left him nothing but confused and hurting.

Slowly, letting Dylan know he was unwilling, Val untangled himself from his lover and stood up. But when he crawled onto the bed and held out his arms, Dylan shook his head. Instead of coming to Val, he sat down on the edge of the bed just out of touching distance, his expression somber.

"You lied." Val let his arms drop.

"What do you mean?"

"There's something wrong. I can see it. So just say it." Dylan was leaving him, he was almost certain. Sure, he was here now but...

"Okay." Dylan's gaze dropped away. He didn't speak for a long time.

The tension in Val's gut wound itself tighter and tighter until he just couldn't take it anymore. He slammed his fist down on the bed. "Stop dragging it out, man. If you're leaving just fucking say it already."

Dylan's hand settled on Val's ankle and squeezed. "Calm down, Valentine. I'm not leaving." His gaze met Val's. "But I can't stay either."

"What the hell does that mean?" He wanted to pull free of that touch. He wanted to wrap it around him and wallow in it. So he did neither, just stayed still with Dylan's hand on his ankle.

Dylan sighed. "I came back because you called me. And because we were interrupted last night before we finished."

"How did I call you?"

"You went looking for me. Isn't that what you were doing tonight when you went to all those places?"

"How do you know that?"

"You're wearing it, aren't you?"

There was no need to ask what 'it' was. Val nodded, suddenly very aware of the corset pulled snug around his waist.

"When you wear it I can feel what you feel. It ties you to

me like…"

"Like a spell?"

"More like a bond. There's magic, yeah, but it doesn't control you. You can take it off, if you want to."

"So when I wear it, you can see me, know what I'm doing?" That thought made Val shiver.

Dylan shrugged. "Not see you exactly, more like I can feel you." He grinned. "Don't let it creep you out. It's not like I know what you're doing or anything. More like I can sense you. Tonight I felt that you wanted me so I came."

"And if I take it off…"

"If you take it off, the connection is broken. Like I said, you can take it off, if you want to. It's just a way for me to keep you close even when I can't be with you."

"And why can't you be with me?"

"You believe that I'm Eros."

It wasn't a question, but Val nodded anyway.

Dylan—or Eros—smiled. "I am responsible for making matches. It's what I do, gold-tipped arrows and all that. You know the drill."

Again, Val nodded.

"If I stay with you, I'd be ignoring that responsibility and the world would fall into chaos. It happened once before."

Val recalled a scrap of a myth about a time when Eros had shirked his responsibilities and the world of mortals and immortals had indeed fallen into chaos. People didn't fall in love, relationships crumbled and the fabric of life was torn apart.

"So what happens now?"

"That depends on you."

"Me?"

"You're the one who has to choose. You can come with me, live with me and give up your mortal life. Or you can take off the corset, break our bond and keep your mortal life."

Even though his pulse was pounding, Val laughed. "You

sound like Monty Hall. Is this the mythical version of Let's Make a Deal?"

"Maybe. Except I'm telling you what's behind door number one before you choose it."

"And what's that?"

"Keep your life as it is. Go to Greece with Mac, become his lover. He's a good man, Val. He'll treat you well. You can build a life with him, if it's what you want."

"I don't think I love him."

"Do you want to? I told you, I can do that for you, just say the word."

But he didn't say the word. Instead he rolled his next question around on his tongue and considered not asking it. But he had to ask it.

"Can you make me fall in love with you instead?"

Did you already do it?

"I could, but I won't."

"Why not?"

"Because a heart given freely is a greater gift than one I could steal." He grinned. "That sounds corny, I know, but it's the gods' truth, Valentine. The choice has to be yours. I won't make it for you."

Val thought about his family, especially his mother whom he'd always been close to. How could he leave her forever and not even say good-bye?

He thought of his friends, the ones he'd known for years and a few, like Eddie, he'd met only recently but who were important to him nevertheless. He would miss them a lot. And wouldn't life be lonely with no friends?

Last he thought of his studies, the Latin and Greek, the poetry and mythology and literature he loved and his plans to share that love with others as a teacher. What would happen to those plans if he gave up his mortal life to be with Dylan?

He met Dylan's gaze. "If I go with you, could I ever come back?"

Ties That Bind

"You could come back to visit, if you want. A lot of people do, at least at first."

"Why only at first?"

Dylan sighed. "As an immortal, you won't grow old. You'll stay the same as you are today, or whenever. The same won't be true of your family and friends. A lot of people find that too sad so, after a while, they stop coming back."

Yeah, he could see how that would be sad, watching the people you love grow old and die. Of course, wasn't that part of life anyway?

"Thank you for telling me all that."

"It's only the truth. And I want you to make the choice that will make you happy."

Val took a breath and felt the corset holding him tight, supporting him. "I want to be with you."

He saw the quick flash of joy in Dylan's eyes, saw it just as quickly tamped down.

"Are you sure, Valentine? You need to be sure because…"

"I'm sure. Take me with you to Olympus or…wherever. It's what I want, to give you my heart, if you want it."

Val held out his arms. This time Dylan came to him, stretched out beside him and pulled him close.

They kissed, a long slow meeting of lips and sharing of breath that left Val feeling a little dazed.

"I want it, I want you." Dylan laid his cheek against Val's. "Your gift humbles me. I'll make you happy, I promise."

"You already do." Val molded his body against Dylan's. "I want you inside me right now." He took a kiss.

"Getting awfully bossy, aren't you, Valentine?" Dylan's hand slid under Val's shirt and traced the edge of the corset. "Take off your clothes and lay on your stomach. I want that pretty ass on display for me." He gave said pretty ass a light swat. "Do it now."

Val scrambled off the bed. He toed off his shoes and shucked his clothes, all but the corset, leaving them in a heap on

142

the floor. When he turned around he found Dylan already naked, stretched out on his bed watching him.

"Not much style in that strip tease." Dylan grinned but his gaze burned and his cock stood proudly at attention, nearly as thick as Val's wrist and flushed dark with blood.

Val's prick stiffened in response. "I'll do better next time."

"Yes, you will." Dylan wrapped long fingers around his own shaft, stroking lazily as his gaze raked over Val's body. He held out his free hand. "C'mere, Valentine. I want you under me."

Val crawled onto the mattress, lay down on his stomach and eyed his lover. "God, you're so beautiful." And he was, with his dark hair loose and tumbling around his face and all those long, lean muscles. Val's cock twitched. "Please, touch me."

Dylan smiled. "How do you want me to touch you? Like this?" He stroked a hand down Val's spine, his touch so light Val barely felt it.

"Not like that." Val squirmed. "I want your cock up my ass. Please?"

"Well…" A fingertip traced the edge of the corset. "Since you're looking so delicious and you asked so nicely." Dylan rolled over. "Spread your legs for me, baby. Show me how much you want it."

Val spread. His cock, trapped against the mattress, ached to be touched. But when he slid his hand down, it was batted away.

"No touching. In fact…" Kneeling between Val's legs, Dylan stretched out above him, his prick pressing against Val's crease. He took Val's hands in his and stretched his arms out to either side. "Keep them there and don't move or I'll stop." He thrust his hips against Val's ass. "I love seeing you like this, all laid out, so wanton and slutty. You make me so horny."

Lips ghosted over the back of Val's neck. He shivered and a small whimper escaped. Soft open-mouthed kisses were pressed to each shoulder. "Mmm, you taste so good. Gonna taste you all over then fuck you till you scream."

God, yes.

A series of small nips and licks trailed down his spine, raising goose bumps all over his body. Hands framed his waist as Dylan licked along the edge of the corset. Then lower. Strong hands parted his ass-cheeks and a warm, wet tongue licked along his crease.

Val's hole fluttered, his internal muscles clenching spasmodically. He loved getting his ass eaten out but had known only a single lover who was willing to do it.

"You like that." Dylan lapped at Val's opening. "Your little hole is flirting with me, Valentine, begging for my tongue. Is that what you want? Want me to tongue-fuck your sweet little hole?"

"Yes. Please?" Val lifted his hips, his body begging for what it wanted.

"Uh-uh, baby, stay still or I'll stop." Another lick. "I want you to say it for me."

"Please," Val begged. "Please, lick my asshole. Let me come for you while you fuck me with your tongue."

Humming softly, Dylan licked from Val's balls to the top of his crease, then back down to swirl around and dip inside his hole.

"Oh, God." Val buried his face in the pillow and fought to remain still. His cock, leaking steadily now, had left a wet patch on the sheet, and Val could smell his own arousal.

Dylan's thumbs spread him open, Dylan's tongue slid into his ass, tasting and teasing and ramping up his need. Licking and slurping noises blended with low, satisfied hums and murmurs as Dylan ate him out.

Val's pricked throbbed, his fingers curled into the sheets and he bit down on the pillow to keep from screaming. And the slow, sweet torment went on and on.

"Please," Val gasped, sure he was going to blow his load without Dylan's permission.

"Please, what?" Dylan paused and rested his cheek against Val's ass. Warm breath puffed against his drenched hole. "You want to come, Valentine? You ready to cream for me already?"

"Yes. Need to come." Val shifted, trying for some friction, unable to stay still.

"Okay. I guess you've been good long enough." Dylan gave his hole one final lap then crawled up to press his cheek against Val's. "Where's the lube and condoms?"

"Nightstand. But…" Val hesitated.

"But what, baby?" Dylan rolled over and opened the nightstand.

Val propped himself on one elbow and watched his lover. "I was thinking that well, since you're…you know, immortal and all…"

"Yeah?" Dylan cocked a brow, the suggestion of a smile playing around his mouth.

"Well, since you're immortal you probably don't get diseases, right?" Val felt his face growing hot. He'd never asked for this before, had never been serious enough with anyone to want it.

Dylan nodded. "No, no diseases."

"That's good. So, do you think…?"

"Yeah?" Dylan waited, a wicked gleam in his eyes.

"Oh hell." Val turned his face away, cheeks burning. He hated asking for stuff like this.

"Don't turn away." Dylan lay down beside him and pulled him close. "Are you trying to ask me to fuck you bare? Is that what you want, baby?"

"That's what I want," Val whispered. "I never had anyone do that before. Never wanted to."

"And I'm the only one who will ever do that to you." Dylan cupped his cheek and looked into his eyes. "You belong to me now. You know that, right?"

Val nodded. Something clutched tight in his chest at that look in his lover's eyes, and he knew he had made the right

145

choice.

Kneeling between Val's legs, Dylan got him ready, first slicking and stretching his hole before he dripped lube over his shaft and positioned himself at Val's entrance.

Leaning over Val's back he touched their lips together. "I love you, Valentine. I always will."

"I love you, too." Val closed his eyes.

Dylan pushed. After a moment of resistance, the head slipped in. He paused, waiting. "Okay, baby?"

"Okay. More. Give me all of it."

He loved this moment, savored it, the feel of being penetrated, taken and filled. He loved the burn and stretch and the feel of another man's cock, Dylan's cock, deep inside him.

When his lover hilted, balls resting against Val's ass, they both stilled. Then Dylan began to move. Long, slow thrusts rocked him, setting up the sweetest ache inside his ass and just enough friction for his dick against the sheet.

Val moaned and pushed up, meeting Dylan thrust for thrust, tiny sparks flaring along his spine, delicious pressure building in his balls. Gradually Dylan sped up, shoving in deeper and faster, pushing Val closer and closer to orgasm. But just as Val opened his mouth to say he was close, Dylan pulled almost all the way out, leaving Val's body grasping and empty except for the head just inside his ass.

Val whimpered and shoved back.

Dylan pushed him down. "Be still, baby. Gods, but you're so hot and sweet." He dropped a kiss on Val's shoulder. "Inside you is like satin, so hot and tight around my cock. I love it. Can't wait to shoot my load in your ass."

"Do it," Val groaned. "Come inside me. Let me come for you, come with you. I need it."

"Me too." Dylan thrust deep, fucking Val's ass, taking them both to the edge with a series of fast, hard jabs. His rhythm faltered, his thrusts becoming erratic.

The sheet rubbed against Val's prick. Dylan's cock dragged

over his gland. "Oh, God, gonna come. Can't wait."

"Come for me now." Dylan shoved in deep, holding himself just there at the peak of his thrust as his cock throbbed, filling Val's ass with heat.

With a cry Val came, muscles clamping down, warm sticky come spilling from his trapped cock to puddle on the sheet beneath him.

Afterward they both lay still, gasping, Dylan still inside him. Back slick with sweat and front sticky with come, Val tried to catch his breath.

"I love you, my pretty Valentine." Dylan kissed him softly, just a light brush of lips.

"I love you too, my Eros."

Ties That Bind

Laura Baumbach

Rough Ride

The world swirled, spinning out of control. James' vision was filled with a dizzying, white blur dotted with occasional glimpses of Bram's laughing face and the dark outline of nearby trees that ringed the hilltop.

The early winter sun was just rising and its dim efforts put a warm, golden glow on the surrounding snow-covered woods and hillside. Barely sunrise on a Sunday morning, they were the only two people braving the cold and ice.

The glow spun and looped as James Justin was carried down a steep hard-packed slope at what he swore were speeds higher than his car ever achieved on the road. Seated on one side of a double inner tube, he bounced and slid, spinning and flopping along, leather-gloved hands clinging to what felt like too flimsy, rubber handles on either side of the giant tube.

The other side of the tube was amazingly steady, its high lip and deep hole filled to overflowing and weighed down with

149

his lover, Bram Lord's massive bulk. The tall, broad, beefy man wore a dazzling grin and his pale blue eyes matched the blue threads in the Norwegian print wool sweater that was stretched over his broad, barrel chest. The ends of a red fleece scarf loosely wrapped around his neck whipped in the wind.

Bram's cheeks were a cheery red from the cold, and his honey blond hair was tousled over his forehead, creating the perfect canvas to highlight James' favorite feature on his lover, Bram's charming and oh-so-seductive lopsided smile. James caught glimpse of that smile as he rose a foot in the air.

Soaring over a particularly big hump in the long slick trail, James bounced hard and lost his grip on the tube. Airborne, James yelped and scramble for a new hold, but his groping hands meet empty space for several long seconds before a pair of strong restraining arms plucked him from his free fall.

"Holy shit!"

He landed with a thunk and a thud sprawled across Bram's lap and chest. His breath slammed out of him, James grunted and concentrated on not smacking noses with Bram.

The tube twisted, jetted off another small ramp of snow and hit down hard. Suddenly unbalanced, both James and Bram were thrown off the rubber ring. They rolled and slid a dozen feet down the ice-crusted run, James tightly clasped to Bram's chest. They came to a stop in a mound of snow, the empty twin tube skittering pass them, a blur of twirling black.

Relieved, James rested on top of Bram's heaving chest, then unexpectedly found himself buried in the mound of snow as Bram rolled them over, pinning James comfortably under him.

Snow clung to Bram's hair and eyelashes, his breath a frosty mint puff of warmth only inches from James' panting mouth. His pale blue eyes crinkled at the corner with laughter. His handsome, broad face was an enticing combination of light morning stubble and soft, tempting lips.

"Jesus! That was crazy. You did that as a kid?" James

smacked one gloved fist into Bram's shoulder then hung on tightly to the sweater under his fist. "What were you, suicidal?"

"Nah, just *tough*, baby." Bram shook his hair and snow flew in all directions, most of it into James' face.

"Asshole." James sputtered, chuckling. He shook his head to brush off the flakes, but only made more fall down from the surrounding snow.

Bram's laughter was soft and carefree, the deep joyous sound echoing off the surrounding woods and vibrating through James' body. Pressed chest to chest, each wiggle of Bram's large, heavy body on top of his pushed James deeper into the chilly snow bank.

The unexpected touch of icy cold touched James' skin and he yelped and squirmed, rubbing their lower abdomens together in his startled frenzy.

"Shit! Get up. Snow's going down the back of my pants!" He wiggled some more to try to slip out from under his lover.

"Lucky snow." Pinning a struggling James in place, Bram slid one muscular thigh between James' legs and did a little wiggling of his own.

James' cock responded despite the cold, but as he started to protest, Bram's hovering lips sealed over his own. The kiss was slow and thorough, a languid exploration of his mouth that left him much more breathless then the ride.

The snow that had worked its way down his jeans began to melt and a slow stream of freezing wetness divided its efforts between soaking into his pants and trickling down the crack in his ass. The sensation was uncomfortable, but oddly exotic and arousing.

His cock strained against the confines of his boxers, hard as the icicles hanging from the nearby branches. A thick shaft that gave the nearby tree limbs some competition for size rubbed between his legs and over his cock.

Locking his gaze on Bram's, James felt his heart slide up into his throat. God he loved this huge mountain of a man.

Ties That Bind

Surrounded by the soft morning light, the sound of the birds and the shushed fall of new snow, James felt a sense of peace and security descend around him. He knew he'd never been loved by anyone else the way Bram loved him, cared for him, and understood him. This was what finding true love was really like. Looking into Bram's love-filled face, James felt his heart lock onto Bram's. They were suddenly bound forever, souls united in this single, shushed moment on this isolated park hillside. It was awe-inspiring and exhilarating. And sexy as hell.

"Want to do it again, Jamie?"

James had to swallow past the lump of emotion in his throat before he could push down his arousal to answer.

"I don't know. That was a hell of a rough ride down." James stroked his gloved palms over Bram's shoulders, hungry to touch the man any way he could. He chuckled, arching his back to shift the snow still packed under his butt, bringing their groins into closer contact. "I'm not sure it's worth the bruises."

Bram smirked, kissed the tip of James' chin and the corner of his mouth, a light, seductive caress. "Okay." He let his words tumble into James' parted, waiting mouth. "Then how about I take you home and give you a different kind of rough ride?" Bram quickly kissed him then tugged at James' lower lip with his teeth. He released it, his stare heated. "I promise any bruises you get will be worth the ride."

"You won't even have to close your eyes if we go too fast." Bram tossed his scarf over James' head but, instead of draping it around his lover's neck, he used it to blindfold James. "And I'll make this ride last a lot longer than the one we just took. What do you say, Tiger?"

The outside world disappeared behind a blanket of soft warmth, isolating James, making Bram's voice his only tangible connection to it. He instinctively leaned into Bram's body. James' pulse rocketed and his cock jerked. He panted, feeling the wisps of warm air from his mouth grow cold, their moisture condensing and clinging to his face, captured in the scarf ends that lay on his cheek.

Slowly and deliberately, he tugged the fabric loose until it fell free to his shoulders. The expression on Bram's face was hot enough to melt the entire hillside. James' cock hardened, chafing against the confines of his jeans. There was a tightness in his chest. A flush of warmth shot though his limbs as need flowed though his veins along with the growing desire. It only took a look from Bram to get him hard. There was no doubt he was in love.

James laced his hands behind Bram's neck and pulled his lover down for a searing kiss, overcome with the need to show some of the depth of his emotions to Bram in something stronger than mere words. He poured as much of that emotional heat into the kiss as he could, his own lips tingling, scorched with wanting. When he pulled back, Bram was panting and James could barely huff out his answer. "You're on, Caveman."

James let Bram pull him to his feet, and dust him off. Against James' better judgment, they retrieved the evil snow tube for future excursions and then walked back up the hill holding hands.

* * * * *

Chest hairs crinkling under his touch, Bram ran his hands down James' chest, the unmarked skin smooth, supple, warmed by the heat of flames from the their bedroom fireplace. James was stretched out beside him on the floor by the hearth, lean, lithe and deliciously naked in the flickering light. The down comforter under them trapped their body heat and separated them from the drafty floor in the old house. Under the dancing, golden hues of firelight, the beige cover looked like small mounds of snow from the sledding hill.

Bram traced the line of chest hair down the center of James' rib cage, following the trail over his lover's taunt, concave belly to the dip of his navel. Gooseflesh erupted on James' abdomen and Bram watched it ripple outward to cover

153

every inch of pale skin. Then just as quickly, it melted away.

Bram used one fingertip to draw circles around the shallow dip of navel, his eyebrows rising as a tiny shudder and a breathy moan resulted. He loved how responsive and open James was in bed, how easily affected his lover was by a single touch. Even now, months into their relationship, he found it difficult to grasp just how amazingly fortunate he had been in pursuing James after the first night. Casual sex in a back alley way with a stranger didn't often lead to long-term commitment and love. But it had for him. For them.

As emotionally shy as James was, James would never have pursued him. If he hadn't asked James out a second time that night, he'd have lost out on the man who was rapidly becoming the center of his world. The cold, empty loneliness he'd come to accept as the way his life was going to be had drained away after the first night James had spent with him. It changed everything forever as far as Bram was concerned.

After his parents' deaths and his only sister's debilitating accident, Bram was certain his future held only work, friends and the occasional one-night stand. Now his life held the promise of so much more, all of it at his fingertips right now, quivering, needy and waiting for his touch.

He straddled James' slim hips, his own naked ass and thighs delighting in the warmth that radiated up off his lover. He settled over James so their cocks bumped, the majority of his weight resting on his knees and calves. His scrotum nestled up against the base of James' jutting cock.

"Christ, Bram!" It was that breathy, strained moan that always made Bram's passion burn impossibly brighter.

"Tell me what you want, baby. You know all you have to do is ask."

"Jesus!" That struggling, growly sound was going to be the death of him yet. The first droplets of precum oozed from the tip of his cock.

"Sorry, can't give you that. He's busy. Try again."

Ties That Bind

James groaned and writhed, unable to move more than a twitching wiggle. The scarf from earlier was again over his eyes, but this time his wrists had been captured in the long ends as well, tied behind his skull so his head rested on the soft bonds. His elbows were bent, arms high, drawing the flesh of his torso taunt and leaving him open for exploration. Bram had been doing just that for the last half an hour or so. Exploring, touching, tweaking, tasting and teasing.

Bram watched James pull in his lower lip and bite it, hips bucking under his ass. Bram knew his lover was struggling to ask for what he wanted, still fighting his insecurities and natural shyness. Bram wasn't going to make it easy for him. Far from it. Time to speed up this joy ride just a little.

"I want to taste you, Jamie. But do I want this hole?" He curled over to lick the tip of James' cock, lapping the bead of cum off it in a slow, wet stroke of his tongue, wiggling the tip of the wet muscle into the leaking slit. "Or do I want a taste of this one?" He paused just long enough James would be left guessing where he was going to lick next, then dropped forward and sucked the edges of James' belly button. James gasped and jerked, a strangled sound coming from the back of his throat.

Bram slid his hands up James' sides, his hand span wide enough to cover a large portion of James' ribs, holding his lover down. He loved the feeling of James moving under him, squirming with want, burning with need, vulnerable and open. He was always conscious of the size difference between them, aware he dwarfed the shorter, slender man, his own iron muscles and ripped, construction worker body shouting power and strength.

He could easily crush James, force his will on him, dominant and subdue with bruising strength. And James would let him. James' own craving for rough domination in the bedroom was intense. But Bram instinctively knew how much James needed and could handle, and he gave it willingly, lovingly. Neither of them was into whips, chains, servitude or humiliation, but James craved strength and Bram had plenty to share.

He rimmed the shallow navel, mixing sharp, quick nibbles followed by slippery strokes of his tongue, teasing its edges until James' arms jerked up and the muscles of his abdomen fluttered in protest.

James finally moaned a low, hesitant, "Suck me, please… just…God, Bram, suck me!"

"Okay, baby." Bram licked his way up James' torso to latch onto a taut, dusky nipple standing tall and swollen. "Love it when you beg like that. So hot. Needy. Love when you tell me how much you need me."

James gasped and jerked again, trying to raise his knees, but Bram's ass effectively pinned him in place.

Pulling the teat out from James' chest, Bram let it slip from between his teeth, scraping it as it popped of his mouth with a wet, sucking sound. James tossed his scarf-encased head and groaning, rolling his hips in frustration, but said nothing. Bram grinned and worked a trail of wet kisses across to James' other teat and treated it to the same. His hands caressed the tender flesh of James' underarms and sides.

Hunched over, Bram's cock slid alongside James' shaft in an irregular dance of missed steps and fleeting touches that had James' arching his back in an apparent effort to gain more contact. Bram ignored the unspoken request, waiting for James to voice his passions. Bram knew this was the hardest part of communicating in their lovemaking for James—asking for what he wanted with words.

"Bram?" Head thrashing on the comforter, James pulled his arms outward, the small gesture tightening the knot that kept his eyes blindfolded and his wrists restrained. Sweat covered his skin, making it glisten, the firelight shimmering in the beads of moisture that pooled in the curves of his upper lip and throat. Sweat trickled down his temples into his dark curls, matting them and adding a freshly fucked look to his appearance that made Bram's breath catch in his throat.

"Say it."

"You know!"

James was begging. Blindfolded, bound, flush and writhing under him. The way Bram liked his passionate, shy lover. Needy, erect and desperate for Bram was also a nice plus. But James had to ask for what he wanted.

"What? Not what you wanted sucked?" Bram mouthed the areola around the swollen nub he'd just released, teasing the dimpled tip with his tongue. His chewed the stiff peak roughly, gauging his pressure by how fast James' groin lifted to slam into his ass.

"You have to tell so I get it right, Jamie." Still astride James' stretched-out body, he tightened his thighs and captured James' hips, stilling them. Groans of frustration filled the air and Bram noticed James' fingers were clenched in his hair. "Tell me, baby. Let me hear you say it."

"God!" James bit his lower lip then choked out a raw, "Suck my cock! Eat me! Damn it!"

A flush rippled through Bram's chest, sending a glow of warmth all the way to his toes. Every time James let a little of his reluctance to ask for his own needs during sex fall away, Bram felt a burst of pride. James was an amazing man. The perfect man for Bram.

He ran his hands lovingly over James's body, then leaned over and kissed James' parted, panting mouth. A soft kiss that was meant to be nothing more than a simple reward, but James responded with a hunger that fanned Bram's barely contained passions. Suddenly it was an all consuming kiss, full of stroking tongues, gasped breath and low, needy moans from both of them.

Pulling back, Bram let his lips brush over James' mouth and chin as he said, "Suck your cock. Oh, yeah. I can do that."

He uncurled from over James' body, using his hands to propel backward, sliding on his knees until he was comfortably positioned to take James' cock in his mouth. His knees gripped James' thighs tightly, forcing them closed when he knew James' wanted to spread wide for him. A rush of savage power and possessiveness surged through him, the urge to take, claim and own his lover, but he tempered it. By the time the primal emotions flowed out in his touch, it was muted from savage want to a firm confidence.

He took a moment to take in the sight of James stretched under him, James' cock straining up to curve over a quivering belly, skin slick and warm, bound and vulnerable, but most importantly, trusting. A sharp pressure squeezed his chest and stole his breath. His cock ached with the need to take what was his, but his heart ruled. Pleasuring James came first. Without another word, he grabbed a small ice chip from the wine cooler by end of the bed, slipped it into his mouth and sucked the head of James' cock in after it. He was rewarded with a bellow of surprise and three more inches of cock shoved down his throat.

God, he loved his man.

* * * * *

Surprised his back could arch that far off the floor with his legs trapped by Bram's weight, James unlocked his spine and melted down onto the comforter. Bram's mouth followed him, lips retreating to the head of his cock then swallowing it to its base. Icy cold slid along his cock's length, the extreme temperature difference searing the moment into his fevered brain.

"Ahh! Jesus!"

The wet heat slid down his shaft in one fluid motion as the chill melted away. James gasped and arched, but Bram backed off, controlling the action, teasing, prolonging the pleasure, driving James wild. Bram always seemed to know just what James' needed, how much he could take, and when it was time to let him explode with passion. And Bram did make James explode, time and time again like it was the first time, every time.

Ties That Bind

Bram knew what turned him on and what made him vulnerable, helpless and crazy with desire.

Like the blindfold that took away the persuasive power of his pleading stares.

Or the tied wrists that stopped his hands from taking what he wanted or touching himself.

Or Bram making him ask for what he wanted using words, making the illusion he was an unwilling participant drop away. Making him surrender to Bram's will. Making him admit he liked having sex and making love with the massive, loving man. And God knew he loved it and Bram. There was no one like his caveman. Rough, raw, demanding and primal, Bram was made for him.

James' heartbeat pulsed so hard he could feel it hammering through the sides of his swollen shaft, the ribbons of surface veins vibrating to the thundering rhythm in his chest and head. The flat of Bram's tongue pressed against the vessels as if his lover was counting the beats. The wet, pliant muscle then turned stiff, the tip traced over Bram's favorite spot, the one that made James gasp and groan like he was doing now.

The tongue lavished attention on that spot until James heard his own voice crack and mumble out an incoherent plead for more, less, anything to end the delicious torture. And Bram moved on, tongue jabbing into the weeping slit on top, curling under the rim of the flared head, while his lips caressed the sides of James' cock, sucking and massaging every centimeter of dusky flesh.

Saliva, warm and slick, swathed his cock in layer of heat, then swirled and rushed hard forced into a whirlpool effect by Bram's swish and suck. It was a trick that never failed to startle and delight James, the sensations never the same twice. The mental vision of what Bram looked like, bent over him, lips wrapped around his dick, face bobbing up and down the glistening shaft, eyes half-lidded in a sultry gaze was enough to make James want to rip the blindfold to see if reality matched his fantasy.

He had to see. Had to see the lust and want in his lover's eyes that matched his own rising emotions. His arms moved, but were drawn up short, the ends captured in an unyielding hold. James tossed his head in protest.

"No." It was simple, one small word, a denial of James' desire to see, but it sent jolts of pleasure from the pit of his lower abdomen straight up his cock. James felt it pulse harder.

His body burned. His skin felt raw. He could tell his teats were standing up. The bitten, worried flesh overly hot, bared in the cooler air of the bedroom, swollen in parody of his jutting cock. They begged to be kissed again, suckled, pinched, teased. He arched, thrusting out his chest to let them plead their own case, as words failed him again. He felt a quick swipe of a wet thumb bathe them in moisture, intensifying their heat, but the touch disappeared too quickly to be satisfying, serving only to notch up his frustration.

His asshole spasmed, clenching and unclenching, empty and unhappy. He needed more, wanted to be filled, filled with his lover. He wanted the man inside him, any part of him.

"Fingers!" James gulped for air, suddenly glad *and* disappointed he couldn't see the pleased reaction he knew would be on Bram's face. "I-I want...your fingers...up my ass."

The lips caressing his cock moved up his length until they held only the head in Bram's mouth. Rustling sounds of movements alerted James that Bram was shifting position only seconds before his legs were spread wide. A press of warm flesh and the tickle of hair on his inner thigh signaled Bram's desire to move from outside his legs to inside of them.

Free to move, James bent his knees up, letting his legs fall open, exposing his ass. A blunt pressure nudged his opening. Bearing down, James tried to capture it and suck into his body, but pressure breached his opening and plunged deep into his channel in one slick stroke. Just as he adjusted to the sudden, delicious intrusion, a new sensation exploded in his ass. A sliver of icy cold skated around his clenched hole then it wormed its way into his ass beside the thick finger wiggling and stroking the hot lining of his gut. The burn was unbelievable, startling, exotic and unexpected. In his mind he saw the half-moon sliver the icemaker downstairs produced and envisioned its smooth, slender curved shape sliding into his ass.

"Fuck! Holy fucking shit!" His cock lost a little of its hardness but was pulled back to instant iron glory by a few deep plunges ands twists of Bram's finger in his ass and a bit of wet, firm lip pressure under the crown of his dick.

The buzz of orgasm burst to life in the pit of his abdomen. Tendrils of heat sizzled along his nerves and zapped every cell in their path to life. James rode Bram's finger like it was the his lover's cock, squeezing it, milking it with his muscles, clenching his cheeks so tight he could feel the knuckles of Bram's hand buried between them. The ice had melted, but a chill trickle of water oozed from his opening when a second finger was inserted. It dripped down his crack like spilt cum.

Suddenly he felt a thickness alongside his cock, Bram's mouth stretching to accommodate more than just James' shaft. It was warm, satiny and throbbing, and James couldn't help but envision Bram's cock head stuffed into his lover's mouth beside his own. His orgasm raced up from the depth of his gut and exploded into Bram's mouth, scalding over his cock and his lover's tongue. And whatever else was there. He bucked up hard to jam as much as he could down Bram's willing throat. He didn't need to thrust back and forth to divide the stimulation between his cock and ass. Bram's hand followed his movement, the man's fingers packed hard into James' ass, grazing his hidden gland, stroking his grasping channel. Bram's meaty fist spreading the tight ring at his opening until it burnt as if on fire.

The instant his orgasm began to fade, his body relaxed and sagged. The warm wetness encasing his cock abruptly disappeared and the fullness in his fluttering ass went with it. His muscles screamed and tried to recapture the hand, but it escaped. Before he could protest, a new, bigger pressure shoved into the void as Bram's cock slammed up his ass so far his lover's balls settled into the spread crack of his butt cheeks. It was like being impaled on a telephone pole.

"Jesus! Oh yeah, fuck me, fuck me hard!"

It felt so damn good James' still half-hard cock nearly shot a second time.

"Christ! Bram! God, I love you!"

* * * * *

There was nothing like the feeling he got when James let loose and called his name. It made Bram feel like the king of the world with superhero powers. It was exhilarating unlike anything else! Possessiveness surged through his veins and took lust and passion to a new height. His cock was as hard as steel, thick and needy, encased in James' heat, burrowing its way to the core of his lover's body and soul. There was nothing like making love with Jamie. It was nirvana. Pure ecstasy packed into one hundred forty-five pounds of wiry man.

Words almost escaped him at this point but a guttural growl rolled up from deep in his chest. "Fuck, what you do to me, baby!"

Sliding in all the way to his cock's base, Bram slammed into James' ass, burying himself in his lover's clinging heat. The groan that rolled off his lips was again more growl than sigh, a deep, primal sound that vibrated through his down his spine. Even his hips shook. He thrust harder, roughly taking everything James could give him, enjoying the exquisite pleasure of James' ass gripping his shaft, stretched to its limits, while James buck up for more.

The comforter was thick and warm under his knees, but the touch of James' ass on his thighs was scalding. Bram grabbed hold of his lover's hips, dragging James closer, plunging his cock in deeper. Once he was as deep as he could get, he ground his hips in a circular motion as he thrust. Even so often James would grunt and jerk, telling Bram he'd managed to hit

162

the spot that made James thrash with need. Like now.

"That's it, baby, tremble for me. I never get tried of feeling you under me, shaking, rocking my world like this." The need to see into James' eyes, to meet his lusty gaze, to see the raw emotion James let loose during their lovemaking was too powerful and urgent to ignore anymore. Bram bent down and kissed James hard and long. Then one hand twisted in the bit of scarf over James' eyes and pulled the scarf down behind James' head leaving his wrists tied. Bram's cock surged and he almost shot at the glazed, sultry expression on his lover's face.

There was nothing like seeing that vulnerable, wanton, needy stare and the turmoil that swirled in those sapphire eyes. He kissed him again, hard, thrusting in long strokes, grinding his hips on the final shove and striking James' hidden nub of prostate on the slide in. He was reduced to grunts and gasps. He felt a sizzling jolt of pleasure race down his spine as James licked his dry lips and gazed up at him through half-lidded, sex-glazed eyes.

"Fuck me, Bram. I want to cum!"

His chest ached, and his balls tightened, the sound of James' raw, choked voice pushing him toward the edge. Pulling the ends of the scarf over James' head, Bram pulled his lover's captured hands down and wrapped them around James' own cock, a layer of the soft fleecy fabric between cock and palm.

"Look at us, baby. Watch me slid inside you, feel my dick up your ass, hammering your hole, rocking us both to ecstasy." He grabbed James' hips and yanked him hard, rolling his hips and grinding his groin against James' spread cheeks, stretching his opening until he felt it spasm and clamp down around his rod. "Look at your hands, your cock. Tied together, hot and happy." He kissed James, quick and hard, then leaned up. "Just like us."

"Fuck, fuck, fuck, *fuck*! Bastard, fuck me! " James thrashed and whimpered, legs bent back and tied hands milking his cock at a fierce pace. "Do it, oh yeah, do me, *Bram*!" His gaze locked on Bram's and the vulnerable, desperate need to be loved was so plain to see Bram felt tears burn the back of his eyes.

"Love you." Bram came, shooting long splashes of cum deep into James' hot, clinging channel, letting its clenching muscles wring every drop out of him. "God, baby, oh, yeah, take it from me!" Christ, he would never get enough of this man!

Hot stands of milky white hit his chest. He ran one hand through the spurting trail dotting James' torso, using the slippery pools to wet and stroke James' swollen teats. He loved the choked sounds the man made at the back of his throat as he work his fingers over the hot nubs.

James shuddered and bucked, his hand groping for Bram, his mouth working but nothing more than strangled grunts and harsh breaths escaped accompanied by the rhythmic slap of sweaty flesh on flesh. It was all music to Bram's ears, the symphony of a well-loved lover.

* * * * *

"You going to untied me any time soon?" James wiggled his fingers where they rested on his bare torso, wrists wrapped in knots of bright fleece spotted with drying smears of creamy wetness.

"Not sure yet." Bram ran one of his massive hands over James' wrists and up his arm, the palm rough, his flesh hot, leaving a scorching trail behind. He followed the path back down again, coming to rest with his palm on the curve of James' naked hip. "I kind of like that look on you—well-fucked, exhausted and helpless under me—can't go wrong there in my book, baby."

He lay on his back with the big man at his side. Head propped up on one arm, Bram leaned over him, their bodies pressed together, stretched out on the wrinkled and bunched down comforter, the firelight making early winter shadows dance around the room.

The air was thick with the scent of cum, sweat and

164

firewood, a heady, delicious, comforting smell that soothed James' raw senses. Making love with Bram fried all his nerves on a regular basis but when they went at it rough and unbridled, when Bram fucked him harder and deeper than James thought he could stand it, the big man totally in control of all of James' responses, James was drained senseless. He was sore, achy and gloriously sated.

"You really are a caveman." James snorted and twisted his wrists. He wasn't really in any hurry. He enjoyed the pressure on his flesh, the drying stains reminding him of his climax. The ache in his ass was almost as thrilling now as it had been when Bram stretched and filled him, massaging his insides with his satin steel cock until he burned as bright as the flames beside them. His ass clenched at the memory.

"But I'm your caveman." It was a smug growl of triumphant, sexy, deep-throated, teasing. It vibrated right through Bram's chest and into James. No one thrilled him, understood him or cared for him the way Bram did. Not even his own family. His chest was suddenly too small to hold his heart.

"There's no way I'll ever forget that." His chest tightened and his eyes burned. He didn't know how much happiness could hurt until he met Bram. "Or regret that."

"No regrets? Not one?" Bram cupped James face. The firelight caught in the man's eyes and James could literally see the joy and satisfaction he heard in Bram's voice shining there.

"It's been a hell of ride since day one, lover." James could barely rasp out the words, his throat was so tight with emotion.

"A little rough-going some days?" Bram soothed a thumb over James swollen lower lip, a spark of renewed passion in his husky, raw voice.

"Yeah, a little." James raised his bound hands and pulled the thumb from his lip, holding so he could lick it between words. "But remember, with you—I like it rough."

Ties That Bind

J.L. Langley & Dick D

One Good Favor

Evan looked out the passenger side of his truck, trying to keep his mind off Buck. It was probably a good thing Mark was driving. Every time Evan started thinking about his horse he got all depressed. Buck should have had a few more years in him. Why'd he have to go and die while they were on the road? Right in the middle of the season no less. Evan pulled his hat down further over his eyes. The sun was making them all watery.

It was bad enough Evan lost a friend and companion, but he was going to have to come up with the dough to buy a new horse, too. Not just a new horse, but one trained for roping. He didn't have time, or the heart, to break in a new mount. He wanted Buck back. Hell, he still had that box of sugar cubes in the glove box for Buck.

"Quit brooding, Evan. Everything will work out. If you need it, you can use some of my prize money. This is one of the best horse ranches in the country. Two Spirits Ranch is known for their roping and barrel-racing stock. Damn lucky we were in New Mexico anyway." Mark made a left hand turn onto a dirt road.

"Easy for you to say. Dotty is in the trailer behind us." Evan looked out the back window, checking on Dotty, Mark's horse. Dotty was a good girl. She probably missed Buck too.

Michael Martin Murphy's "Wildfire," came on the radio. *Damn.* Talk about timing. No way could he listen to that song right now. Buck had been given to Evan by his parents on Evan's tenth birthday. Evan blinked back tears—damned sun— and reached for his truck radio and flipped channels, finding a classic rock station.

Mark groaned. "I miss Buck, too. Hell, he's been with us since we started, but we don't have time to dwell on it. Listen, I talked to the owner's son, Adam, and he's waiting on us. He's said he'd even set us up some calves to practice on. They have a small practice arena on site."

Thank God for small favors. Evan nodded. He wanted to be mad at Mark for his cold, pragmatic attitude, but Mark was right, they didn't have time for a pity party. "It cost me five hundred to have him picked up from the stables and cremated. I still have twelve grand in savings, but it's going to be tight. Buying this truck last season really put a crimp in things. I guess I can have my mom and dad wire me more if I need it."

"Nah, no need. I've got about ten grand in savings. We'll make it. It shouldn't be more than around ten to twelve grand. Assuming you get a good one and we win some prize money, you'll be back on track in no time. I won't even charge you interest." Mark chuckled, punching Evan in the shoulder, then taking another left.

Evan chuckled too. Interest was a standing joke with them. Mark's parents weren't very understanding about Mark roping for a living. Anytime Mark borrowed money from his folks, he got charged ten percent interest. Needless to say, Mark hadn't borrowed from them in years. "I should say not. I bought that damned saddle for you last season when yours got stolen."

"Wow." Mark's eyes widened, then a slow smile crept across his face.

The sheer awe in Mark's voice told Evan he wasn't talking about the no interest comment. Evan glanced forward to see what his friend was looking at. "Whoa." The place was huge and picturesque. It was a scene right out of a picture book, or a contemporary western movie. A white vinyl fence ran all around the property, right up to the front gates. Over the entrance was a sign that read Two Spirits Ranch branded into an oblong piece of wood. It was everything Evan dreamed of having one day. A big white house on a hill came into view as they drove up the winding dirt road. Barns, corrals, stables and what must be the small arena Mark mentioned dotted the left side of the property a few hundred yards before the main house. *Small, my foot.* It was easily the size of any arena Evan had ridden in, bigger than the corral where they practiced on Evan's parent's farm. Quarter Horses, Appaloosas and Paints milled about the pastures.

"Yeah, I knew it was big, but damn. If we can't find you a horse here we might as well pack it up and go home."

Evan watched a black horse with white socks and a white diamond on his forehead run by as they drove over a cattle guard. *Oh man.* He was beautiful. Evan stared, turning back over his shoulder to watch the horse out of the back window until the trailer blocked his view. "I'm more concerned about affording one. I've no doubt I can find one I like." He was starting to get a little excited. He loved Buck, but he hadn't gotten to pick him out. Actually, he'd never gotten to buy a horse. The possibility made the tightness in Evan's chest ease a bit, but then guilt set in, wilting the budding excitement. He felt like a traitor.

A dark man with long black hair, a gray cowboy hat, mirrored Ray-Bans and a light blue shirt waved to them as Mark pulled the truck to a stop in front of the corral. "I bet that's Adam. He and his brother run the place, now that their father retired."

Evan unbuckled his seat belt and opened the door. Traitor or not, he had to have a horse. Buck would understand.

He and Mark met the man at the fence.

"Mark Hammond and Evan Marshall?" The man asked as he approached. He was tall and lean, with a cowboy's build. When he got closer, Evan realized he was also Native American and very handsome. He appeared to be a little older than Evan and Mark, maybe in his early thirties.

"You must be Adam Two Spirits?" Mark extended his hand. "I'm Mark. This here is Evan."

"I am. Nice to meet you both." Adam shook Mark's hand then Evan's. "I've seen the two of you rope. Last year up in Albuquerque. You're damned good." Adam dipped his head at Evan. "Sorry about your horse. Was it the buckskin you rode last season?"

"Yeah, that was him. Thanks."

The black horse Evan had watched while coming up the drive strode up to a fence catty-cornered to the corral Adam had climbed out of. He stuck his head over, nudging Evan with his nose. His eyes were the palest blue Evan had ever seen; what Evan had heard referred to as wall-eyed.

"Well, hello beautiful." Evan held his hand out to the horse, letting it smell him.

The horse sniffed Evan's hand then nuzzled his face against it like a giant cat.

Evan smiled, petting him with one hand and bringing his other around to rub the black nose. He loved the velvety feel of their noses.

Adam sighed. "Just ignore him." He shoved the horse's shoulder. "You, away, pest." He turned towards another set of buildings and motioned for Evan and Mark to follow. "Let me show you the roping horses I've got that are ready to go." He pointed to a gray building just inside the fence.

Evan patted the black beauty one last time and followed,

almost reluctantly. Oddly, a sense of belonging settled over Evan. He liked this horse. They seemed to have an instant rapport. Which was just Evan being silly. Of course he liked the horse, he'd yet to meet a horse or dog he didn't like. Hell, he hadn't met one that didn't like him. He'd always had a way with animals in general. As a kid, he'd wanted to be a veterinarian.

As he got to the gate where Adam and Mark were entering towards the stables, he glanced back at the horse. It wasn't there. Oh well, he was here to find a horse, how silly would it be to settle on the first one he saw, just because it was the prettiest horse he'd even seen. For all he knew the horse wasn't even for sale, and Evan needed a roping horse, or one that was at least somewhat trained for roping.

"Evan, are you looking for anything in particular, other than being trained for heeling? You're a heeler right?" Adam asked as he opened the white gate and held it open for Evan and Mark.

"Yes, sir, that's right. I don't really care what it looks like as long as it's mostly trained and has a good disposition." Evan stepped just inside the gate.

The black horse came around the corner of the building they were heading toward. He hurried over to Evan.

Evan grinned and petted the horse. He couldn't help it. He liked the blue-eyed beauty. "What about this one?"

Adam snorted and shoved at the horse's side. "Go away." He looked back at Evan. "Believe me, I'd love to sell him to you."

"What's his name?"

"Uh…Genghis Khan." Adam led them into a large stable with around twenty stalls.

"Genghis Khan?" Mark asked with a chuckle.

Evan followed with Genghis Kahn keeping pace beside him. The horse kept rubbing his face against Evan's arm, trying to get attention. He was a real character with a nice temperament, like a great big puppy dog. Evan wrapped his hand up under Gus's neck and patted him.

"Uh, yeah. He's definitely a tyrant with delusions of world domination." Adam stopped at a stall, holding a roan quarter horse. "This is Miss Kitty. She's seven years old and—"

When Evan stopped, Genghis Kahn rested his chin on Evan's shoulder. Evan chuckled and scratched his cheek. "Is he rope-trained, Adam?"

Adam groaned and turned toward Evan and the horse. "Yeah, he helps train the— he's normally a header." He cut his attention to the horse. "What are you doing?"

Genghis Kahn snorted at Adam, put his forehead in the middle of Evan's back and started walking, nudging Evan forward.

Adam threw his hands up. "Okay, fine, you don't think Miss Kitty is right for him."

Evan chuckled, letting the horse nudge him along. They stopped in front of a stall holding a brown and white tobiano paint. It was a fine looking horse and came right up to see him, but Evan had made up his mind. He wanted the pest behind him. It didn't even matter if he wasn't used to heeling, Evan was sure any horse this smart and personable could handle what Evan needed from him. Yeah, okay, logically he was going to have to ride him first, but... "I want him."

Adam's eyes widened, then he sputtered. "But, no, I can't —"

Gus—that's what Evan was going to call him—started flipping his head up and down, neighing and pawing the stable floor with his right front foot.

"Evan, shouldn't you look around?" Mark asked.

Evan petted Gus and peeked around at Mark.

Mark stood next to a bewildered Adam with his brow scrunched. He tipped his straw hat back and scratched his head. "I don't think Adam wants to sell this one."

Adam held his hands out, a frown on his face. "I'm sorry Evan I can't—"

Gus's tail flicked, hitting Adam in the cheek, making him sputter and bat the hair away.

"Fine. You bring a saddle?" Adam asked.

Evan nodded, his spirits soaring. This was right. It felt good. Something told him Gus was going to ride like a dream.

Mark frowned. "Uh, should I go get it and saddle Dotty?"

Adam sighed again. He stepped up next to Evan, grabbed Gus's chin in his hand and stared at him for several seconds.

Gus jerked his head away and nuzzled against Evan.

"Go get your tack," Adam looked back at Mark, "and your horse and meet me in the arena around the side over there." He pointed out the end of the stables toward the main house.

Evan patted Gus's neck a few times in affection and trotted off toward the truck with Mark right behind him.

"Evan, shouldn't you look more first?" Mark asked, opening the trailer.

"Nah, there is something about him. I don't know what it is. I just have this feeling."

Mark smiled.

"What?"

"I think Adam is gay."

Evan tried his damnedest not to let his mouth fall open, but he wasn't sure he was entirely successful. "What?"

Mark shrugged. "Just a feeling. Maybe you could ask him out or something?"

Evan just stared at his friend.

"Well, okay, maybe not. I was just trying to cheer you up and I figured—Nevermind. Let's go test your new mount out and see if he'll work."

Evan laughed, feeling joy bubble out of him. "You nut. I'm cheered up, I don't need a date. I miss Buck, but Gus is beautiful, don't ya think?"

Mark shook his head and chuckled. "Yeah. I think Buck would totally understand. He was gay, too, ya know."

Evan wasn't even going to ask.

173

"He never made a pass at my Dotty."

"He was a gelding." And besides that, Dotty was fixed.

Mark shrugged. "She's still a pretty thing. Aren't you, girl?"

Laughing, they got Dotty out and saddled. Then Evan threw his saddle over his shoulder, grabbed the blanket and bridle and headed back toward the arena.

When he got there, Adam had his hands on his hips, glaring at Gus. "Have you lost your damned mind?"

Gus snorted, stomping his right foot.

"Fine, you better call me the first chance you g—" he glanced up at Evan and smiled. "The first chance you get after your first event and let me know how he rode. If you decide he won't work out, you can bring him back and I'll fix you up with another."

* * * * *

Three months later...

"...get sperm from Gus."

Evan jerked the cell phone away from his ear and stared at it, hoping he'd misheard his friend.

People milled in and out of the stables, caring for their horses. Neighs and snorts bounced off the walls. One of the mares a few stalls down carried on, destroying her empty water bucket by banging it into the wall. The place was pretty loud, but for the life of him, Evan couldn't come up with any other sentence that both made sense and sounded like what he thought he'd heard. He leaned back against the stall door, returned the phone to his ear and waved to one of the barrel racers as she walked by with her horse in tow.

Out of the corner of his eye he saw a dark blur, then Gus stuck his head over the stall door. Nuzzling in, Gus rested his face next to Evan's ear and knocked Evan's felt hat crooked. Even still, Gus was close enough Evan could feel the downy soft peach fuzz covering the black nose on the back of his hand. Evan leaned into the familiar heat, trying to collect his thoughts. "What did you say?" He idly petted the stallion's nose.

"I need you to collect semen from Gus." Mark let out a long suffering sigh, like he couldn't believe he was having to repeat himself. "Alfred Cooper offered me twelve hundred to breed Gus to his mare, Rosy. That will make back the eight grand you paid for him."

"Mark, I am not jerking off my horse."

Bo Graf, one of the bulldoggers, stumbled on his way down the aisle. His mouth hung wide open as he looked back at Evan. Glaring, he shook his head and continued on his way, looking over his shoulder at Evan the whole way.

Great, they already treated Evan like an outcast because he was gay, now there were going to be rumors of bestiality, too. Evan pointed to the phone and shrugged. "I've already made the money I paid for Gus back in prize money."

"There is this thing on Ebay. I'm going to order it. All's you have to do is hold it and get him to—"

"Mark. No. You can't just do this stuff out of the blue. You need specialists and people who know what they are doing. It's all very clinical." Evan ran his hand down his face, trying not to laugh. He should have gone back to the motel room with Mark. Every time Mark got online, he came up with these harebrained ideas. Last month he tried to buy a rope with a metallic gold cord woven throughout it. Evan was going to have to hide Mark's laptop again.

Gus nibbled at the phone, catching Evan's fingers between his lips.

"Cut it out." Evan batted at the stallion with his free hand.

"Evan, this could be a profitable venture. Gus is unique. There aren't a lot of wall-eyed, black quarter horses with four white socks and a white star on the fore—"

Chris, a fellow team roper and friend, stepped in front of him, rope in hand. "Mark left this sitting in the back of my truck."

Evan nodded and held out his hand. He needed to get a handle on this or his header would be taking out ads for stud service. "When Gus and I are done with the rodeo circuit we'll talk about breeding him. Right now he's the best roping horse on the circuit and I'm not about to—"

Chris scoffed. "You mean the orneriest."

Gus snorted at Chris, blowing snot all over Evan in the process.

"Ah, damn." Evan held the phone away from his ear and took off his hat. He waved it around, trying to get the horse boogers off. "Hold on Mark, I—"

Gus snatched the phone and danced backward in the stall, throwing his head up and down.

Doubling over with laughter, Chris nearly dropped the rope.

"Shit." Evan wiped the mucus off his cheek, plopped his cowboy hat back on his head and held his hand out through the open space above the stall door. "Give me the phone."

Turning his head away, Gus gave Evan a perfect view of his long, sleek, black, muscled neck as if to say, "I can't hear you."

Oh, please don't make me beg in front of Chris. "Don't ignore me. I said give me the phone." Evan snapped his fingers, leaving his hand out. "Don't make me come in there."

Gus side-stepped and hovered his mouth over the water bucket—the water bucket Evan had just filled—hanging from the side wall of the stall. Gus twitched his ears, making one go forward and the other back as he stared at Evan.

"Whoa." Evan held up his hands in surrender. This would be the second phone in three months that Gus had killed. If Evan didn't know better, he'd swear Gus was jealous of Evan talking on the phone. The last time Evan had been trying to get directions to a date's motel, Gus had snatched the phone, flipped it up into the air, let it fall, then stepped on it. "Come on, boy…please don't."

Evan leaned over the stall door, slow and easy. He wasn't afraid of startling Gus, Gus did not startle. But Evan knew damned well his horse would take any fast movement to mean "play time." And if Gus thought Evan was playing, he'd drop the phone in the water for sure. "Please give me the phone… Pretty please, with sugar on top?"

"I swear to God that horse has you by the balls. Never in my life seen a grown man plead with his horse." Chris barked out between guffaws.

"Shut up, Chris." Evan grabbed the bars on each side of the stall door and hefted himself up. He threw one leg over the top and held his hand out to Gus. "Come on, Darlin', give me the phone. That's a pretty boy, give me the—" The toe of Evan's boot got caught on the top plank of wood. There was no time for him to get it loose; he pitched forward, off balance. Closing his eyes, he held his hands out to break his fall.

Chris scrambled forward and grabbed him by the belt.

Hooves clicked, a puff of air passed Evan's cheek and his face landed hard against warm hair.

"Fuck me." Chris whispered.

Evan opened his eyes and saw nothing but black. He was suspended in the air, with his nose mashed into Gus's back. "Ow."

Chris hauled him upright by the belt. That's when Evan realized his other leg was caught between Gus and the stall door. He pushed at Gus, making him move over just a tad.

"He saw you falling and tried to break your fall. Shit, that horse is too damned smart."

Evan smiled, patted Gus's rump and hugged the horse's back, not surprised one bit that Gus had kept him from face-planting. Gus *was* smart. And loyal to a T. He'd saved Evan's stupid ass from falling a couple of times in the last three months. "Thanks, honey. Now give me the phone." Evan crawled the rest of the way onto the stallion's back, straddling him. He scooted up until he was practically on Gus's neck, laid down flat and stretched his hand out as far as he could.

Gus flipped his head and let go of the phone.

Ties That Bind

Evan heard the plop sound that water makes when something is dropped into it and felt a drop on the back of his hand, then Chris burst into laughter again.

"Damnit, Gus." Evan groaned and dropped his arm, lying limply on his horse's back. "We're really going to have to have a talk about your hatred of cell phones."

* * * * *

Damn, that guy was hot.

Ever since Evan had seen him two months ago in Dallas, he'd been seriously rethinking his stand on approaching men in honky tonks. The man was tall, broad-shouldered with a nice ass in a pair of painted-on Wranglers. Too bad the gray cowboy hat was always pulled down so low over his eyes. Evan was betting those eyes were coal black to match that swarthy skin. And boy did that tanned skin look nice against that green shirt. Then again, it had also looked great in the red shirt he'd worn in Denver, the last time Evan had seen him.

Evan took a swig of beer, tearing his gaze away from the bar and looking out at the dance floor. The last thing he needed was to get caught checking out the hot cowboy four barstools down. *I wonder if he's dark all over.*

He glanced over again and noticed the cowboy looking back at him. Evan dipped his chin.

The man returned the gesture and took a drink of his beer before looking away.

Evan told his libido to chill the hell out. *Then again, maybe I should go over and... And what?* He knew better, especially in this part of the country. Tulsa was way more conservative than, say, Dallas or Denver. Gay bars...okay, picking up men in honky tonks was a no-no. His gaydar wasn't good enough for that. Hell, Mark was better at picking out gay men than Evan was, and Mark wasn't even gay.

Hmmm... Maybe he should have Mark take a gander at the guy? He was either a rodeo cowboy or a rodeo follower, because he'd been at the same bars Evan and his buddies had gone to in the last couple of months. All of those bars had been regular, good-ole-country-and-western bars, which in all likelihood meant the man was straight. Weren't they all? At least 'till you got a few drinks in them.

Mark slid up next to the bar, a longneck in hand. "Rumor has it…" He looked around and leaned in close enough Evan could smell his woodsy aftershave. "There is a gay bar six streets over, near that Love's store we filled up at when we came into town."

"And how did you find this out?"

Mark chuckled, his eyes dancing with laughter.

Ooh, this must be good. Evan pushed his friend's shoulder. "Well?"

"Jeff Benson, Brett Lahr and Dodger Craig wandered in by accident last night." He shook his head and took a drink of his beer. "Damn, I'd love to have been there and seen their faces when they figured it out. Bunch of homophobic assholes."

Oh, now that had to have been a sight. "Bet they hauled ass out of there." Evan grinned.

"Oh yeah. Tracy Wade was with them. He said they didn't let any grass grow under their feet after Lahr noticed all the guys were dancing with each other."

Evan winced. He suspected Tracy was gay himself. Good lord, if his buddies found out… Hell, Evan could be wrong, but it was hard not to notice Tracy scoping out other men and trying to pretend he wasn't. It was surprising his friends hadn't caught him at it. Unlike the other bull riders Tracy hung with, he seemed like a nice guy. He'd never actually spoken to Evan, but he always waved when he walked by. According to Doreen, Mark's on-again off-again girlfriend, and her friends, he was shy and didn't talk much.

"What was that for?"

"What was what for?"

Mark took a swig from his bottle. "That grimace?"

"Nothing." No way was he telling Mark what he suspected,

Mark would be trying to set him up with Tracy. Evan had been on too many of Mark's blind dates not to know a disaster waiting to happen.

"Hey, what'da ya think of the cowboy over there in the gray hat?"

Mark scoffed. "Which one of the fifty in here are you referring to?"

Evan elbowed him in the ribs. "To your left about four barstools down, smart ass."

"Eh. He's okay. I wouldn't do him, but—"

Evan elbowed his friend again, trying not to smile. "What do you know about him?"

Mark chuckled. "Well, if I were a betting man—"

"You are. What do you know?"

"Well, I'd be willing to bet he's gay, or at the very least open to the possibility."

Damn. How did he do that? More to the point, how the hell could he be so sure? "Quit being an ass, you can't know that by just a glance."

Mark shrugged and took a swig from his longneck. "I'm not being a smart ass. I have no clue who he is but I've seen him before and the way he watches you when you aren't looki —"

"What? He watches me?" Evan leaned forward past Mark's shoulder to peek at the man in question. He was staring off toward the band. "You're so full of it." Mark had to be shitting him. Wasn't he? Hell, maybe Evan *should* go talk to the guy. Oh what was he thinking, Mark *was* fucking with him.

"Would I do that?" Mark asked, feigning innocence.

"Yes."

Laughing, Mark shook his head. "Get out of here, go by the bar I told you about. I'll find my way back to the motel before tomorrow."

Evan cocked a brow. "Oh?" He surveyed the bar, trying to find the source of his friend's good mood. Not that Mark wasn't cool, he was, but still… The man must be planning on going home with some cowgirl.

"Doreen."

Evan's gaze shot back to Mark. "Yeah? Y'all are back together?"

"For tonight anyway." Mark wrinkled his brow, staring at the floor. "Not sure how I feel about that, actually. I don't think I want anything permanent. Doreen's fun and all, but…"

But when they'd dated before, she was as carefree and easygoing as Mark. Mark needed someone to take him by the reins and give him focus. The man was all over the place. He needed a strong hand, someone to ground him. He needed stability. Doreen wasn't that person, she needed to be taken care of as much as Mark did. Lord knew Evan tried to take care of the man, but it was damned near a full time job, and Evan couldn't do it full time. Mark and his scheming plumb wore Evan out. He slapped Mark on the arm.

Mark snapped out of his daze. "Get out of here." He shoved Evan toward the door.

Evan glanced back at tall, dark and handsome one last time. If he couldn't have that, he might as well take what he could get. He held up his arms in surrender. "Okay, I'm gone. Have fun."

It looked like every country and western bar Evan had ever been in. It smelled the same too, like cigarette smoke, beer and sawdust. The band was decent, although a bit loud. They were playing an old Alabama song at the moment. It was easy to see how those bull riders would've come in and sat down before noticing there were no women. No, that wasn't true. Evan noticed right away that there were only men on the dance floor, but maybe he was looking for it. It could probably be overlooked if one were headed straight for the bar. The bar ran perpendicular to the doorway and was the first thing you noticed upon entry. Not to mention the place was dark and cloudy with smoke. Although the name of the bar, *The Neon Rainbow*, should have been a dead giveaway. Then again, he supposed an Alan Jackson fan wouldn't think much of the name, since Alan had a song called "Chasing that Neon Rainbow."

Evan sauntered in and took a seat at the big, dominating wood bar. If it weren't for the assortment of neon signs around the mirror behind the bar, the place would've brought to mind an old saloon.

"What'll it be?" The bartender wiped down the bar in front of Evan.

"Bud Light."

The man dipped his head and walked off down to the end of the bar. He bent over and came up with a longneck. As he headed back, Evan pulled the billfold out of his back pocket.

"Five dollars." The bartender twisted off the cap and slid the beer across the smooth dark surface right to Evan.

"Thank you." Evan tossed a five down on the bar and put his wallet up.

The bartender took the money and stepped away, already talking to another patron.

Evan snagged his beer and turned on his barstool, surveying the crowd. Two big ole rough-looking cowboys two-stepped their way past and Evan grinned. He could just imagine Benson and his group of friends sitting down, ordering a drink then turning to find a very similar sight to the one Evan was now watching. *Oh, to have seen the look on their faces…* Evan took a drink, still smiling. He got a vision of them looking like cartoon characters with their eyes popping out of their heads and chuckled.

The back corners of the room were pretty dark. A short, stocky cowboy pulled another tall man toward the back wall. Hmm, there looked to be back room, well not actually back, more like a side. It was across the dance floor on the other side of the bar. The two men he just saw disappeared behind a black curtain. Evan had heard about them, but he'd never been in one before. Most the bars he went to were pretty much just a place to drink and meet people. If couples wanted to get to know one another better, they usually went to the restroom, although Evan had been in a few places where people didn't even bother trying to make it that far. He'd always been too picky. Anonymous sex wasn't his thing. He took a long pull from his bottle as he watched another couple, who were hanging all over one another, practically fall into the room.

Damn, that was kinda hot, maybe he'd had more beers at the other bar than he'd thought. Evan shook his head and drank down the rest of his beer. He'd been too long with nothing but his hand if he was thinking sex with a stranger was appealing.

Turning back to the bar to set his empty bottle down, Evan caught a glimpse of gray and green in the mirror. His gaze locked with the reflection's. Did the guy wink at him? *Gray hat and green shirt.* Evan dropped the bottle and whipped his head around so fast his neck popped. *Ack.* He stretched his head side-to-side as he searched the crowd. The bottle continued to clatter behind him on top of the bar, then stopped. Evan heard someone say "whoa, buddy," but his attention centered on the vision at the edge of the dance floor.

The tall man in a green shirt and gray hat had turned around and was walking away.

Hot damn. It was the same man. Evan would recognize that frame anywhere. He'd been lusting after it for months now. A pang of excitement shot through him at the prospect of his cowboy showing up here and what it meant. If he wasn't gay, then why else would he be here? Had he followed Evan?

Evan stood and hurried after him.

The gray felt drifted away, barely visible over a sea of darker hats, then it disappeared altogether into the crowd on the dance floor. *Where did he go?*

A knot formed in Evan's stomach. He couldn't lose the guy…not now. Making his way across the dance floor, he dodged couples left and right. When he made it to the edge of the sawdust-covered wood planks he searched the tables.

In the corner booth, two guys were making out, both were bare-headed. There were a couple of men standing around a table, but all of them had on dark hats. A man in a gray hat sat at the table next to that one, but it wasn't his cowboy, the guy was wearing a denim shirt. Another light-colored hat, Evan couldn't tell if it was white or gray because it was under the blue neon bathroom sign. Even from that distance Evan could tell it wasn't who he was looking for anyway. Tall, dark and handsome was nowhere in sight. Where could he have gone? The restrooms were the opposite direction from which the man headed. *Did that mean…* Evan glanced toward the black curtain. It was still swaying back and forth.

The unease of seconds ago grew into a tickle way down deep in Evan's belly. He was certain the man had winked at him. Which meant he'd come here to find Evan, didn't it? Evan's prick began to fill, well on its way to hard. God, he'd had a hankering to get himself a piece of that man since he's laid eyes on him a few months ago in Dallas.

No time like the present. Evan headed toward the back room, his chest getting tight with anticipation. If he were completely honest with himself, he was a little nervous too. He'd never done this before. But if his cowboy were in there waiting for him… He hesitated just a few seconds, then pushed through the heavy black material.

The smell of sweat and sex hit him before he let the curtain fall closed behind him. The sound of skin slapping against skin wafted up over the sound of the band. In the dim light he could make out bodies writhing together, some against the walls of the narrow, long room, others in the middle of the floor.

Evan stepped around a couple just inside the door, screwing against the wall, and made his way through the narrow room, trying not to look as shocked as he felt. This was the stuff he fantasized about, but he'd never had the guts to do anything like it. He was just a small town boy. Grunt and groans filled the narrow space. Evan stepped over the feet of a guy who knelt on his knees giving a blow job, and walked deeper into the room. It was dark, with only a single dim, red-colored bulb near where he'd entered. Evan was having a harder time seeing the farther back he went. On the other hand, there weren't many light-colored hats, most men seemed to prefer black, like Evan's Resistol.

Spotting a pale shape, Evan stopped and squinted. The man leaned against the wall, stroking himself, watching the couple next to him. Turning his head he caught Evan's gaze. He grinned and dipped his chin. It wasn't the right man.

Shaking his head, Evan averted his attention toward the other wall. Thank God it was dim in here 'cause he knew, sure as shit, he was blushing. He was hard as a fucking rock, too.

Where are you? Evan started walking again, trying not to make eye contact. He was in here to find one man in particular. If he didn't find him… well, he might stay and watch the goings on, but he was dead set on locating his mystery man. After all the nights of fantasizing about the man as he jerked off, Evan was determined to at least talk to the guy tonight.

Searching back to his left, Evan spotted another pale-colored hat. It appeared to be hanging on the wall. The men next to it were ripping at one another's clothes. Was that a green shirt, that guy just unsnapped? Evan squinted, stepping a little closer. His foot caught on something, a boot from the looks of it, and he pitched forward.

An arm wrapped around his waist and a warm, hard body pressed up against Evan's back, keeping him from falling.

Evan gasped and grabbed the muscled forearm looped around him.

"Looking for something, cowboy?" A soft, deep voice purred into his ear.

Evan shivered as the hot breath caressed his cheek.

Ties That Bind

The man started walking them toward the wall as his hand snaked down, pressing Evan's hips back against him. He moved forward, nestling his front to Evan's ass. There was no mistaking the hard prick touching Evan.

"I'm looking for *someone*." Evan whispered and glanced down to see if he could make out the color of the man's shirt under the red light. He couldn't. Turning his head, he tried to glance over his shoulder, but the man's head was too close, all he saw was the couple kissing next to them.

"I'd say you found him." The gruff voice rasped into Evan's ear making his cock throb. *Damn, that voice.* Not much of a drawl, but it was deep and sexy. He sounded like Josh Turner. God, Evan loved the country singer's voice. How many times had he jerked off to Josh's "Your Man?"

He maneuvered Evan up next to a wall. "Put your hands on the wall."

Evan hesitated. What if it wasn't his cowboy?

The man nipped Evan's neck, hard enough that the pressure shot right through his body, leaving goose bumps in its wake. "Put your hands on the wall." He said again in reprimand.

Oh God, Evan loved a commanding, confident man. His cock jerked and his stomach tensed. His body got all shivery.

The warm whisper of breath touched Evan's cheek, then his companion bent and kissed the skin of Evan's neck, exposed above the collar of his Texas flag shirt. Their hats hit and Evan's fell from his head. He reached for it, but his savior caught it first and held it up toward the wall.

There was a peg about a foot over their heads to the left of them. Evan stared as his hat came to rest on the peg. *Nifty.* It made sense, this *was* a western bar and cowboy hats *did* tend to get in the way.

Before Evan could drop his outstretched hand, his wrist was seized in a strong, warm palm. His other wrist soon joined it, then both were pushed above his head against the smooth, cool wall.

A light-colored hat brim appeared out of the corner of Evan's eye as the man licked up the side of his face from his jawbone to his cheekbone. "Be still, Tex." He pressed his hips against Evan's ass again, mashing Evan's own throbbing prick into the wall.

The pressure on his cock felt good. Evan groaned and pushed backwards a little. He straightened his arms so he could press further back against his companion, letting the man's warmth sink into him, feeling the hard prick against his ass cheek. It was like a branding iron garnering all of Evan's attention. It felt huge. Evan groaned and rocked back.

"Mmm... You like that?" The man reached around and squeezed Evan's cock through his jeans.

Evan gasped and thrust into the touch. His dick twitched, begging for attention. The sounds and smells of sex surrounded them, adding to the excitement. Evan was too caught up in the feel of his cowboy touching him to speak. He should ask the man's name, find out why he hadn't approached Evan before. Maybe Mark was right and he'd been watching Evan. At least Evan hoped it was his cowboy. At this point it didn't really matter, he was too far gone to care. His balls were so tight, he wanted to come...needed it.

The hand left his prick and fumbled with his belt. The heavy buckle jangled free, hitting Evan's hip, and the nimble fingers started working on his pants. He should help, but his wrists were still caught and held against the wall. He was certain he could get away if he wanted to, the grip wasn't that tight, but he didn't want to. The need for someone else to take charge for a change was overwhelming.

The warm hand wormed into his briefs and wrapped around his cock. "So fucking hard." The thumb swiped over the head, smearing precome Evan hadn't even known was there. "Tell me you want it." The sexy voice rumbled in his ear.

Evan nodded, dipping his head back and letting it fall on

the other man's shoulder. He stared up at a pale, felt cowboy hat brim and a dark chin. "Yes." He'd never had a lover take over so completely, it was exciting. Somehow he'd known his mystery man would just sweep him away and take what he wanted, what they both wanted.

His cowboy released his hands and let go of his prick. He pushed Evan's pants and underwear down over his hips. "Spread your legs to keep your jeans from falling all the way down. The Great Spirit only knows what's on this floor."

Evan spread his thighs and reached for his throbbing cock as he heard the clink of a belt buckle and rustle of clothes.

"I didn't say you could move your hands, Tex." The sound of something—a condom wrapper?—being torn came from behind Evan. Then his cowboy's breath danced across his cheek and his hat brim once again appeared in Evan's line of sight. "Put them back on the wall."

Evan shivered and his balls drew tighter at the smooth, cocky voice. It was a difficult command to obey with his prick already dripping. The room was fairly warm, but the air felt cool on his heated skin, more so where precome had trickled from the tip and down his shaft. The hairs on Evan's legs stood out and a tremble raced up his spine. He slapped his palms against the wall. "Hurry."

"Mmm… That's a good boy."

Something wet slid up Evan's crease to find his hole. It was small like a finger.

"Relax."

As Evan let out the breath he was holding, the finger slipped in. It didn't hurt, but it had been awhile since he'd done this.

Cowboy pulled his finger free, then his hand appeared and tapped at Evan's lips. "Get them wet." He pushed two long fingers into Evan's mouth.

Evan's eyes widened, but he sucked both fingers, getting them good and wet. It was such a primal act. The taste was tangy, not what he'd expected. Evan's cock jerked again. Damn, he was so hard. He moaned around the fingers, wishing like hell his cowboy would grab his cock again.

Pulling his fingers from Evan's lips, the taller man grabbed his hip with the other hand. His wet fingertips trailed across Evan's ass before pushing against his hole. When they slid in, Evan groaned and moved back toward them, his body on fire. *Fuck, that feels good.*

"That's it, move with me."

Sweat dotted Evan's forehead, he squeezed his eyes shut and concentrated on the feel of those long fingers in his ass. His cock bobbed up and down as he moved.

His cowboy moaned in his ear and pulled his fingers free. The tip of the cowboy's cock touched him, sliding up and down the crack of his ass. When it found his hole, it pushed slowly and steadily inside.

Evan's breath hitched. The slight stinging feeling he expected was way more intense than he'd anticipated, but not enough to make his erection flag. His companion was freaking huge.

"Breathe, Evan." An arm wrapped around Evan's chest, rubbing softly. That sexy-as-sin voice crooned to him, telling him to relax and telling him how hot he was. Then his cowboy's free hand wrapped around his prick and squeezed. Denim touched Evan's bare ass and his lover stilled. He licked up Evan's neck to his jaw. The pinch of pain receded as tall, dark and handsome worked Evan's cock with one hand and slipped his other down Evan's chest to his hip.

The tingly feeling intensified in Evan's ass and his cock jerked against the palm holding it. Pleasure coiled tight in his balls. Damn, he couldn't believe he was doing this.

"Ready?"

"Oh, hell yes." He pushed back.

A groan flooded his ear then his partner started moving, thrusting hard and fast.

Evan thrust too. Sweat trickled down his chest making his shirt stick to him. His cowboy let go of Evan's dick and clutched his hips in a punishing grip. He fucked Evan hard and deep, all the while maneuvering Evan until he was bent over with just his hands on the wall for support.

Using the wall as leverage, Evan shoved backward. He was so close. He needed more. If he could only— His lover moved just right, the head of his prick rubbing against Evan's gland.

Evan's whole body tightened. He actually felt faint for a moment. He reached down with one hand and tugged his cock. Once, twice…that was all it took, his balls drew up, his ass clenched and his cock spewed. He barely heard his partner groaning out his own release.

Bent double, Evan panted, trying to get his wits about him as his cowboy's cock slipped out of him. He heard the jingle of a belt, saw his companion's hands fastening his pants, then all the other sounds came back to him. He was in the back room of a bar, dripping with come and his ass hanging out.

Evan stood.

A hard arm encircled him. Denim pressed against one ass cheek and his lover slid almost beside him.

Evan saw a flash of white, or gray, as the man pulled off his hat. He caught Evan's chin and melded their lips together. Evan squeezed his eyes shut and threw himself into the kiss. It was rough and possessive and took Evan's breath away.

Their tongues tangled as they filled one another's mouths with moans. Then as suddenly as it began, it ended.

The tall, dark stranger kissed one of Evan's eyelids, then the other. "Pull up your pants, Evan, the floor likely has cum all over it." He stepped back, releasing Evan, and put his hat back on his head.

Shit! Evan reached for his jeans, jerking them and his underwear up over his hips. He knew damned well his own spunk was on the floor. He buttoned his fly and fastened his belt, trying not to think about it. Then it dawned on him. The

man had called him by name. He knew Evan, even if Evan
didn't know him.

It was way past time they talk. Evan looked up, to thank
his lover and finally ask the man his name.

His cowboy was nowhere in sight.

* * * * *

At least the music was good. Who was he kidding? Evan
sighed, his shoulders slumping. His mystery man was nowhere
in sight. Evan had been here for a good three hours and there
was no sign of his tall, dark and handsome cowboy. He should
just call it a night. Every time he'd seen the tall drink of water,
he'd come into whatever bar they'd gone to shortly after Evan
and his friends. They'd gotten into town earlier in the afternoon,
so he hadn't had a chance to look for a gay bar.

Besides, he was tired. Okay, fine, he was brooding. He'd
been hoping to run into the man again. He couldn't stop
thinking about that last night in Tulsa. It was like the man had
read Evan's mind, like he'd known him forever. Hell, the guy
had even known Evan's name. Evan could still feel that huge
cock in his ass a day later. He wasn't sore exactly, but there was
a nice reminder of the night before every time he moved.
Damn, that had been amazing.

A tall, familiar-looking cowboy, a bulldogger Evan
thought, walked by on his way to the bar and mumbled rather
loudly, something about faggots masturbating horses. *Asshole.*

Evan took another swig of his beer and slumped back
against the bar, he was getting maudlin. He should really go
check on Gus before the stables locked up at midnight, but he
had to wait for Mark. Traveling all day yesterday, then spending
the evening getting Gus settled into the rent stables and today's
qualifying round had him beat.

Riding the circuit and rooming with Mark kept Evan from
being lonely and helped with money, but on the occasion that
one of them found a bedmate for the evening or just wanted to
be alone, it sorta sucked. Like now. Tired or not, Evan's truck

was their only transportation and he couldn't very well leave Mark here and go back to the motel.

Mark was two-stepping with Doreen. He didn't look ready to leave anytime soon.

Someone bumped into Evan's arm, sloshing his beer. He brushed the splatters of beer off his shirt and looked up a nicely muscled blue-plaid-clad arm to an equally impressive chest, then met glaring hazel eyes under a black cowboy hat.

It was Jeff Benson, one of the bull riders. If he didn't have such an attitude problem he might actually be a good-looking guy. The buckle bunnies seemed to find him pleasant enough, but he hadn't spoken two words to Evan in the three years he'd been on the circuit. He never missed a chance to glare at Evan, though.

"What are you doing here, fag?" Jeff snarled.

Evan held up his beer and tipped his head. Just because Jeff was an ass didn't mean he had to be. Mama always said politeness was the best way to deal with rude people. *Oh fuck that.* So he was gay, big deal. It didn't give Jeff or anyone else an excuse to act like a dickhead to him. The man should apologize for spilling Evan's beer. Besides, a good fight would likely get him out of here, where he was tired of being. "Having a beer... asshole."

Jeff's eyes widened. Apparently, he hadn't expected Evan to stand up to him.

Why did macho—more brawn than brains—cowboys think gay equaled sissy? It was a stupid mistake on their part. Evan had grown up on a farm, just like most of them, and was no stranger to hard work and hard living. He'd been in more than his share of fights growing up. He stood straighter and moved his bottle to his other hand, in case he had to take a swing.

"Pfft." The bull rider shook his head. With one last glare, he ordered himself a beer and ignored Evan. Which was probably for the best, Evan didn't know if he had enough bail money in the rodeo fund right now.

He finished off his longneck and looked at his watch, still keeping tabs on Jeff out of the corner of his eye. Damn, today sure seemed longer than normal. He and Mark had qualified for the next round but they'd ridden late in the day. They'd gotten a decent time, but by no means their best.

"I know that look." Mark sidled up to the bar between Evan and Jeff, holding up a finger at the bartender. "Bud Light." He tossed a few bucks on the bar and grinned at Evan.

"What look?"

"The Evan Marshal I'm-bored-and-ready-to-leave-look."

Evan chuckled. "I had no idea I was so transparent."

Mark shrugged. "Well, I've been your friend since we were in elementary school." That much was true. They grew up about a mile apart from one another and started roping together in junior high school. "Go on and get outta here, I'm going back to Doreen's room. I'll catch up with you tomorrow at the arena." Mark waggled his eyebrows and took his beer from the bartender.

Mark glanced over his other side at Doreen, who was sitting at a table on the edge of the dance floor with her friends.

Evan looked too and noticed that Jeff was gone.

Mark turned his attention back to Evan, a big grin splitting his face.

"All right, if you're sure Doreen is taking you back to her motel, I'm leaving."

"Hmmm…" Mark's face scrunched up and his brow wrinkled. "Maybe you should look around, see if you can find some company?"

Evan leveled a stare at his buddy. Mark knew his rule about hitting on men in honky tonks.

"Fine." Mark nodded. "I'm sure. Go."

Evan slapped Mark on the shoulder. "See ya tomorrow." Before Mark decided to say something else, Evan hightailed it out of the bar.

Ties That Bind

On the way back to the rent stables, Evan detoured by a convenience store to buy Reese's peanut-butter cups, peppermints and a sixteen-ounce bottle of Coke.

Not surprising, when he got to the stable it was empty of people. It was late, about thirty minutes before the stable locked up for the night. Everybody had gone out to celebrate their wins or moved on if they hadn't qualified.

This was one of the nicer rent stables on the circuit. It smelled of sweet feed, oats, hay, sawdust, leather…horses, it smelled like horses. Evan loved the smell, it reminded him of home.

The stables had painted cinderblock box stalls in the center of the building and nicer, wooden stalls along the perimeter of the building. Evan had paid the twenty extra dollars and rented one of the bigger stalls on the far wall. He'd had to skimp on his last couple of meals to afford it, but Gus was worth the extra money.

As close as it was to closing time, the lights were also dimmed. It was almost cozy. Gus might be asleep. One thing about Gus, there was no sleeping standing up for him. He sprawled out and got comfortable. Evan grinned. His horse was truly unique and it wasn't only his unusual coloring. Although not many horses were blue-eyed.

Evan walked down the aisle where Gus's stall was and blinked, he could swear there was someone standing in the stall. "Hey!" The person had black hair, Evan could only see the top of his head. "Hey! What are you doing?" His stomach tightened and heat raced up his body. Clinching his fists, Evan ran. What was that man doing with his horse? His boots clicked on the cement, echoed loudly and nearly kept time with his thundering heartbeat.

When he got within ten feet of the stall, Gus stuck his head out over the door as far as he could get it, looking for Evan.

Evan didn't slow down. He grabbed the latch and threw

the sliding door open.

There was no one in there but Gus.

Hmmm… Okay, he was seeing things.

Gus butted his head up against Evan's chest, looking for attention.

"Hey, boy." Evan chuckled, patted the black neck and leaned on the doorframe. "Man, my imagination is running away with me." *Whew,* that gave him a scare. Evan let himself take a deep breath in an effort to calm his racing pulse.

"Got something for you." He held up the bag of peppermints and Reese's. After dropping the peanut-butter cups into his shirt pocket, he balanced his drink on the part of the sliding half-door that was still sticking out and tore open the bag of candy for Gus.

Prancing in place, Gus flipped his head in greeting to Evan.

It was nice to be loved. Evan pulled out two mints and began unwrapping them. A hot puff of air blew over his cheek as Gus stepped closer, then a warm, wet tongue lapped over his jaw.

Okay, maybe there was such a thing as too much love. "Ugh. I hate it when you do that. You're not a dog, dang it." Bending his head to the side, he rubbed his face on Gus' shoulder. "You are so strange sometimes."

Gus snorted, but didn't move back. He nuzzled Evan's chest, nipping at the pocket.

Evan sighed. His horse thought he was a lap dog.

Grabbing Gus's halter, Evan maneuvered his head out of the way and continued to unwrap the candy.

Butting his head back in, Gus snagged the Reese's package out of Evan's pocket.

"Hey, that's mine." Evan snatched the chocolate back and held out the peppermints in his palm. "This is yours."

Gus lipped the candy out of his palm and began crunching it loudly.

Ties That Bind

Evan patted the horse's neck then unwrapped his own candy. He peeled the paper off one cup and ate it. Leaving the other one in the wrapper, he put it back in his pocket and grabbed his Coke. He needed a place to sit down. There should be a stool somewhere in the stable. Ah, there at the end of the row. He pointed his finger at Gus, "stay here," and headed down to the silver stool, half visible around the corner of the end stall.

As Evan reached for the stool, it moved.

A brown boot stepped into view. "Hey, cocksucker."

Evan jerked his head up.

Jeff Benson tossed the metal seat to the side, away from the glossy white cinderblock wall, as Dodger Craig and Brett Lahr walked around the corner.

Shit.

"What? You not gonna say anything?" Jeff spat a stream of snuff-laced saliva right beside Evan's foot.

Jerking his boot back, Evan scowled up at the bull rider. What the hell was the S.O.B. up to? He'd hardly done more than glare at Evan the whole time they'd known one another. Damn, this must be about Evan calling him an asshole at the bar. Well then so be it, 'cause Evan wasn't apologizing. Jeff had been rude first. "What do you want, Benson?"

Dodger laughed. "We want your sorry faggot ass out of here, that's what we want. There's no place for faggots around here. Rodeo is for real men."

Brett nodded his agreement.

Jeff spat again. "And take your creepy assed wall-eyed horse with you."

It looked like they were cruising for a fight. Damn it all to hell, Evan wished Mark was here to back him up. His stomach knotted up a little at the thought of getting his ass kicked, but he sure as shit wasn't backing down. Evan could hold his own, but he doubted he had much of a chance with all three of them. "I don't think so." Evan fisted his hands and balanced his weight.

Ties That Bind

"You do whatever the hell you think it is you have to do, but I'm not going anywhere. I have as much a right to be here as the three of you...so you can kiss my ass." Hey, if he was getting his ass kicked anyway, he was certainly gonna let them know what he thought of the situation.

Benson jerked back like he'd been slapped. Then he actually hesitated, clearly stunned by Evan's boldness. "Damn, you got a mouth on you. When are you gonna learn? You don't talk to your betters like that, queer."

Fury built up inside Evan. Really, it shouldn't have, he knew lots of people thought they were better than him or that something was wrong with him because he was gay, but he was tired and on the irritable side. Not to mention he still smelled like beer where this asshole had spilt his drink earlier. Evan hauled back his arm and popped Benson right in the nose. Blood flew, splattering the front of Benson's blue plaid shirt and part of the stall wall next to them.

Benson's hat fell off as he stumbled backward.

Lahr and Craig caught him, pushing him back upright.

Evan wasn't stupid, he didn't give them time to recover, much less think. He waded in, fists flying.

Cowboy hats littered the concrete floor and blood covered Evan's knuckles. He got in several good punches to all three of them, before Lahr and Craig grabbed his arms and held him.

"You fucking fag." Benson wiped blood from his chin, then hauled off and punched Evan right in the gut.

The air left Evan's body in a whoosh. It was like falling off a horse and landing flat on your back. His lungs seized up, refusing to let air in as Evan doubled over...or rather tried to. He couldn't move much with Brett and Dodger holding him. His black felt hat fell to the ground in front of him and Jeff kicked it aside. Evan heard the cowboys laugh but it sounded like they were in a well. Damn he hurt.

Benson didn't give him any time to recover before he popped Evan with an uppercut to the chin.

Ties That Bind

Everything went black for a few seconds and nausea clawed its way up Evan's belly into his throat. Benson just kept coming at him, fists flying as the others held him up. They laughed, calling out for Benson to hit him again.

Evan lost track of how many times the bull rider punched him, he concentrated on staying conscious.

A loud staccato of rapid clacking sounded behind them and Lahr, or was it Craig, yelped and dropped Evan's arm.

"What the—" Benson's eyes widened.

Angry horse sounds came from behind them, then the other cowboy hollered. Evan's other arm was freed and he began to fall. He tried to brace himself, but an arm slid around his waist, keeping him from hitting the cement. Slowly, he was lowered to the ground. He looked up into a pair of pale blue eyes, set in a handsome, tanned face, then everything went black.

* * * * *

God, his head hurt. What the hell happened? He hadn't drunk that much last night.

"Evan? Evan, can you hear me? Are you awake?"

Evan recognized the deep voice, but he couldn't place it. Where had he heard if from? It was low, deep and almost comforting, if it weren't for the urgency.

Something warm caressed Evan's cheek. Then the sexy voice said. "Come on, Evan. Open your eyes so I know you're okay."

Peeling his eyelids open with what felt like Herculean effort, Evan gazed up into pale blue eyes. *Amazing.* Evan blinked, getting his eyes to come into focus. The rest of the man's face was just as spectacular as his eyes. His short black hair, long narrow nose, almond-shaped eyes, high cheekbones and flawless tanned skin attested loud and clear to the man's Native American heritage, but those eyes… "Who are you?" Evan's voice was rusty and barely there, but it sounded awed, even to his own ears. *Ouch.* Speaking also made his head hurt worse.

One side of the man's slim lips turned up. "How are you feeling?" He brushed back Evan's hair, his touch lingering.

"Like shit." Evan stared for several seconds. The man was...well for lack of a better word, hot. Then it dawned on him. This was his cowboy. He wasn't wearing the familiar gray hat, but this was him.

His cowboy lowered the rail on Evan's bed, captured Evan's hand and took a seat next to him. He wore a red western shirt that looked familiar. Why did the shirt look familiar? The last Evan had seen him he'd been wearing a green shirt, not red. Evan glanced around and spotted the gray felt hat on the chair across the room. *Wait!* Brett Lahr had been wearing a red shirt. *Shit!* Evan's memory rushed back to him, he'd been in a fight. This man must have helped him. *Wait!* He was in a bed. Evan glanced around. He was in a hospital room, not the stables.

"Shh..." He rubbed the back of Evan's hand, then brought it to his lips and kissed it. He whispered something. It sounded like "You're okay, love," but Evan had to be hearing things. He didn't know the guy that well. He wanted to but... They'd only had sex in the back of a bar.

Evan's attention drifted upward and caught the pale eyes watching him. God, the man had beautiful eyes. They were the same color as Gu— "Gus!" Evan started to get up, managing to get his shoulder off the bed, before a wave of dizziness overcame him. His head felt like it weighed two tons and hurt like a son of a bitch, but he had to go back to the stables. What if—

"Relax." The man let go of his hand and pushed his shoulders back to the bed. His face was just inches from Evan's, his hands pinning Evan to the bed. "Your horse is fine." His breath smelled like peppermints.

Evan's breath caught. Even as badly as he ached, his cock was threatening to harden. Was this incredibly sexy man always going to affect him like this? "Are you sure? I left his stall door—"

"I saw to him myself. Everything is fine, other than those assholes deciding you'd make a good punching bag."

So he had been in the stables and came to Evan's aid. "You helped me."

Sitting up, he smoothed Evan's wrinkled forehead with his fingers and dipped his chin.

Evan hadn't seen him, he was sure of it. The last few days he looked for this man everywhere he went, hoping to see him again. Evan must have been out of it when his savior intervened. "Thank you, but I wish you hadn't brought me here. I don't have the money to—"

"It's taken care of."

Evan started shaking his head.

"You are in no condition to argue." His cowboy grinned unrepentantly and arched a brow, daring Evan to argue further.

He was too tired to argue this right now, so Evan gave in. "How long have I been here?"

"We've been here for several hours and this is the first time you've been coherent enough to make sense. You took a hell of a hit to the head. You're probably not going to remember this when you wake next time. You don't recall waking up last time, do you?

Wow. He'd woken up before? He didn't remember. "What's your name?"

Before he could answer, a petite woman with red hair in a pair of navy scrubs and a white lab coat opened the door. She smiled when she saw Evan. "Ah, looks like you are awake again. Can you answer some questions for me, Mr. Marshall?" She didn't wait for an answer, but instead pulled out a flashlight and proceeded to blind Evan.

Blue Eyes squeezed his hand.

Evan yawned, and wished he hadn't. His head throbbed something fierce and the penlight piercing his skull wasn't helping matters.

200

Ties That Bind

Finally the doctor put her light up and asked him all sorts of questions, what day it was, who the president was? It seemed sort of silly, but Evan answered her without hesitation. Apparently, from what he gathered, he hadn't answered her correctly when she'd asked earlier in the evening. Funny, he didn't remember her or being asked questions.

"Can I have something for this headache?"

"Sure, I'll send the nurse in with some Tylenol. We don't want you having anything too strong. You can sleep, but we want to make sure we can wake you up. Are you still nauseous?"

He'd been nauseous? Evan yawned again and shook his head. "No." He was just tired.

Cowboy asked the doctor a question, but Evan didn't pay attention, he was feeling very drowsy all of a sudden. He closed his eyes and listened to the soothing, sensual tones of his rescuer's voice. A man could get lost in that voice. It had sounded like heaven whispering naughty things in the heat of passion.

"Evan?"

Mark? Evan blinked his eyes open, he must have dozed off. Sunlight streamed into the window across the room, silhouetting Mark.

"Hey buddy." Mark came forward, holding his hat in his hands. His brown hair was mussed and he had stubble on his cheeks. He looked like he hadn't slept. "You okay? Tracy Wade called me. He rooms with Brett Lahr and said Brett came in pretty banged up, talking about how they jumped you in the stables. I checked the stables and went back to the motel looking for you. I just happened to drive by here and see your truck in the parking lot. Did you drive yourself?"

Evan blinked, squinting his eyes against the light. "No. I— my truck is here?" The man from the bar must have driven his tru—. Evan glanced around the room. A hollow, sinking feeling settled in Evan stomach. He was gone.

"Who's Aaron?"

"What?" Evan turned his attention to his header.

"Someone named Aaron checked you in."

Evan frowned. That was a damned good question. "The cowboy from the bar."

* * * * *

Damn it. He had to get his head out of his ass and back in the rodeo. He'd been cleared to ride and Mark had driven them to the next stop on the circuit. They needed the prize money. And to get it, they had to qualify and ride this time since Evan missed the last rodeo due to that concussion. Of course, he still had the money in his account from buying Gus because apparently Adam Two Spirits hadn't cashed the check, but Evan wasn't going to count on that money. He needed to call Two Spirits Ranch again. Hopefully, he could get a hold of Adam this time.

Evan pulled the curry comb across Gus's shiny black coat, trying to get his head in the right space for roping instead of looking for Aaron. "I tell you, Gus, I'd wonder if he was all in my head if Mark hadn't seen him at the bars, too. He always disappears before I can talk to him. There is just something about him…"

Gus leaned into the combing, like a giant cat, forcing Evan to push at him.

"Not only did he save my ass, but he apparently stuck around to make certain I was all right." And because of that, Evan had a name. *Aaron.* Fat lot of good it did him though. "Why would he do that? Now I'm positive it was him that night in the bar." Mark was convinced he was a stalker.

Evan argued he didn't fit the bill. Stalkers didn't rescue their stalkee, then disappear. And he *had* disappeared. Evan hadn't seen him at any of the local bars he'd dragged Mark to last night. He'd even stayed and watched most of the qualifying rounds to all the other events today just to watch for Aaron.

"Umm, Evan?"

Evan jerked his attention toward the open stall door.

Ties That Bind

Tracy Wade stood there, his black hat in one hand, his rope in the other. His reddish brown hair was mussed and the leather on one hip of his black chaps was dusty. A yellow riding glove stuck out of the pocket of his red, white and blue shirt under his open black riding vest. He must have just ridden. Evan didn't pay much attention to the bull riders. Well, no, that wasn't entirely true, they made good fantasy material, but they hated his ass, so…

Tracy glanced around the stables. "Can I t-talk to you for a minute?" Tracy shifted forward, leaning in and making his spurs clink. Sweat dripped down his right temple onto the hay-covered floor.

Odd, he didn't remember hearing Tracy had a stutter. Maybe it was just nerves. And well, if Tracy were nervous… Evan looked around too. It was fairly busy, but no one paid them any mind. Tracy had never spoken to him before. Not that Evan expected Tracy was gonna cause problems. From all accounts, it wasn't Tracy's style, but it still made Evan a little leery. "Sure. What's up?" He motioned with the curry comb for the other man to come closer.

Clearing his throat, Tracy stepped closer and put his hat on his head, pulling it low over his eyes. "I, uh, well—" Tracy held out his hand. "Guess I should introduce myself f-first, yeah? Rude of me. S-sorry." He spoke with slight drawl. *East Texas? Louisiana?* He also had a crooked grin that was cute as hell. It gave him a boyish look, even with the stubble on his cheeks. No, not boyish, that wasn't the right word…mischievous.

Evan, unable to help himself, grinned back and put the comb in his other hand to shake Tracy's.

Tracy had a nice firm grip, big hands, slim fingers. "Tracy Wade. I'm a friend of Mark's, well more D-doreen's actually, but I know your header, too."

"Yeah, I know. Nice to meet you officially. Thanks for calling Mark last week and letting him know where to find me."

"Welcome." Nodding, Tracy took his hand back and

gestured toward Evan's face. The bell on his bull rope clanked faintly. "You, uh, doing okay?"

Evan touched his cheek, the bruise was still healing, but he didn't quite have a black eye anymore. "Yeah, I'm good."

"G-good, good. Man, I just wanted to tell you, I had nothing to do with that." Tracy rubbed his empty hand down the back of his leg where his chaps met his jeans. "The guys have never done anything like that before. I—" He shook his head. "I'm sorry man. I h-heard them mouthing off, but I didn't think they were serious. If I'd 've known—"

Well damn, Evan felt bad watching the kid squirm. "'s alright. Heck, I appreciate you just letting Mark know where to find me."

Tracy nodded. "You b-bet. Least I could do after I found out. I didn't actually know you were in the hospital, I just felt like I had to let someone know what Brett had said when he came in. Brett rooms with me on the road." Frowning, he cast his gaze to the ground. "Makes me reconsider the arrangement now." He added softly.

Evan wasn't sure what to say. The thing was, if Tracy's buddies even caught him talking to Evan, they'd likely lay into him. Evan glanced around again. Maybe he should get the guy outta here. But he really wanted to know what Lahr said. Maybe Tracy had heard what happened after Evan blacked out? What if he knew something about Aaron? "Would you like to get something to eat or—ow! Gus, get off my foot!" Evan shoved at his horse.

Gus flipped his head up as he stepped off Evan's foot. He swished his tail, smacking Evan's side with it.

Thank God for boots. It still didn't feel all that great, but it could have been worse, he supposed. He rested his hands on Gus's back and shook his foot out. "You big oaf."

Gus snorted and jerked his head around, nipping at Evan.

"I'd heard he was a character. Doreen and Mark talk about him and his antics all the time." Tracy chuckled. "I hear he has a thing for cell phones."

Evan groaned and tossed the curry comb on top of the bag he carried his gear in. "Speaking of, I need to go buy a new one. You wanna see if we can find a cell phone store? I'll buy you dinner."

"Sure." Tracy smiled.

Gus cocked his head and his ears shifted backwards, dropping close to his head. He eyeballed Evan as if to say, "I'll kill that one, too."

Evan sighed and pointed at his phone-hating horse. "You even look at my new phone, I'll…" He glanced up at a laughing Tracy and shook his head. "Cool. Let me just get my stuff and lock him in here." Evan turned to grab his bag.

"He sure is pretty." Tracy's stutter seemed to have disappeared. Maybe it was just nerves at first.

After cleaning the curry comb out and tossing the hair in the corner of the stall, Evan hefted the strap up onto his shoulder and turned.

"I've never seen a horse with blue eyes." Tracy reached forward to pet Gus.

Gus's lips came up, his ears went back, and he opened his mouth.

Tracy jerked his hand back, barely keeping it from being bit.

"Gus!"

Gus turned toward Evan and licked the side of his face.

"Ugh." Evan shrugged his shoulder against his face, wiping it off.

Tracy laughed so hard he ended up leaning against the stall door. "He thinks he's a dog."

"Tell me about it. Sorry about that, I don't know what got into him. He's never tried to bite before." Evan shooed Tracy out of the stall and closed the door. There was a puff of hot air on his cheek, then his hat was plucked off his head. "Gus!"

Evan pulled up to the bar and cut the engine. "Tracy, thanks for going with me. Are you sure you want to be seen with me? It might not be a good idea, given what your buddies think."

Tracy turned, putting his arm across the top of the truck seat and leveled a stare at Evan. "Honestly Evan, I don't give a d-damn what they think. I'm beginning to wonder why I ever became friends with the whole lot of them." He nodded his head once to emphasize his point.

Grinning, Evan dipped his chin in return. "Then let's go." He opened his door and got out, grabbing the new phone off the clip on his belt. "Wonder where Mark and Doreen are?" He'd gotten the same phone number again, but he'd have to reprogram all his contacts. Changing numbers had been appealing, thinking maybe the one he had was bad luck, but then he'd come to his senses and realized that it was Gus that was bad luck where the phones were concerned. The salesman had looked at them like they'd sprouted another head when Tracy suggested the man show them the "horse-proof" phones.

Evan dialed his header's number as he met up with Tracy at the front of the truck.

"You guys ride tomorrow?" Tracy tipped his hat toward a couple of giggling women as they came out of the bar.

"Yeah, we qualified this morning. You?"

"Qualified y-yesterday. I drew Bodacious."

Evan let out a low whistle. Bodacious was one tough customer. That was the bull that put Larry Kincaid in the hospital last month.

"'Lo?" Mark answered his phone as they reached the door of the bar.

With the loud music it was hard to hear, so Evan covered his free ear with his hand. "Where are you?"

"In the back, towards the bathrooms." Mark hollered into the phone.

"'k. We'll be there in a sec." Evan hit end, flipped his

phone closed and replaced it on his belt. "They're toward the back, near the bathrooms."

They began weaving their way through the crowd. The bar was busy. Evan saw lots of familiar faces, but not the one he was looking for. He'd asked Tracy about Aaron, but according to what Brett told Tracy, it was Gus that came to Evan's rescue.

Tracy waved to someone and elbowed Evan. "There they are."

Mark, Chris Johnson and Gayla Buchanan sat at a little table, but Doreen was standing on the chair beside Mark, waving her arms at them.

"Looks like someone's had a bit to drink, eh?" Evan chuckled.

"Certainly looks that way." Tracy stopped and looked around. "There's the bar. You w-want something?"

"Nah. I'm good. Go ahead."

As Tracy walked away, Mark pulled Doreen off of the chair, so she could sit in it.

"Going somewhere, Tex?" A low, husky voice asked from right behind Evan.

"Aaron." Evan whipped around and came face-to-neck with his cowboy.

Aaron's eyes and upper face were shielded by his gray felt hat, but his lips were turned up slightly on one side. He seemed taller face-to-face like they were. His shoulders seemed wider too, stretching the blue denim shirt to capacity. Evan would be willing to bet the shirt did great things for those pale, almost translucent eyes. He sure wanted to find out, but first he had to get them out of here.

"We need to talk." Evan looked around for a place they could have a bit of peace, quiet and privacy. He didn't see any, and no way in hell was he going to the bathroom with Aaron; he didn't trust himself to keep his hands off him. And in a place like this, that was liable to get them both killed. Even now his fingers were itching to reach up and touch the wide, muscular chest in front of him.

"Do we now?" Aaron's lips twitched. "Won't your friend mind?" He put a lot of emphasis on the word friend.

"Friend?" *Oh*. He thought Tracy and Evan were together. Well they were, but not like he implied. "Nah, Tracy won't mind. He's just a friend."

Aaron bobbed his head, his lips turning up in a genuine grin. "Come on then." He turned and walked away.

Evan's gaze zeroed in on his nice, round cowboy ass. Damn, the man filled out a pair of Wranglers well. He glanced back at Mark. He should tell someone where he was going, but Aaron wasn't waiting around and Evan wasn't about to lose him again. He hurried through the crowd, following the gray hat. Thankfully most people preferred black hats. It made Aaron easy to find in a crowd. With the way Aaron vanished, Evan was afraid to let him out of sight. He watched as the gray felt hat disappeared out of the bar.

When he reached the exit, he couldn't find Aaron in the crowd coming into the bar. "Shit." Looking around, he pushed through the throng, apologizing as he went. If he'd lost Aaron again… His gut tightened. What was it about this man that affected him so? After a brief but pleasant fuck, he wanted to get to know Aaron better. He hadn't had delusions about having an honest to goodness relationship in ages. His lifestyle didn't make that a viable option. But Aaron turned up everywhere Evan did, so he must follow the rodeo, right? And that made them getting to know each other better possible… didn't it? Provided Evan could ever keep Aaron from disappearing.

He took off at a fast clip toward his truck. He could stand up in the bed and get a better view of the parking lot.

Evan's steps faltered, Aaron was leaning against the truck.

How did Aaron know that was Evan's truck? Mark's words about Aaron being a stalker popped into his head. Okay, he was being goofy. Evan chuckled to himself. It wasn't real hard to find out, it certainly wasn't classified information. Most folks, even the buckle bunnies who followed the circuit, knew who belonged to what vehicle.

When Evan drew within arm's reach, Aaron grabbed him by the lapels of his black western shirt and pulled him close. He tilted his head, slanting his lips over Evan's with fierce and commanding pressure. Their hats hit, knocking Evan's onto the back of his head and making him have to grab for it.

Aaron tasted of mint and honey, fresh, warm and sweet all at the same time. Evan leaned into the big body, pressing Aaron flat up against the pick-up door.

Before Evan knew what hit him he was swept away, moaning into Aaron's mouth. At that point his hat could have fallen off and blown away and he wouldn't give a rat's ass. The kiss was rough, almost painful, then their tongues tangled and it slowed down a bit, turning into a barely banked passion. His cock hardened and that same tingly, excited feeling he got before he roped coiled in his gut. He never wanted it to end.

Aaron's chest was warm under Evan's hand and his heart raced to match Evan's. He actually moaned into Aaron's mouth and moved closer. It was, without a doubt, the most amazing kiss he'd ever shared.

Aaron pulled back first.

Evan stood there dazed, staring at Aaron's chin. It took all he had not to beg Aaron to continue.

Holding on to Evan's shoulders, Aaron looked around the parking lot, turning his head left and right. "That was stupid. I completely forgot myself. Seems to happen a lot when you're around."

"Huh?" Evan glanced up, fixing his hat, and met Aaron's gaze. Oh, well this was for the best. They needed to talk. Evan was determined to see Aaron again. He hadn't had many lovers and none he particularly wanted to get to know better, but he damned sure was going to find out what was between himself and his ever-disappearing cowboy.

"This is not exactly a good place to be doing this. You've already been beat up once."

Evan shook his head, but he fished for his keys anyway. "Everyone on the circuit knows I'm gay. I don't hide it." He got his keys out and hit the remote door locks, unlocking the truck. "Where to?"

Aaron gave him a downright naughty grin. "Your motel." His voice dropped an octave.

Evan imagined those pale eyes lighting up from the shadows of his gray hat brim. His cock throbbed, remembering that husky voice whispering right into his ear. He wanted that again. "Let's go."

Aaron chuckled, already heading around the truck to the passenger side.

"What do you do?" Evan asked as he pulled out of the bar parking lot.

"I work with horses. Training them. Mostly roping, but I've trained barrel racers too. How long have you been competing?"

"About five years now." Unfortunately, the motel was only a block away and it didn't give much time for conversation, but Evan didn't think Aaron was going anywhere any time soon, at least he sure hoped not.

When they pulled up in front of the motel room and got out, Evan locked his truck and handed Aaron the room card while he unhooked his phone from his belt. He needed to call Mark and tell him to make himself scarce for the night. Doreen wouldn't mind Mark staying with her and, hell, Mark owed him one.

As Aaron pushed the door open, Evan dialed the phone.

Shaking his head and smirking, Aaron closed the door behind them. "You and phones."

What was that supposed to mean? Evan barely had a phone nowadays, with Gus around. "I just got th—"

"Where are you?" Mark shouted over the background

noise of the bar.

"At the motel. Listen. Can you stay with Doreen tonight?"

Aaron nudged Evan over to one of the two beds in the room, pushing him to sit on the edge and began pulling off Evan's boots.

Mark laughed into the phone. "Oh man. You took someone back to the motel, didn't you?" Tracy, and it sounded like Doreen, made "woo hoo" noises and catcalls in the background, then it sounded like Mark gave someone a high-five.

Evan rolled his eyes but couldn't help grinning at his juvenile friends. "Yes."

Tossing Evan's second boot behind him, Aaron stood and pulled Evan to his feet. He arched a brow as he unfastened Evan's belt buckle and jeans.

Evan's prick perked right up at the proximity of Aaron's hands to his groin. He swore he could hear his heart pounding in his chest.

Waving goodbye in Evan's face, Aaron reached for the phone and his pale eyes lit up with a wicked gleam. He took the phone from Evan and lifted it to his own ear. "Bye, Mark." He pushed disconnect and tossed it onto the bed behind him, then he took Evan's hat and tossed it aside. It was a bold move, but it fit Aaron. Had it been anyone else, Evan probably would've been upset.

He caught Aaron around the back of the neck and pulled him in for a kiss.

Aaron obliged, exploring Evan's mouth as his hands continued to divest Evan of clothes. He got Evan's shirt unbuttoned and halfway off his shoulders and nipped his way down to Evan's collarbone. Damn, it felt good. Who knew being bitten could be hot?

Riiiiing.

Growling, Aaron lifted his head and glared toward the phone.

Ties That Bind

Well shit. Evan really needed to get that, or Mark was going to worry, and Evan damned sure didn't want his buddies coming back here to check on him. "I need to—"

Aaron shook his head. "I don't think so, Tex." He tugged Evan's shirt the rest of the way off and, quick as lightening, he snagged Evan's wrists. Using the shirt sleeves, he tied Evan's hands in front of him. "You talk on the phone entirely too much." He kissed Evan on the chin and shoved him.

Falling back onto the bed with a gasp, Evan looked down at his wrists. This wouldn't keep him bound.

"Evan is fine. Go away."

Evan glanced up in time to see Aaron hit end on the phone and toss it over his shoulder. It hit the floor with a thud and a clack. Damn, that was a new phone.

"Put your hands over your head and relax, babe." Aaron got down on his knees between Evan's legs where they hung over the side of the bed. Keeping his eyes on Evan, he unbuttoned Evans jeans. "Well?"

Oh God. Those blue eyes were something else. At first it was kinda creepy, since Gus had eyes that color, but now… with heat in Aaron's gaze? Gus was the last thing on Evan's mind. Evan groaned and put his hands over his head, his cock jerked, trying to get closer to Aaron's long, tanned fingers at they parted the fly of his jeans.

When Aaron pulled Evan's jeans and underwear down, his cock slapped his belly, leaving a wet spot.

Aaron growled, stood up and took off his gray hat. He set it on the other bed, then bent over and licked the drop of cum off Evan's belly, teasing his tongue around the tip as he did. It was exciting to watch and even more so to feel. Evan swore he was going to come right then and there. He shifted his hips up a little, hoping his cowboy would take the hint and suck him.

"Mmm… not yet." Pulling Evan's pants down to mid-thigh, Aaron stepped back. His gaze raked over Evan. "That is a pretty sight. You all bound and at my mercy. I reckon that rope of yours would look lovely tied around you." He reached down and unsnapped his pants. His fingers were mesmerizing. Slowly he unhooked the snap and zipper. It was almost a caress.

God, Evan wanted those hands on him so badly.

"Scoot into the middle of the bed, but leave your pants where they are and keep your hands over your head." Aaron hooked his thumbs in his waistband and pushed his pants down. His prick fell through the slit at the bottom of his denim shirt where the buttons didn't reach. It was a thing of beauty and bigger than it had felt the other night. The man would make a stallion self-conscious.

Evan wiggled his legs onto the bed and shimmied into the middle, never taking his eyes off Aaron. It wasn't easy to do with his hands tied over his head and his legs hobbled together, but he managed. It also made his dick wag and bop against his hip.

Aaron sat on the edge of the bed and tugged his boots off, watching every little movement of Evan's cock. His gaze was so heated Evan fancied he could actually feel it. He shivered.

If this was what it was like to be tied up, Evan liked it. The anticipation was about to kill him, but Lord was it sweet. It made him ache. If anyone had told him he could feel this comfortable in front of someone else, he'd have never believed it. Aaron was something special.

Aaron stood and began unbuttoning his shirt.

Evan's prick leaked a little more. His breathing was so audible he could hear it over the rustle of clothes, and Aaron continued to strip.

His chest was tanned and powerful. Aaron's stomach was corded with muscle ending in a v at his groin. The only hair on his body was a black patch above his cock. He was breathtaking. If he'd had long hair, he'd have been the picture-perfect Native American. That and different eyes. Evan had never seen anyone so dark with eyes that light. Personally, Evan liked the short hair and the pale eyes. It made Aaron unique.

Ties That Bind

By the time Aaron was naked, Evan was writhing. The harsh, normally itchy motel bedspread actually felt nice against his ass. It distracted him from the tightness in his balls. Even the air on his cock as it moved felt delicious. Maybe being tied wasn't so good after all, he wanted to touch himself.

"Damn, you look good squirming around." Aaron climbed onto the bed and lowered himself until his breath caressed Evan's hip.

Evan shivered.

Grabbing Evan's cock, Adam rose up on his elbow and swallowed him down in one smooth motion, moaning all the way down and adding a vibrating sensation.

"Shit." The sensation traveled all the way up his spine. Evan arched up off the bed.

"Mmm…" Aaron looked up at Evan, letting his dick slip from his mouth. He swirled his tongue around the head and down the shaft with his piercing blue gaze locked to Evan's. Inserting his finger into his mouth he sucked then pulled it out.

Evan moaned.

Taking Evan back in his mouth Aaron trailed the spit-slicked finger over Evan's balls. It almost tickled.

Aaron continued to suck him and play with his balls until Evan's whole body was tense and ready to explode. If Aaron didn't stop soon, Evan was going to come. Not that that was a bad thing, but he was dying to feel that huge cock in his ass again. "Please."

After swallowing around the head of Evan's cock and constricting his throat one last time, Aaron released Evan's cock and sat up. "You ready to ride, Tex?"

Excitement shot right through Evan. His cock jerked at the invitation. He tried to ask, "Condom?" but it came out as a whisper.

Luckily, Aaron heard him. He nodded, got off the bed and went digging through his pants, giving Evan a nice view of his ass. "Get your pants off, but keep your wrists tied."

Ties That Bind

Evan hurried to comply, flopping and floundering ungracefully, but it couldn't be helped.

Aaron came up with jeans in hand, pulled a foil packet out and tossed the jeans back down. "Lube?"

"The red duffle bag in front of the dresser." His voice sounded raspy and rough, even to himself.

Aaron got Evan's duffle and dumped the contents onto the other bed. He quickly located the tube of lube and tossed it onto the bed next to Evan. Ripping the foil package open, he climbed onto the bed. Lying down on his back, he rolled on the condom then looked up at Evan. "Get ready cowboy."

Evan didn't need any more encouragement; he straddled Aaron's hips. "What about this?" He held up his hands bound with the black shirt.

"Oh, leave them. I like you being the one bound. Maybe we'll try a bit of leather next time, maybe a lead rope." Aaron retrieved the tube of lube and saturated his fingers with it before tossing the tube away. "Come here." He jerked his chin up and gripped Evan's hip with his dry hand. His slick fingers touched Evan's ass cheek before slipping in between.

Aaron started with one finger, pushing it in slow and steady.

Evan was so ready he sank down, hissing out a breath as Aaron pushed in.

"Great Spirit, that's something." Aaron maneuvered Evan's hips with his other hand, encouraging Evan to move. "You look amazing." His deep voice sounded even more sultry than normal. The expression on his face as he watched Evan made Evan even more turned on than the feel of that long digit sliding in and out of him. "More?"

"Oh God, yes." Evan planted his bound hands on Aaron's chest, leaning forward just a tad.

Aaron added another finger.

"Oh fuck, that feels good."

"Yeah? Then this is going to feel even better." He found

215

Evan's prostate, rubbing his fingers over it.

Incredible. It felt incredible. Evan pushed down, using his strong thigh muscles to move himself up and down. Thank God for all the hours on horseback. He could do this all day.

Aaron added another finger and pushed in hard.

Okay, he couldn't do this all day. His thighs were fine, but his balls were so damned tight he was going to come any minute. He rode Aaron's fingers, a tingle traveling up his back. Closing his eyes, he dropped his head back and just felt.

"Fuck, Evan." Aaron's fingers slipped out and he tugged Evan downward. The tip of his prick slipped up Evan's crease, missing his hole.

Evan tried to reach back to help, but remembered his hands. As it turned out, he didn't need to because Aaron tried again, using his hand to hold his dick still this time.

Damn he was big. Evan took a deep breath and pushed out as he lowered himself. By the time he was seated on Aaron's hips, sweat was trickling down his temples.

Aaron had his eyes squeezed shut. He, too, was sweating. If Evan didn't know better, he'd have though he was in pain. Reaching out, he used his shirt to wipe at Aaron's forehead.

Aaron blinked his eyes open. Catching Evan's gaze he smiled. "You okay?"

"Oh yeah." He was way better than okay. Aaron's cock was so damned big it was already nestled up against Evan's prostate. Evan had never been one for size, but damn… This burning pleasure was pretty damned intense.

"Evan?"

"Yeah?"

"Move, babe."

"Yeah." Evan started slow, raising up almost all the way until he could feel the tip of Aaron's dick almost slip out, then sank back down inch by inch.

They both groaned.

He did it again, teasing himself, enjoying the feeling of

being filled until it was just too much.

Aaron's hands squeezed Evan's hips and he shook with his effort to be still. The patience and restraint was Evan's undoing. He couldn't remember anyone caring enough about his pleasure to try holding back. He leaned forward, resting his elbows on Aaron's chest, his hands and shirt balled up under Aaron's chin.

Aaron's control broke, he let go of Evan's hip and wrapped his hand around the back of Evan's neck and mashed their mouths together. His tongue thrust into Evan's mouth just as he thrust up into Evan's body.

Evan kissed back and slammed himself down to meet Aaron. The kiss grew almost punishing, their teeth coming into play, mashing their lips.

Aaron continued to fuck him hard and fast, his hands slipping back to Evan's waist. The slap of skin was loud, echoing over the grunts and moans.

Evan sat back up, impaling himself over and over. The pleasure rushed over him, making his cock throb and bounce in time to Aaron's body-jarring thrusts.

"Come, Evan." Aaron grunted out through gritted teeth.

His stomach tightened, his balls drew up and that was all she wrote. Evan came so hard he saw stars. Semen hit his lower abdomen and Aaron's in a hot stream.

With a hoarse yell, Aaron followed him, shoving up into Evan one last time and stilling.

The white spunk on Aaron's tanned skin was one of the most erotic things Evan had ever seen. Evan stared, his body feeling loose and relaxed.

After a few seconds, Aaron grabbed the shirt holding Evan's hands and wiped the come off of him and Evan. Then he tugged it loose from Evan's arms and tossed it onto the floor.

Without a word, they crawled under the covers and got comfortable. After a few minutes Evan rolled onto his side and rose up on his elbow. "We should tal—" He yawned.

Aaron grinned. "You talk way too much as it is, babe." He tugged Evan forward onto his chest.

Evan nuzzled his face into Aaron's neck and settled in, feeling relaxed and at ease. Maybe a nap was in order before their talk. Aaron didn't act like he was any hurry to leave.

Wrapping his arms around Evan, Aaron kissed his forehead. "We should ride like that more often, Tex."

* * * * *

Evan woke to the sound of the door closing. *Shit! Aaron.* He sat up in bed, blinking his eyes open.

Mark stood right inside the room, looking around. "So? Where's this mystery man?"

"God dammit!" Evan jumped out of bed. He ran to the bathroom, already knowing he wouldn't find what he looked for. *Nope, no Aaron.* Then, he ran to the front window and threw open the curtain. "Son of a bitch!" Evan's eyes watered at the bright sun. Damn it, he'd slept the whole night through and they hadn't talked. And now Evan was more sure than ever he wanted, no he *had*, to see Aaron again.

There was a soft clunk sound and then Mark started laughing.

"What? This isn't funny. He left…Again."

"Shut the curtain, Evan." Mark, still cackling, reached for the thick, rubber-backed fabric, preparing to close it.

Evan looked out the window again.

An older woman, probably in her early sixties, stood to the left of the motel room window, her mouth hanging open and her hands out. At her feet lay an ice bucket and small squares of ice littered the ground by her feet. He glanced down. *Oh man.* He was still naked. Groaning, he fumbled for the curtain, but Mark slung it across. It made a rattling sound as it slid over the window, blocking out the woman's shocked expression. At least he wasn't still covered in cum. That was something, right?

Mark flopped down on the made up bed. "Oh damn, that

218

was great."

Evan growled at him as he rummaged through his bag. He was down to his last pair of jeans. They were going to have to do laundry before they moved on. It would kill two birds with one stone. It'd be great for getting his mind off Aaron and back on roping, as well as get him clean clothes. Jerking on his pants, Evan hopped around to see the clock on the nightstand between the beds. "What time do we ride?" Maybe Aaron would be in the stands? Evan sighed, yeah, he definitely needed to do something to distract himself.

"Seven-thirty in the morning." Mark stretched his hands over his head and yawned.

"You got quarters?" He really wanted to go look for Aaron, but he knew it was pretty pointless. "We need to go check on the horses, then do laundry."

"Shit. Aren't you going to feed me first?"

Evan growled at him again and grabbed himself a t-shirt. "After we check on the horses." He wondered if Aaron— "We'll grab something on the way to the laundry mat. Hey speaking of, is there one here on site?" He could brood over Aaron later.

"I don't know." Mark picked up a pillow and tossed it in the air and caught it. "So what happened to your, uh, date?"

"I don't know." Evan sat on the unmade bed and put on his socks and boots. "We were supposed to talk."

Mark laughed. "Uh huh. Didn't do much talking, huh?" He missed the pillow this time and it hit him in the face.

Evan debated picking it up and smothering him with it, but decided it really wasn't Mark's fault he was in a mood. He should have known Aaron was likely to disappear again. Why was the man always...*Oh God.* Was he already with someone? Evan hadn't even considered that before. Ugh. He got a queasy feeling. Why hadn't he thought of that before? Why else would the man be so secretive?

"What? No matter how hard you stare at your other boot,

it's not going to put itself on your foot." Mark rustled around for a second, then he was sitting on the edge of the bed across from Evan, waving his hand in front of Evan's face. "Hey buddy? You okay? You look like you've seen a ghost?"

"Yeah. I was just thinking." Evan shook his head, trying to clear it. This wasn't a big deal, it wasn't. He barely knew Aaron. It was better he realized something was up now than, say a week down the road, or even tomorrow for that matter. "I was just thinking. What if he's married or something?"

Mark frowned. "It was a one-night stand, right? Does it matter?"

"Okay, let's go." Evan put his other boot on, smoothed his pant leg down and stood up.

"Evan?" Mark didn't move. *Damn it.*

Figured. Evan didn't want to listen to the whole "stalking" speech again. Mark didn't normally meddle in Evan's love life, but if he thought someone was bad for Evan, he didn't hold his tongue. Evan sighed. Mark was his best friend, and Evan didn't mince words either when he thought Mark was making a mistake. "You remember the guy from the bar?"

"The guy who took you to the hospital?"

Evan nodded, then set about gathering his clothes to take to the laundry mat.

"Have you lost your mind? I told you there was something up with that guy from the beginning. Otherwise, why on earth would he keep running off? He could be a—"

Shaking his head, Evan groaned. "Stalker? Do you know how silly that sounds? If he were a stalker, he wouldn't be disappearing."

Mark sighed and got up from the bed. "Fine. But it's still suspicious. Maybe you're right, maybe he is in a relationship." He, too, began gathering his clothes. "Wait." Mark stood up from digging through his duffle bag. "Do you want to get to know this guy better?"

Evan shrugged, trying to convince both he and Mark that

it didn't matter. He wasn't upset, really, just a little disappointed. He should have asked questions first. It was his own fault. "Yeah, kinda. It's weird, it's like we know each other. There's this strange comfort level."

"Strange comfort level?" Mark gathered up his bag and went to stand by the door.

"Yeah, strange 'cause it's not. I mean, we just seem to click really well." Evan zipped his own bag. "We moving on after we ride tonight?"

"Yeah." Mark opened the door, holding it for Evan. "I don't know what to tell you. If you really like the guy…try talking to him first next time."

Evan heaved the strap of his bag onto his shoulder and headed out the door. "Thanks, smart ass." Like he hadn't already realized that was what he needed to do.

Evan was pretty pleased with their time. They were in fifth place going into the finals, not bad at all considering the concussion and Evan having to switch horses mid-season. But no matter how hard he tried, he couldn't get his mind off Aaron. "I think he has someone else, Gus. Why else would he disappear all the damned time? I tell you, that man would put Houdini to shame."

Gus snorted. That seemed to be his response to everything nowadays. Especially Evan's love life. Actually, come to think of it, that was pretty much Evan's opinion of his love life, too.

"That was a-awesome man. Y'all done good."

The stables were pretty much empty this time of night, but Evan recognized the voice. Smiling, he glanced up from unsaddling Gus as Tracy stepped into the stall, grinning from ear to ear. "Thanks."

"You meeting up with Mark and Doreen at the bar?" Tracy leaned against the stall. He wore blue jeans, boots and a tight black t-shirt with a tan hat. He didn't appear to be riding tonight.

Gus stuck his neck out, trying to bite again.

Tracy jumped back.

Evan groaned and smacked Gus on the shoulder. "Yeah, headed there after I finish up here. Mark conned me into brushing down Miz Dotty—" he pointed to the next stall over, where Mark's mare was housed, "and Gus by myself." That wasn't entirely true, Evan preferred to spend time with the horses. He'd actually volunteered. "When do you ride?" Evan worked the cinch free, then the girth. He tossed both straps over top of the saddle and pulled it off Gus.

Tracy spit right outside the stall then reached forward, grabbing the saddle blanket as it canted sideways. "Tomorrow night. Y'all gonna be around or are you headed on to the next stop?"

After Evan threw the saddle over the stall wall, he took the saddle pad from Tracy. "Thank you. We were planning on heading out tonight. You needing a ride to the next stop?"

"Nah, I'm good. I was just w-wondering." Tracy glanced at his watch. "Listen, I gotta go. I promised to meet some people at the Lone Star Bar before I catch up with Doreen, Mark and Gayla at the Wagon Wheel. I just wanted to drop by and tell you congrats." He slapped Evan on the shoulder. "I'll see you l-later on, okay? I'll buy you a drink."

Evan squeezed Tracy's shoulder. "Good deal, I'll take you up on that drink. And thanks again."

Tracy left and Evan stepped up in front of Gus, unbuckling his bridle. "He's a nice guy, Gus. Stop trying to bite him."

Gus shook his head. *Ornery horse.*

"Yes, he is." He patted his horse's neck before grabbing the halter off the peg on the wall. After fastening the halter, he grabbed Gus's brush out of his bag. Running the bristles over the sleek black coat, Evan hummed.

Gus closed his eyes and let out a heavy breath. It was one of the things Evan loved about Gus. He never seemed to mind

222

Evan's off-key humming and singing. Buck had always started getting fussy when Evan decided to belt out a tune. Actually Buck wasn't the only one; when Evan was a kid he'd had a dog, Joe, that howled every time he tried to sing. Going Christmas caroling with Joe had seriously sucked.

Gus snorted and pawed at the ground.

"What the—?" Evan jumped back to keep his feet from getting stepped on. "Easy bo—"

"I thought we told you we don't want faggots around."

Evan snapped his attention toward the door.

Benson, Craig and Lahr stood crowded around the stall door.

Evan's stomach clenched up and his shoulder muscles tightened. Out of instinct, he glanced around seeing if anyone else was in the building. There wasn't that he could see. *Great.*

"Why are you still around? Didn't you learn your lesson last time?" Craig asked.

Evan sighed. Nothing he could say was going to keep him from getting his ass kicked. No way in hell was he promising to "be good" and leave. "Just do whatever the fuck you think it is you gotta do. I'm not going anywhere."

Benson stepped closer to Gus.

Gus shook his head, blowing out and getting spit on him. Benson scowled.

If Evan hadn't been so nervous he'd have laughed, hell maybe he did, he didn't know. His gaze focused on the revolver Benson pulled out of his jacket and leveled on Gus.

* * * * *

Un-fucking-believable. Evan huddled further into the corner of the horse trailer. He was scared shitless, cold and getting a headache from trying to figure out how to get himself and Gus out of this in one piece. He looked up at Gus. "Any ideas, boy?"

Gus continued studying their scenery outside the two tiny windows on each side of him. *Great,* he was enjoying the ride and Evan was having a nervous breakdown.

Ties That Bind

Evan laughed, or tried to; it came out as a croak. He really was having a nervous breakdown. Of course Gus was acting normal, he had no idea how grave things were. Before now Evan would have said the likelihood of more trouble from these three assholes was slim. They were bigots, not crazy. Surely they had to know if something happened to Evan, they were going to be the first suspects. Didn't they? Evan may not have pressed charges on them for assault and battery, but everyone knew who'd beat Evan up, and why. And what the fuck? Where they that stupid? Before now Evan wouldn't have thought so. Assault and battery was one thing, but murder... Did they really have it in them?

The truck came to a stop.

Shit. What now? Evan jumped up and ran to try the door again, if he could get it open... It was locked. Hell, he'd known it was, because he'd tried it after they first made him load Gus and shoved him in afterward, but he had to try. It wasn't in his nature to give up.

A truck door opened and voices followed.

Lahr, it sounded like, asked what they were going to do now.

Someone—Dodger Craig, Evan thought—whined that horse theft was still a hanging offense in Texas.

If Evan hadn't been sick with worry, wondering if they had a plan, he'd have laughed. Maybe they were that stupid. They obviously hadn't planned this out. Which could be a good thing, or a bad thing. If they suddenly came to their senses, things were looking up. Assuming they didn't panic. If they panicked then all bets were off. They could just as easily act first and think later.

Evan patted Gus's rump. At this point he could only think of three options. Unfortunately, the trailer wasn't big enough for him to turn Gus around and haul ass when they opened the door. That left him with trying to reason with a group of obviously unreasonable men, or fighting like hell. Maybe he could even get a hold of the gun and turn the favor in his direction.

The men continued to talk, Benson telling the other two to shut up as they walked around the trailer. Evan couldn't see them, but he could hear their voices moving. When the clank of the lock echoed through the trailer, Evan made his decision. He really had no choice but to fight. With any luck he could take them by surprise as soon as they opened the door. A small voice in his head said that might not be a great plan, they could shoot first and ask questions later, but Evan ignored it. If he was going to get shot, he was going to do so trying to defend himself and Gus.

A small shiver ran down his spine and he was so close to heaving. Could he really do this? And what was taking them so long? They seemed to be taking forever getting the lock off the trailer. *Come on, Evan, this is it.* He crouched down a little, preparing to run at the door. His limbs felt shaky, like he was about to crawl out of his skin.

The door handle creaked as it was turned and pulled out of the latch. Moonlight appeared through a tiny crack.

That was all Evan needed. He ran at the door, hitting it as hard as he could, making it burst open. There was a loud bang and the door flew back at him. Someone yelled, but he didn't stop. He just kept going, shoving through the door to the outside. His foot landed right smack dab in the middle of whoever he'd knocked over with the door when he ran out of the trailer, making the man huff out a breath and groan in pain.

Turning around, Evan took in the location of the other two men and looked for the gun.

Lahr and Craig stood on the other side of the trailer door, stunned. There was no sign of the gun.

Gus was backing out of the trailer in a hurry. *Good. Hurry, boy.*

Evan ran back toward the trailer, right at the two surprised cowboys. He reached Lahr first. Drawing back his fist, Evan belted him right in the nose. Blood spurted everywhere and Lahr let out a hellacious, gurgling yell.

Shit, that hurt. Evan shook his hand.

Craig tackled Evan from the side, knocking him to the ground before Evan could do anything else. They rolled around the ground, wrestling for position, with Craig shouting out a stream of curses at Evan.

Evan landed on a rock. It hit him in the middle of the back and pain flared up his spine. "Ah." Using all his might, he flipped them over again and pinned Craig to the ground, straddling his hips to keep Craig from rolling them again.

"You son of a bitch." Craig popped Evan in the jaw.

Evan jerked back out of reflex but the blow still caught him enough to hurt.

Someone yelled behind them, then someone grabbed Evan under the arms and began hauling him off of Craig.

Evan flailed his arms, nailing the assailant in the face, making him let go. Evan fell back to the ground, but Craig scrambled out from under him and caught him in the chin with his boot heel.

Everything went white for a few seconds, long enough for the two men to jerk Evan to his feet.

A shot ran out and everyone froze. A muted thud followed.

Craig and Lahr let go of Evan. As one unit, the three men whirled around in the direction of the shot.

Benson held the revolver in one hand and rubbed his gun arm with the other.

On the ground, a few feet in front of him, lay Gus.

"No!" Evan ran forward, not even caring if Benson shot him too. Everything seemed to slow down, taking him forever to get to Gus. It was like he was running in quicksand. He hit the ground, his knees skidding to touch Gus's belly.

The other men started yelling all at once, but Evan didn't hear a word that was said. Gus's chest rose and fell in a hard, heaving motion. He lifted his head, looking at Evan as Evan ran his hands over the short hair on Gus's neck and chest looking for a wound. "Hang on, boy."

"Fuck man, we gotta get outta here."

"We're going to jail."

"Shut up. We aren't going to jail. Get your ass in the truck, both of you."

Truck doors slammed and the truck started.

No. They couldn't leave. Gus needed help. Evan jumped to his feet.

The back tires threw dirt and debris and the trailer fishtailed as the truck sped away.

"Wait!" Evan watched the tail lights fade away, feeling helpless. He had no idea where he was, it didn't matter anyway. Aaron had broken his phone when he'd tossed it the other night.

His shoulders slumped and a knot formed in his stomach. Tears streamed down his face. *Please don't let Gus be hurt badly.*

There was a flash of light and Evan saw his own shadow on the ground. *A flashlight?* Evan turned around and froze.

"Son of a bitch, that hurt." Aaron stood where Gus had lain, naked, rubbing his shoulder.

"Wha—" Evan looked around. *Where the hell had Aaron— Where was Gu—* "Wha—"

"Whoa. Evan, you okay?" Aaron grabbed Evan's arms and pulled him down to the ground, making him sit.

Evan studied the ground behind Aaron. "What the hell is going on? And where is my horse? Why in the fuck are you naked?" Okay, yeah he was shouting, but damn it, he was scared. Something was way off.

Aaron rubbed his right shoulder again, then pulled his hand away and looked at the spot. "That left a scar." He shook his head and crouched down in front of Evan. "You okay? You look a little pale."

Evan stood up. "Ya think? They shot my horse." He

walked past Aaron, looking around for Gus. Why was Aaron here? How'd he get here? Evan felt like a horse had kicked him in the head. Gus was hurt and…gone. Aaron was here and…

Naked? *Oh God!* They'd brought Aaron here to pay him back for helping Evan.

Evan spun around and came nose-to-neck with Aaron. He grabbed Aaron's shoulders. "Are you okay? Did they bring you here? What happened? We've got to find Gus."

"You better sit down." Aaron touched his cheek like it was the most natural thing in the world to do. He acted like there was nothing wrong, like he had no concern for anything but Evan. It was tender and loving and Evan found himself leaning into the caress before he snapped out of it. They were in the middle of nowhere, out in the country somewhere away from civilization, with no phone, no truck, and Gus needed help.

"Aaro—"

"No really. Sit down, Evan, I've got to show you something." He stepped away and pointed at the ground. "Sit, babe."

"We've got to—"

"Sit down."

The stern voice had Evan obeying, even though he didn't want to. He sank to the ground, sitting in the cool grass.

A flash of bright white light surrounded Aaron.

Evan squinted and brought his hand up to shield his eyes. *What the…?*

The light went out and, in the pale moonlight, Gus stood where Aaron had been seconds ago.

He couldn't say anything. He wanted to, but he couldn't seem to get his mouth to work. This was unreal.

There was another flash of light, then Aaron was coming forward, crouching down in front of Evan again. The moonlight caught his pale eyes, making them glow. They were…uncertain, worried. "Come on, Tex, say something." Aaron tipped Evan's chin up, staring into his eyes.

It made sense, in a strange sort of way. The eye color, the fact that Aaron was never around when Gus was. The man Evan had thought he'd seen in Gus's stall... "I...you..." This was the strangest night of Evan's life. On the bright side. "There's no one else is there?"

Aaron smiled. "No Evan. Just you."

"Why?"

"You looked so sad. I had this crazy urge to cheer you up." He leaned forward, nipping Evan's lip before he kissed it. "I knew I had to have you."

* * * * *

Epilogue

Adam's rope hit the ground about a foot behind the calf's legs as his horse turned away. Evan could see his frustration from here. This was the third time the mount he was training had done that.

Mark shook his head, but he had a smile on his face. His horse had gotten it right all day and his time heading was damned good.

Cupping his hands around his mouth, Aaron shouted out at his twin. "You suck."

Adam stopped pulling in his rope long enough to flip Aaron off.

Upon arrival at Two Spirits Ranch a month ago, Evan'd learned quickly that the twins never missed an opportunity to rib the other. He was still somewhat amazed that he hadn't noticed Aaron's resemblance to Adam when he'd first seen Aaron at the bar. Actually, Evan hadn't realized they were twins until he seen Adam again. Adam's long hair and sunglasses had gone a long way in masking the resemblance.

Evan chuckled. "They'll get it eventually, Mark just got lucky with that moun—Wait. Mark's not riding one of your family members is he?"

Aaron groaned, but there was a grin just visible under the

229

shadow his gray hat cast on his face. He jerked his head to the side, indicating he wanted Evan to follow, and turned his mount away from the practice arena. "Most Anasazi would never allow themselves to be saddled. It's why no one knows of our shapeshifting abilities. Hell, it's part of the reason historians believe we died out. My people are good at hiding. No way were they going to be captured and made into a white man's faithful mount."

"You didn't seem to mind." Evan pulled his hat down lower, shielding his eyes from the sun.

"Only because I wanted to be bound to you, Tex." Aaron reached out and tugged on Evan's reins, pulling them both to a stop. He leaned over, grabbing Evan behind the neck and drew Evan forward. His lips touched Evan's briefly, but it was enough for the familiar excitement to ignite.

Evan groaned at the loss of those warm, sure lips.

"What about you? You don't mind spending your off season here with me, training horses?" Aaron nudged his horse into motion again.

What was to mind? Evan had the man he loved, a place to live with said man, and steady pay. "As long as you don't mind traveling with me during the season."

Aaron stopped again, the sunlight caught him just right, showing off those pale blue eyes. "Nope, not now that those psycho ass bull riders are gone and I don't have to worry about them beating you to a bloody pulp and shooting me."

It wasn't likely they'd shoot Aaron now, even if they were around. Benson, Lahr and Craig had disappeared from the rodeo after shooting "Gus." The best Evan could guess is they were afraid of him pressing charges. For all they knew, they'd killed Gus. After the shooting, Aaron had remained in human form and called home for another horse to be brought to Evan.

Mark was told Gus died from the gunshot and that Aaron had felt so bad for him, he'd loaned Evan his own horse for the remainder of the season. Which was partly true. It *was* Aaron's horse, Trixie, Evan had ridden. Explaining that Aaron's family owned Two-Spirits Ranch was a little trickier; Evan had wondered if it would raise questions, but Mark had allowed that to pass as a strange coincidence. He also hadn't noticed the resemblance in the twins. Apparently, Superman wasn't the only one who could hide his identity with a pair of glasses.

"Think they'll ever show back up?" Evan reached down and patted Moe's neck. Moe wasn't Gus, or Buck for that matter, but he was a good horse. And by the time the season started up, Evan should have him trained for roping.

Aaron shrugged and pulled Trixie to a halt again. "If they do, they'd best be smart enough to stay away from you." The glint in those pale eyes was downright murderous.

Evan stopped, too, then leaned over and kissed the snarl right off that tanned mouth. Some things didn't change, horse form or human, Aaron was a possessive, protective bastard… and Evan loved that about him.

Ring.

Evan drew back from their kiss.

Aaron blinked, then glanced down at the phone on Evan's belt.

Evan looked down, too. Aaron's hand came into view, headed straight for Evan's phone. *Oh shit!* Evan heeled Moe and took off as he grabbed his phone.

Aaron gave chase. "Coward!"

Welcome to ManLoveRomance Press

MLR Press provides you with some of the very best in gay erotic romance and fiction. Join us. We have something for everyone. From lust-filled, stolen moments to long, lazy afternoons of lovemaking, we have the man-on-man mayhem you're looking for wrapped up in solid plots with heroes you can love with a passion. Maybe even hate with a passion—but passion will always be a part of it. Meet our authors and see our catalog at www.mlrpress.com.

Ties That Bind

Visit these authors at MLR Press at
http://www.mlrpress.com

or their author sites here:

JetMykles
http://www.computerotika.com

J.L. Langley
http://www.jllangley.com

Dick D.

Kimberly Gardner
http://www.kimberlygardner.com

Laura Baumbach
http://www.laurabaumbach.com

Ties That Bind

Lightning Source UK Ltd.
Milton Keynes UK
16 March 2011

169345UK00001B/13/P